"You asked for a transfer? Without even telling me?"

Alex's voice was shaking. She stared at her husband. He looked the same, but she suddenly felt as if he were a stranger.

Cam watched her in silence, and several more charged moments passed before he answered. "You met Perchinsky at the Christmas party, remember?"

Cam's boss. Alex nodded, wondering what the connection was.

"Well, Perchinsky's been an addict for over a year. He put one of my guys in jeopardy, and I blew the whistle on him. Last Monday I testified at orderly room proceedings. Perchinsky was discharged from the force and he's facing jail time. Now I can't stay on Drug Squad. I have to get out, get far away."

Alex shook her head, frowning in confusion. "But I don't understand, Cam. You did the right thing. Why should you have to leave? You love your job."

"Yeah, well, that's all changed now."

"So if I want to live with you, I'll have to give up *my* job at the hospital and move to this—this place, this Korbin Lake."

"I'm afraid [...] ne. All I can tell y[...] me with me, Alex?"

Dear Reader,

In the coal-mining valley where I grew up, a girl had two career
choices: she could be either a teacher or a nurse. I chose to be a
nurse, and I actually went off to nurse's training for all of a week
before I realized that although the idea of medicine fascinated me,
nursing just wasn't where I belonged. Storytelling wasn't a career
option in those days, in that place, and it took many years before I
knew myself well enough to try.

That early enchantment with the healing arts never faded, however.
It made me an avid reader of all things medical, but...a little
knowledge can be a dangerous thing. When the idea for this series
occurred to me, I was elated—here was a chance to create an
entire medical dynasty, to perform operations and deliver babies
and prescribe remedies. But then it dawned on me that romance
writing didn't exactly qualify me for brain surgery.

That's when my good friends stepped in, many of them involved in
medicine. With excitement and enthusiasm and generosity, they
answered questions, read parts of the manuscripts and gently
corrected both my terminology and my surgical skills.

I've had the time of my life researching and writing these books.
(The next one will appear this summer.) May you have just as
much enjoyment reading them.

Love always,

Bobby Hutchinson

SIDE EFFECTS
Bobby Hutchinson

Harlequin Books

TORONTO • NEW YORK • LONDON
AMSTERDAM • PARIS • SYDNEY • HAMBURG
STOCKHOLM • ATHENS • TOKYO • MILAN
MADRID • WARSAW • BUDAPEST • AUCKLAND

ISBN 0-373-70723-1

SIDE EFFECTS

Copyright © 1997 by Bobby Hutchinson.

"The most fundamental principle of medicine is Love."

—Paracelsus (1493-1541)

ACKNOWLEDGMENTS

My deepest gratitude to the medical experts who so generously and patiently answered questions, advised, read, corrected and made gentle suggestions that prevented me, a nonmedical person, from committing unintentional surgical mayhem on the bodies of my poor characters.

Particular and heartfelt thanks to Pat Ford, RN, MN, to Dr. Greg McCloskey, to Monica Adamack, BSN, to Richard Adamack, EMA 3, ALS 2, and to Ross Holloway, Unit Chief, Infant Transport Team.

CHAPTER ONE

ST. JOSEPH'S Medical Center sprawled in Vancouver's watery June sunshine like a gigantic gray toad, solidly situated on a large and expensive chunk of land smack in the center of the city's downtown core, a few short blocks from both skid row and some of North America's most breathtaking and expensive beachfront real estate. The hospital had none of the attractive patina aging sometimes endows on even the ugliest architecture.

St. Joe's had aged badly, its vast assortment of buildings patchworked haphazardly onto the original six-bed infirmary founded in 1914 by Mary Margaret Constantine, an intrepid and invincible sister superior with the Angels of Mercy.

It was eight minutes before eleven on a Tuesday morning, and the emergency room was abnormally quiet.

Emergency physician Dr. Alexandra Ross had been at work almost four hours and she'd only seen one other patient besides the one she was presently treating. The first patient had been what the staff called a "man-down," an alcoholic from the nearby skid row area who'd suffered a seizure with resulting lacerations and minor head injury. She could hear him in one of the observation cubicles, intermittently cursing and begging the nurses for a drink.

This quiet time was undoubtedly just a lull before the hurricane struck, Alex mused as she looked at the X ray and assessed the young and healthy specimen of muscular manhood sitting in the wheelchair in front of her.

He wore purple jogging shorts, a green headband and a white T-shirt. His bare right foot was propped on the chair's extended footrest, and the middle toe was obviously fractured.

"It's a clean break, Mr. Siddon. We can either anesthetize you to set it or—" She cradled the man's wide, long foot in one hand, steadying it, and gave a sudden sharp pull on the crooked toe. Just as Alex had known they would, the clean edges of the bone snapped into place and the toe was straight again.

"Or we can just do this," Alex purred.

"Ooowww. Son of a bitch—" The young man turned red in the face and glared up at Alex from the wheelchair. "Damn it all, Doc, that hurt like hell."

"Sorry, Mr. Siddon, but that was so much easier on you than having to undergo anesthesia just to set a toe, don't you agree?"

She grinned wickedly at him, and after a moment, he attempted a white-lipped smile and nodded.

"All we need to do now is bind this to the next digit, to keep it steady while it heals." She swiftly wound a length of gauze around the injured toe and the one next to it and secured it with tape.

"Now, I'll just give you a prescription for pain, and then you're out of here in time for lunch. You allergic to anything?"

He shook his head and Alex scribbled on her pad, ripped a page off and handed it to him. "Take these only if and when you need them. Keep off that foot as much as you can. You'll need a set of crutches for a while, but your toe'll be like new in about six weeks. And don't go running into any more bricks, okay? Now, did someone bring you to Emerge, or shall I have Lorraine call you a cab?''

"My buddy's right over there, waiting for me. Say, you work here all the time, Dr...?" His eyes dropped to the nameplate attached to her lapel, lingering an instant too long on her breasts. "Dr. Ross?"

"Yup, I'm afraid I'm here all of my working hours."

Actually, a large portion of her life had been spent here, she mused. She'd been born in this very hospital thirty-four years ago. She'd interned here, done her residency here, gotten this job in Emerge three years ago, and she'd even met her husband here. There were times when Alex wondered what it was about her and St. Joe's.

"You look awfully young to be a doctor."

It was a comment Alex was accustomed to hearing. "It's the excitement of setting broken toes," she said breezily. "Keeps a person from aging."

Mr. Siddon was now looking at Alex in an entirely different fashion than he had a moment before, taking in the riotous mop of thick golden brown curls reaching past her shoulders, the delicate features devoid of any makeup, the wide mouth, naturally rosy and full lipped. She had thick-lashed dark blue eyes and graceful curves not quite hidden by the white lab coat. He liked what he saw.

"So, Doc, you ever get any time away from this joint, like, say, for food?" His voice was husky, his tone suggestive, the anger of a moment before transformed into heat of a different sort. "I know this great Italian restaurant just over on Robson. I'd love to take you there for lunch."

Alex raised her eyebrows and smiled at him again, a smile totally devoid of any flirtatiousness. It was obvious his toe was better if other parts of his anatomy were kicking in. "Once in a long while they let me out, and when they do, I tend to spend time with my husband."

It was his turn to give her a rueful grin. "Can't blame a guy for trying. He's a lucky man. Tell him I said so."

"Shall do."

The triage nurse, Leslie Yates, interrupted them. There was a note of urgency in her quiet voice.

"Paramedics are arriving with a young male MCA—" it was the term the team used for motorcycle accident "—ETA three minutes. We're set up in two."

"Thanks, Les. There goes our quiet morning." Adrenaline poured through Alex as she hurried with her small group of nurses to trauma room two. Hastily they donned protective clothing, sterile gloves and glasses. The room had an outside port for the ambulance's arrival, and in seconds the attendants hurried in with a stretcher.

Alex glimpsed one scuffed high-heeled cowboy boot. The other boot was gone. A blue stocking covered the foot, and it was immobilized in a pillow splint.

"Blood pressure 80 over 50, heart rate 150, respiration 34 and shallow—"

Voices called back and forth, nurses moved, quick and purposeful. Organized chaos reigned, and Alex assessed the injuries.

Fractured right ankle—

He had a young man's strong, long, muscular legs, dark hair covering the areas not bleeding from cuts and abrasions.

Deep laceration of upper left thigh—

What was left of his clothing had been entirely cut away.

Sandbags surrounded him.

Spinal injuries—

One torn and bloody hand clutched the side of the gurney. The other was wrapped in a loose dressing.

Definite injury to extremities—

His strong, naked torso was half covered in gauze trauma dressing with blood seeping through.

Probable internal injury. Liver? Spleen? Bleeding—

Alex heard the anguished, steady sound coming from him, a raw, choking cry of mingled fear and agony that would have torn at her heart had she not heard similar sounds countless times before here in the ER.

All that registered now was that the sounds were a good sign. At least his air passages were open and unobstructed.

"Let's have a look—"

The trauma team were blocking her from a clear view of the man's head.

"What's the story here? When exactly did it happen?" The first hour was crucial; she needed to know exactly how much time she had left of that hour.

She was rattling off questions and instructions as the attendants stepped aside and she stood directly over the patient.

"Sir, can you—" She looked down into what had been an exceptionally handsome face, torn now and studded with shards of glass. Brown curls, only a shade darker than her own, were matted with dust and blood. The left cheekbone was shattered, and tanned skin lay bare from temple to chin.

For an instant, time stopped.

Alex made a strangled sound and her knees gave way. She had to grab the side of the gurney to keep herself erect, and bile rose in her throat. She swallowed it down, and her voice came out in a wavery, high-pitched cry.

"Wade." The name seemed to well up out of the dizzy sickness building within. "Oh, my God, it's my brother, it's my brother, Wade—"

"Dr. Palmer, you take over here." It was trauma nurse Helen Kramer's authoritative voice that broke the horrified, frozen tableau Alex's words created in the small crowd of people now grouped around the stretcher.

The young intern, Palmer, shot Helen a panicked look.

"Susan, page Dr. Chan or Dr. Murdoch. Get one of them down here stat to take over for Alex." She grasped Alex's arm. "Come with me. Let the rest of the team take care of him."

Alex threw off Helen's hand and bent low over the stretcher.

"Wade, it's me. It's Alex. Listen to me, Wade." His blue eyes, so much like her own, were open, but agony was reflected there instead of recognition.

She didn't think he could see her, and she wasn't sure he heard her, either. A mask of pain contorted his face, and the terrible moaning continued unabated.

"Wade, we're going to help you. Just concentrate on staying with us, okay?"

Please, God, help us keep him alive. Please don't let my little brother die....

The doors burst open behind her, and Dr. Henry Murdoch charged into the room with bull-like authority.

"Get that portable X ray in here now," he began. "I'll need a cut-down tray, and get him typed and crossed. Send for a neurosurgeon—"

Helen again took Alex's arm and gently but firmly led her out of the room.

SERGEANT CAMERON ROSS drove the unmarked police car down the Vancouver streets, automatically choosing the route that would most quickly take him to the court-house in the city's downtown core. He hoped to obtain a search warrant for a house in a quiet, expensive neighborhood where quantities of cocaine were being distributed to dealers by the son of one of the city's foremost politicians.

He drove with the easy grace of a policeman totally familiar with the city, one hand on the wheel, the other curled around a foam coffee cup. He was running on caffeine and nervous energy these days.

After nearly ten years on the RCMP drug squad, he was accustomed to the wide range of emotional reactions his job could produce in any single shift, all the way from mind-numbing boredom to gut-wrenching fear, often in a matter of seconds.

But it wasn't either boredom or fear that was bothering him now. It was more a constant anxiety, a deep, gnawing uncertainty in the pit of his gut that wouldn't go away.

If he could talk about it with Alex, maybe it would ease his tension, but so far, he hadn't been able to bring himself to confide in his wife. Maybe tonight. She was on days at the hospital, and they'd have some time together this evening. He'd tell her the whole sordid story tonight.

Trouble was, he'd wanted to reach some kind of resolution about the whole mess himself before he talked to Alex, and so far, that hadn't happened. He was just as screwed up over it as he'd been two weeks ago. Two long weeks of being wrenched from sleep every hour, his body wet with sweat, stale sickness roiling in his stomach, his mind going over and over his decision and the upcoming hearing. Had it been the only alternative? Even now, in broad daylight, Cam wondered.

Fink, snitch, pipeline. He knew all too well the labels his fellow policemen were using about him. The fact that what Cam had done was make their working lives easier and safer had no bearing whatsoever on the way his fellow members viewed his actions.

The police radio burbled out a steady, nearly indistinguishable stream of sound as Cam stopped at a light, not conscious of either driving or listening, his brain still going over events for what seemed the billionth time.

Along with a small percentage of the other officers on Drug Squad, he'd known for over a year that Staff Sergeant Emil Perchinsky, NCO in charge of street crews and Cam's immediate supervisor, had become a junkie. The word was that Perchinsky had been cutting exhibits with corn sugar to supply his ever-increasing heroin habit.

Perchinsky had become almost arrogant about it, knowing that the strict code of silence and loyalty to a fellow officer would protect him, and it had—until two weeks ago, when one of the young recruits Cameron was responsible for had almost died because Perchinsky, on heroin, loose-tongued and publicity happy, had leaked information to the press about a major roundup that was about to occur. As a result, the dealers knew that an undercover man had infiltrated their organization, and Constable Norm Cardinal had come within inches of being snuffed out.

Cam still shuddered at the memory. He'd managed to warn Cardinal, get him to a safe house, but it was touch and go. The moment he knew for certain the young constable was safe, Cam had made his decision. He'd gone to the inspector in charge of Drug Squad and made a verbal and written statement attesting to the fact that Perchinsky was using.

He wasn't surprised when he was totally unsupported. No one else would give statements, adhering to the strict code of silence among fellow officers, but Perchinsky had cut his own throat by refusing to take a drug test. He was suspended with pay for disobeying a direct order and then, desperate for the heroin he'd filched so easily from the exhibit locker, he'd been arrested on the street buying from a dealer. He was now facing orderly room and criminal proceedings.

Next week, Cam would have to stand up at a formal hearing and testify against Perchinsky. The exhibit locker had been inspected, and it was now common knowledge that quantities of heroin were missing. If convicted— which seemed inevitable— Perchinsky would be discharged from the force, with a fair possibility that he'd do jail time.

And Cam would have to live with the fallout of being the guy who'd fingered a fellow officer. The fact that he was in line for Perchinsky's job made it just that much worse, and it horrified him that anyone could think he was simply jockeying for a promotion.

Cam was pulled from his reverie by his call sign on the radio. "Delta 7, XJA 43-Vancouver."

"Delta 7, 43-Vancouver, fifteenth and Cambie," he responded automatically.

"Delta 7, can you give me a land line?"

Glancing at his watch, Cam swore under his breath. He didn't have a lot of spare time to get the warrant, but he couldn't ignore the request for a confidential call. It could be an emergency with one of his men.

"Delta 7, copy." He wheeled the car into the parking lot of a fast-food chain and jogged to the pay phone on the outside of the building, his portable in his hand. He checked the number on the phone and pushed the button on his portable. "43-Vancouver, portable Delta 7, 435-9512."

In a moment, the phone rang and he picked it up.

"Sergeant, there's an urgent personal message from St. Joe's—"

Alex. Oh please God, don't let anything have happened to my Alex— Cam's very skin seemed to shrink with dread, and his heart hammered against his ribs.

"Your brother-in-law, Wade Keenan—motorcycle accident—critical condition—St. Joe's—your wife needs you—"

Not Alex. Wade.

Cam felt ashamed of the momentary relief that crashed through him. *Hang in there, sweetheart. I'm coming.*

He didn't remember hanging up the phone or racing for the car. He wove expertly through traffic, his entire being focused on getting to her as fast as he could. And still one tiny part of his brain focused on Perchinsky.

Of course he wouldn't be able to tell her now....

THEY TOLD ALEX they'd sent for Cameron, but she couldn't have said how long it was before she saw him loping toward her down the hallway. For a moment, her shocked brain saw him as a stranger, the way she'd seen Wade not long before.

But this man wasn't injured. His tall, strong body was loose-limbed and graceful. Power and sensuality were inherent in the way he moved.

His long, thick, inky dark hair was slicked back, tied with a leather shoelace at the base of his skull. Over his shoulder he carried the battered old brown leather jacket that he claimed was his good luck token. Around his waist was the black zippered pouch that held his .38 police special. His plain gray T-shirt was sleeveless, baring the anchor tattoo on his right biceps. His jeans fitted like a second skin, and his heavy boots clattered on the tile.

His face was hard angles and deep shadows, exotic and dangerous, but his worried brown gaze was gentle, intent on Alex's face, and the tight, hard knot inside her loosened just a little as she bolted into her husband's arms.

"Cameron. Oh, God, Cam, I'm so glad you're here." The iron control she'd exerted for the past half hour backfired on her now, and her body began to tremble in his embrace, harder and harder until she didn't think she could stand.

"Easy, honey. I've got you. Just try to relax. How is he?"

The image of Wade, naked and helpless and broken, flashed again in her mind's eye, and the shudders increased until she thought she'd fly apart.

"Not...not good." She couldn't speak of it yet, not even to Cam. She had to skirt around it, talk of other, more ordinary things until the pain receded a little. She struggled for control, trying to stop the tremors that passed through her, searching for the mundane to avoid the unthinkable.

"How'd—how'd you get here so fast, Cam?"

He understood her need to work up to it slowly. "Susan called the detachment, and they got me on the radio." He folded her into his body, pressing her hard against him, supporting her as her nervous system released some of its shock and tension.

She breathed in the dear, familiar smell of him, the aftershave she'd given him for Christmas, the softener she used in the dryer, the unique body scent she knew as well as she knew his name. Against her stomach she could feel the outline of the pouch that held his gun, a mute reminder of the danger he lived with in his undercover work.

At last the trembling subsided. She tilted her head back, and with dry, burning eyes, looked up into his face. "Cam, I'm not sure he's going to make it. There's spinal injury, internal bleeding, head injuries. Murdoch called in Bellamy, and they made me leave—"

"He'll make it." There was absolute confidence in his deep, quiet voice. "Wade's young and he's in excellent condition. He's also a fighter. And you've told me often enough that Bellamy's the finest surgeon there is. I know Wade's going to come through fine, sweetheart."

She was the doctor—she knew all too well what the risks were, and yet it was his assurances that lifted some of her awful fear and made it bearable. She stood within the circle of his arms, absorbing some of his own enormous strength, and although nothing had changed, everything was easier.

"Has anyone called Thea yet, Alex?"

She nodded, still resting against him. "Susan did. Thea's out on a shoot over in West Van somewhere near the canyon—they weren't sure exactly where. Her agent's gone to pick her up and bring her here."

Wade had lived with exotic Thea Calhoun for more than two years now. The dramatic six-foot fashion model wasn't the kind of woman Alex might have chosen for her younger brother. Thea struck Alex as somewhat superficial, obsessed with her job and the intrigues of its milieu. Alex couldn't help but wonder how she would handle this calamity.

"What about your parents?" Eleanor and Bruce Keenan were in San Diego, where Eleanor, a psychotherapist, was attending a conference.

"Oh, God. I'd better call them right now." Dread filled her, and again the ever-present nausea rose in her throat, along with a sudden fierce and unreasonable anger at her parents. They'd always been so critical of Wade. If he died now, it would be without ever once having heard them say they were proud of him, proud of anything he'd ever done.

"I'll call them for you," Cameron said. "They're staying at the Half Moon Inn on Shelter Island, right?"

Alex nodded, enormously relieved to have him make the call.

"You come and sit down in the staff lounge. I'll tell Helen where you are so they can find you as soon as the operation's over." He loosened his arms, leaving one looped around her shoulders, walking her down the corridor. "I'll be back the minute I've talked to your folks."

To Alex's relief, the lounge was empty. As usual, it smelled of burned coffee and stale egg sandwiches. Her knees felt weak, and she collapsed on the sagging brown sofa. She was still shaky, and icy cold now, as well.

Shock, her medical training automatically diagnosed.

The last, awful glimpse she'd had of Wade was vivid in her mind, and now that she was alone, the tears came. She bent forward, head on her knees, at first fighting the need to cry and finally succumbing.

"Alex, sweetie." Like a minor explosion, the lounge door burst open and a small, slender young woman still in operating-room greens, booties on her tiny feet, hurtled into the room and threw herself onto the sofa, hitting Alex in the rib with an elbow as she wrapped her arms around her and hugged her close, the fierce embrace both clumsy and endearing.

"Oh, God, Alex. How awful for you." The words were filled with compassion, spoken in a rich, deep contralto that should have belonged to a Valkyrie instead of this diminutive, redheaded lady. She was half smothering Alex, pressing her nose into a shoulder that carried the sharp and distinctive odor of the delivery room. "I just this minute heard about your brother. I'm so sorry. I talked to Cameron in the hall, and he said they're still operating."

"Hi, Morgan." Alex returned her friend's embrace, absorbing the love and compassion and caring that Dr. Morgan Jacobsen exuded like a rare perfume. It was suddenly easy, held close in this young woman's arms, to let the flood of words and feelings loose.

"Oh, Morgan, it's so awful, it's—it's horrible to be a relative, just waiting to hear what's happening," she wailed. "I—I didn't even know it was Wade at first. The ambulance brought him in and I looked down and—and then when I went into the OR, John Bellamy made me leave. He hollered at me and said if I didn't go he'd have me carried out, but I wanted to stay. He's my brother, Morgan." For a second, sobs choked her. "I'm so afraid he's not going to make it. There were—" Her throat closed at the memory of the unspeakable damage done to Wade's beautiful young body, and the tears came with a vengeance, cutting off further words.

One part of Alex was astonished at the sounds that came from her throat, high, keening cries and guttural sobs that she couldn't remember making since she was a very small child. Her chest hurt and her nose ran, and she laid her head on her friend's smelly shoulder and cried as if her heart would break.

"That's it, sweetie, that's it, let it all out." Morgan patted and hugged and consoled her during the worst of it, at last absently lifting the hem of her surgical gown to mop at Alex's face, impervious to the suspicious stains that covered most of the garment.

The action, so typical of Morgan, who'd never once in her life had a tissue when she needed it, finally brought a watery smile to Alex's swollen face. "God, Morgan, get that away from my nose. You know, you've got blood on your face—and is that amniotic fluid all over you?"

Morgan glanced down at herself, totally unconcerned.

"Probably. I just delivered the most beautiful little girl you've ever seen."

Alex sniffled and wiped at her nose. "You say that about every single kid you deliver, Morgan."

"Well, it's the truth, every single time." Pleased at having made her friend smile, Morgan's all-encompassing grin lit up her pleasant features. "Now, is there anything at all I can do, people you want me to call, anything you need to be picked up or delivered or paid?"

Alex shook her head. "Cam's gone to call Mom and Dad in San Diego. Someone's gone for Thea."

"Well, if you need me to meet your parents at the airport or take that cat of yours home with me or phone aunties in Alaska or anything, just let me know."

"I don't have aunties in Alaska, you nutcase." Alex took Morgan's small, chapped hand in her own and squeezed it. "And Pavarotti would get you evicted. But thanks, pal." They smiled at each other, all the years of their friendship a strong bond between them.

The door opened again, and this time it was the tall, stoop-shouldered figure of surgeon John Bellamy who entered the room.

Morgan's grasp on Alex's hand tightened, and they both stood up. Alex's eyes flew to Bellamy's face, knowing from personal experience that good or bad news is always signaled first by body language, the lack of expression on a carefully neutral face, the tired smile that telegraphed success.

Bellamy was smiling.

"He's come through the operation with flying colors. He's a tough young man. I don't have to tell you that the next day or so is crucial, Alex, but I think he's going to make it. I'd bet money on it, in fact. I called in Ben Halsey to take a look at what plastic surgery needs to be done on his hands and face—he'll start the procedures as soon as your brother's strong enough." He sobered and cleared his throat. "Now, about his spine . . ."

Alex felt her heart begin to hammer, and dread seeped through her all over again. Was her brother, her beautiful, tall, strong brother with his athlete's body, doomed to never walk again?

CHAPTER TWO

"WHAT ABOUT his spine?" Alex could hardly get the words past the lump in her throat.

"I suspect either a fracture of the cervical vertebrae or a dislocation," Bellamy began. "But there's too much swelling at this point to know whether or not the damage is permanent. As soon as he's stabilized, we'll do a myelogram, but right now it wouldn't tell us much. In the meantime, I've used Cruthfield tongs to ensure proper alignment."

Alex shuddered. Cruthfield tongs were a device inserted into each side of the skull, attached to traction ropes and weights, designed to keep the patient totally immobile. She'd always thought they resembled a medieval torture device.

"You—you don't have any idea yet whether he'll be able to walk again?" She knew the answer, but she felt compelled to ask anyway.

Bellamy shook his head. "It's much too early to tell. As you know, spinal injuries are unpredictable." He went on at some length, detailing possible outcomes, but Alex didn't hear more than a word here and there.

What mattered, she realized, was that Wade was alive. The relief of that simple fact was overwhelming. For the moment, it seemed to her that was all that mattered. She'd deal with the spinal injury when she knew for certain how bad it was, but for now, survival was the issue. In spite of

Bellamy's reassurances, she knew all too well that a high percentage of patients injured as severely as Wade died within the first twelve hours.

Thea arrived soon after the operation was finished, her arresting, asymmetrical features frozen into a mask that revealed little of what she really felt. Alex explained exactly what Wade's injuries were, feeling that if she was Thea, she'd want to know every detail.

Thea listened without saying a single word. She didn't even ask, as Alex had, whether or not Wade would be able to walk.

When Alex was finished, Thea simply nodded and said, in her deep, throaty voice, "Okay, I understand. Take me to him now."

Alex did, and Thea made one shocked, horrified sound when she saw him, but she didn't burst into tears or say anything. She sat down beside his bed and hadn't moved since, not even to go to the bathroom. Her long, wild raven black hair spilled over the scarlet-and-gold designer silk pant suit she'd been modeling when her agent located her. She was wearing it still, perched beside Wade's bed amidst the array of wires and tubes and bleeping machines that surrounded him in Intensive Care.

The rules were strict, and various staff members and Alex herself had tried to move Thea out of the busy area. She didn't refuse; she seemed simply not to hear anyone speaking to her. She constantly touched some part of Wade's face and torso with her long, beringed fingers, and she put her lips close to his bandaged, tonged head and murmured to him for minutes at a time.

With her wild mass of curling hair and what remained of her dramatic makeup, she looked like some exotic animal the staff had trapped and were holding captive in the sterile confines of the small, brightly lit cubicle.

Hours and hours passed. Wade went on living.

Toward morning, there was a definite improvement in his condition, and the tension in Alex eased somewhat, leaving awful weariness in its stead. She knew it was terrible of her, but she was dreading the arrival of her parents. Eleanor and Bruce were booked on the first direct flight they could get out of San Diego, a night flight, and Cameron had promised them he'd meet them at the airport at 5:00 a.m. and bring them directly to St. Joe's.

"I know exactly what they're both going to say when they get here." Alex sighed, glancing at Cam, who'd been at her side since he'd arrived the previous morning. It was now almost 3:00 a.m. of another morning, and he and Alex were strolling hand in hand up and down the dimly lit corridor outside Intensive Care. She'd tried to sit, even to lie down on one of the cots the interns used, but she couldn't be still. Every nerve ending in her body seemed to be vibrating discordantly.

"First, Dad's going to corner John Bellamy and question every single detail of the surgical procedure until John's ready to strangle him. John studied under Dad, so he can't very well tell him just to go to hell, even though it's high time somebody did."

Bruce Keenan was a retired surgeon, renowned in his time for innovative techniques which he refused to recognize were now outdated. The problem was, as Alex knew all too well, her father believed that no one could do anything quite as well as he believed he could himself.

"And Mom's going to resent the hell out of Thea being in there with Wade. She'll go on to me about guilt complexes and opposing personalities and the subconscious reasons we do things. I swear to God all that psychobabble keeps her from really feeling much herself. She's told me countless times that she doesn't think Thea's the right person for Wade, and now I'm going to have to hear it all over again.''

Cameron grinned down at her. "Sounds familiar, huh? It's exactly the same thing Eleanor said about me when we eloped.'' He did his best to turn his deep voice into a parody of Eleanor's tenor, hoping to coax a smile from Alex. "We like him, dear, but are you quite sure he's the person for you? Your values are very different, you know.'' There was the faintest trace of bitterness in his tone. "Your folks just don't believe anybody's really good enough for their kids.''

Alex didn't argue. They'd discussed this before, and she'd admitted reluctantly that he was right. Instead, she changed the subject. "Why don't you go on home now, Cam, and get a few hours' sleep before you have to go to the airport?''

"Nope. I'm not leaving you alone in this joint at a time like this, Alex.'' He shuddered. "God, I despise hospitals.''

She looked up at him, into the unfathomable brown of his eyes, thinking of the differences between them and how much she loved him. She needed him at this moment more than she ever had. "Hey, Sarge, I don't mind hospitals at all. In fact, I happen to have a soft spot for this old dump,'' she said with a strained smile. "It's where I first met you, remember? I thought you were the best-looking outlaw I'd ever seen.''

And looking at him now, she thought so still.

Cam gave her his tight-lipped, crooked half smile, the smile that always made something in her chest swell and turn over.

"You think I'd ever forget that night, Doc? Talk about pleasure and pain combined. I fell in love with you while you were digging that damned bullet out of my shoulder down in Emerge. It burned like all the fires of hell, and I remember your hair shining like gold in the lights." He rubbed his chin on her curly head. "It was shorter than it is now, sort of all fluffy, like a halo, and you had on a blue shirt under your lab coat, and that little gold cross around your neck. I looked into those big blue eyes and then I got a glimpse of your legs, and that was that. I'd have gladly let you go on cutting me up all night if it meant being close to you."

Alex, too, remembered every instant of that first dramatic meeting. Corny as it sounded, it had been love at first sight for both of them. She knew that even if Cameron Ross had turned out to be the outlaw she'd first thought him to be, she'd be with him anyway.

Not that his real job was a walk in the park. Cameron's undercover work with the RCMP drug squad was dangerous. They both acknowledged that danger, and Alex had tried her best to accept it. After a few ferocious quarrels, they'd resolved early on not to let either of their careers become a problem in their marriage, but she still worried when the phone rang late at night and he left without being able to tell her where he was going or what he was about to do.

He still resented the shifts that kept her at the hospital when he was on his days off, and he worried about the addicts who sometimes became violent in Emerge.

Cameron leaned down and pressed a kiss on her straight nose. "I'm staying, but come morning I'll have to leave right after I drop your folks off here. I'm not sure if I'll make it back. David's bail hearing's at ten this morning, and he'll probably need someone to sign as guarantor."

Alex had completely forgotten there was a world outside this corridor, outside this hospital. She'd forgotten everything except her own brother. Cameron's words reminded her that he, too, had a younger brother in trouble—different by far from Wade's problems, but worrisome all the same. She gave Cam a contrite look. "I forgot Dave's hearing was today, Cam. Sorry for being so self-centered."

He tightened his arm around her. "Hey, I didn't expect you to remember. But I *do* need to be there for him. Then I've got to meet someone in New West in the afternoon."

"How d'you think it'll go for David?"

David Ross had been part of a crowd that had rioted after a hockey game, causing untold damage to Vancouver's downtown core. He wasn't one of the people who'd looted and wrecked storefronts, but he'd been drunk and boisterous and rounded up with dozens of others, all of whom were charged with taking part in an unlawful assembly.

It wasn't the first time David had been in trouble, but it was the first time he'd been arrested, and Alex suspected it bothered Cameron, although he hadn't said as much.

Cameron didn't talk about his problems the way she did. It was just one more difference between them, convincing Alex of the old adage that opposites attract. His reticence made life difficult at times—he'd been unusually distracted and short-tempered over the past weeks, and she assumed it was over David. She usually managed to pry it out of him, but lately there just hadn't been time. He'd been working a lot of nights while she worked days, and their schedules meant she was leaving for work just as he came home.

"I hope he doesn't get sent to jail, Cam," Alex said now. "You don't think he will, do you?"

Cameron shook his head and sighed. "He shouldn't. It's a first offense. You never know, though. It depends on who he gets as a judge. If he does get off, I only hope this scares the living hell out of him." His voice hardened. "He's twenty-six, and it's bloody well time he grew up."

Again, Alex's thoughts went to her own brother. "That's what my parents always told Wade, that he should grow up, that he wasn't mature or responsible enough for his age," she said with a catch in her voice. "They never let him forget that he didn't go to university. They're scandalized that he's perfectly happy working at Sports Outlet."

"He also happens to play international rugby for Canada's world team," Cameron remarked dryly. "Being a world-class athlete is an accomplishment very few people ever attain. Wade's traveled all over the world—he's a big hero in Europe. Your folks should be really proud of him."

"You and I know that, but Mom and Dad sure don't see it that way. They feel that playing rugby's nothing short of suicidal. When he's leaving on tour Mom always manages to slip in some little remark about him getting seriously injured during a game."

Alex shook her head, tears once again close. "Maybe mothers really do have some sixth sense that way. She was right about him getting seriously injured, she just had the details wrong."

Neither spoke for a few moments. Both of them were painfully aware that Wade's rugby-playing-days were over, that the horrific extent of his injuries would mean months—perhaps years—of rehabilitation, even with the best outcome possible.

"His life's going to change so totally, Cameron," Alex whispered. Now that it seemed certain Wade would live, the ramifications of his injuries overwhelmed her. "Even if he regains motor function in his legs, it's going to take enormous effort on his part to walk again. It's still not certain whether or not he'll have any vision in his left eye, and he's likely going to lose at least two fingers on his right hand. He still needs so much more surgery." She fought to keep the tears at bay. "I keep telling myself how fortunate we are that there was no brain damage."

Cameron turned and took her in his arms, resting his chin on the top of her head. She could feel his warm breath in her hair, his steady heartbeat against her breasts. She could feel his long-fingered hands cupping the swell of her hips, and his lean, taut body pressing against the length of her, her bulwark against the world.

"Nothing ever stays the same for very long, honey." Her ear was pressed against his chest, and his voice was a deep rumble. There was an edge of something like anger in it. "The very moment we think everything's going great is usually the moment before it all falls apart."

She hit him gently on the upper arm with a doubled fist. "You're such a pessimist, Cam." It was another of the differences between them that sometimes amused her and at other times made her frustrated and furious. They epitomized the old glass of water adage—she saw it half full and Cam knew it was half empty.

"That's probably why you're good for me, Doc. You always see the bright side of things." His voice was teasing, but his face was somber.

She shook her head, and it was a long moment before she admitted, "Not today, Cam. There wasn't any bright side at all today. I was really afraid. I still am."

IF ONLY THERE WAS something he could do to take that fear away, to make Alex feel better, Cam pondered late that afternoon.

Once again, he was in the unmarked car, this time driving toward skid row and the Commodore Hotel to arrest a dealer.

For a few hours today, he'd actually forgotten all about his work, even forgotten Perchinsky and the upcoming hearing—but it had taken the near death of his brother-in-law to bring even a small respite from the thoughts that circled inside his head like a monkey chasing its tail.

He thought now of Wade, and the sting of tears burned behind his eyelids. They weren't close friends, but he liked and respected Alex's brother, and he hoped with all his heart that Wade would recover. Cameron had called Alex several times during the day, and it was a huge relief to hear that Wade was gradually improving.

Cameron thought of his wife, and for a moment his love for her banished all the demons that plagued him. She was the best thing that had ever happened to him, and he still marveled at the fact that she loved him back.

She'd looked absolutely exhausted and as tense as a piano wire when he'd dropped her parents off at the hospital that morning. He regretted not being able to stay with her and offer his support with his in-laws, but he'd had to race over to David's court hearing. Eleanor and Bruce were difficult, censorious people, and Cam knew it would be hard on Alex, explaining all the details and shouldering the brunt of their critical comments.

Alex had always played the role of family peacemaker.

She'd gone home late in the afternoon, and he hoped she was now asleep. As soon as he arrested Martinuk, Cam planned to check on Wade at the hospital and then head home himself.

First, however, there was Martinuk to deal with. In his mind, he went over the meeting he'd just had with one of his informants, Ronald Donald Herring, better known as the Fish.

"Martinuk's holed up in room 210 at the Commodore," Fish had whispered, leaning across the narrow table in the back of the Royal City Café and spraying Cameron liberally with coffee-laced spittle. "He's burned Erinson—says he's gonna do him and then he's leaving town. He's hiding out until he meets with your boy tomorrow. He's got a Chinese gal bringing him food and stuff, so he won't show his face till then. Word is he's heading for Ontario soon as the hit goes down."

Martinuk was a dealer Cameron's men had arrested a month before. Out on bond, he'd failed to appear at his court hearing.

Cameron had sent one of his best young undercover men, Bobby Erinson, to try to establish contact. Erinson, in his role as a local buyer, had managed to identify Martinuk's sources, setting up another meet for early tomorrow morning, at which time Martinuk and his offshore supplier would be arrested—except now it sounded more as if Erinson would get himself murdered.

Cameron was the senior officer in Drug Squad, and his job was to look after his underground people, making sure they were safe.

In order to protect Erinson, Cameron had to get Martinuk back into custody fast. He'd make the arrest himself, but he needed backup, so before he left New West he called the man who used to be his partner and asked him to meet him in the alley behind the Commodore.

The rundown brick rooming house came into view, and Cameron wheeled into the narrow alley beside the building.

He parked and walked over to the blue Chevy where Joe Knox sat, slouched low behind the wheel, a cigarette drooping from the corner of his mouth.

"Hey, Joe."

Without answering, Knox glanced up at Cameron and then returned his gaze to the overflowing garbage cans a few feet away. After a moment he said, "So what's going down, Ross?" There was the faintest hint of derision in his voice.

Cameron had guessed how it might be, had steeled himself against it, but still the bitterness of disappointment ate away at him. He'd come up against the same attitude numerous times in the past two weeks, ever since he'd blown the whistle on Perchinsky, but some part of him had gone on hoping Joe would understand.

Joe knew him, for God's sake. They'd been as close as brothers once. They'd worked these streets together when they both were as young as Bobby Erinson, covering each other's backs, loaning each other money, fellow soldiers in a dirty war.

But it was all there in Joe's face and in his voice, the carefully impersonal tone, the absence of any banter, the refusal to meet Cameron's eyes. It was obvious that Knox had sided with the group of men who'd decided Sergeant Cameron Ross had broken the faith, who'd informed on a fellow officer—a bad narc.

Cameron was suddenly tired of it all, of the years of living on the edge of the city's ugliest subculture. He was sick to death of the constant vigilance, the squalor, the deal making, the corruption, the power—and the twisted code of honor that allowed a senior officer to steal and use drugs, putting every man who worked for and with him in jeopardy, arrogantly confident that his fellow officers wouldn't say a word against him.

He forced himself back to the business at hand.

"Martinuk's up there in 210, Joe. The word is he's burned one of my guys. He's going to move right away, so I'm going in."

Knox nodded once and dragged deep on his cigarette, directing a cloud of acrid smoke at Cameron's face. He didn't offer to come along, or even acknowledge that he'd cover the alley.

Rage burned, swift and hot as a flash fire. Cameron wanted to tear the car door open and drag Knox out, throw him against the building and hold him there while he told him exactly how it had been, why he'd had to do what he'd done. Instead, he turned his back and sauntered away, around the corner and into the dingy, cigar-soaked lobby of the Commodore.

There was an ancient elevator, but he took the stairs instead, two at a time. The second-floor hallway was deserted and dimly lit. Through the thin walls came the sounds of a man and woman shouting obscenities, a radio playing a cowboy song.

Cameron put his ear to the door of 210 and listened.

Inside, a toilet flushed and a door banged, but there was no sound of voices. He could only pray that Martinuk was alone, as Fish had indicated.

Cameron sucked in a deep breath and drew his .38, took two steps back, raised his right leg and kicked the door in.

"Police. Don't move—"

Martinuk, in undershirt, pants, and bare feet, was in the process of opening a beer, and he was alone in the small room.

He let out a bellow of fear and rage and lofted the can.

Cameron ducked and it hit the wall behind him, spewing golden liquid across gray wallpaper. Martinuk lunged for the window and the fire escape, and in two long strides Cameron had him, cuffing him while he repeated the Miranda warning.

"Lawrence Martinuk, you're under arrest. Anything you say can and will be used against you in a court of law—"

Next, he called Knox. "Portable 9, portable 6. Subject now in custody. Call for a wagon. Request backup up here. I'm in 210."

There was no response, but there wasn't time to repeat. Martinuk could have friends in the building, and getting cornered in this hole-in-the-wall room wasn't Cameron's intention.

"Let's go. Move it." Cameron had cuffed Martinuk's hands in front of him, and now he grasped the back of the man's belt, herding him ahead into the hallway.

They stepped out, and simultaneously the doors of 212 and 214 opened. Three men came out, dark, ugly men, their eyes flicking from Cameron's gun to Martinuk.

"Take this bastard—he's all by himself," Martinuk squealed before Cameron cut him off.

"I'm a police officer. First person down this hallway gets shot." He moved slowly, cautiously, holding the dealer like a shield in front of him.

The men didn't speak, but they effectively moved to block the stairwell. A shiver of foreboding went up Cameron's spine.

Knox, where the hell are you?

He moved away from the stairs, stabbing his elbow into the button that summoned the elevator.

Like snakes, the three men edged their way along the hall toward him.

How many could he take before they rushed him?

He could smell Martinuk, pungent with garlic and sweat and fear. The hall reeked of urine. He could hear the creaking old elevator rising painfully slowly from somewhere below him. The men were murmuring amongst themselves. He couldn't make out the words, but he could see the tension building in them.

Hurry up, Knox. For God's sake, hurry—

The three men moved again.

"Hold it right there. One more step and somebody gets it—"

Cameron's steady voice betrayed none of his inner turmoil. At last the elevator doors opened in slow motion. Still keeping Martinuk as a shield between himself and the three men, Cameron stepped back—and stumbled.

The elevator was a good six inches below the level of the hallway. Martinuk heaved his body away, but Cameron still had a tight grip on his belt. He recovered his balance and jerked his prisoner inside the small cage, stabbing at the button that closed the door.

The men moved again, closer now.

The black steel grid slid shut, and the elevator jerked once, stopped, jerked again, and then began to move downward.

Martinuk swore viciously, and Cameron forced his hand to release its death grip on the back of the man's belt so that he could pull his portable radio out of his jacket pocket.

"Portable 9, portable 6." Still no response. "Request immediate backup in lobby." The three men would easily beat the elevator down; they'd be waiting when Cameron stepped off.

But when the elevator doors slid open on the ground floor, the lobby was as deserted as it had been when he came in. No sign of the men.

No sign of Knox, either.

CHAPTER THREE

CAMERON, ICY SWEAT trickling down his spine, heart pounding against his rib cage, again propelled Martinuk ahead of him, out the street doors and into the welcoming dusky summer warmth of the June night.

A pedestrian stopped to stare at the cuffs on Martinuk's wrists. A blast of music came from a bar, and the smell of fish wafted from a dingy café across the street.

There was no wagon waiting.

Knox was leaning nonchalantly against the wall just inside the alley, his cigarette only a butt now. He straightened and ground it out beneath his boot when Cameron approached with Martinuk.

"Where the hell were you, Knox? I called you twice. I damned nearly got ambushed in there!"

Knox shrugged. "Radio must be on the fritz. Never heard a sound."

Cameron deliberately reached for his portable.

"Portable 9, portable 6." The sound of his own voice echoed clearly back from the radio tucked in Knox's belt.

Killing rage swelled inside of Cameron. "That's a crock, Joe. You deliberately hung me out to dry."

Knox looked sheepish, but not the slightest bit repentant. He pulled out a new package of cigarettes, unwrapped them and selected one. He found a match and lit it, avoiding Cameron's eyes. Then he sauntered over to his car and used the car radio to call for a wagon.

Cameron watched as the man he'd once trusted with his life got in his car and, without a backward glance, drove into the street, leaving Cameron alone with his prisoner to wait for the wagon.

It was the beginning of an inevitable ending. On some level, Cam had known from the moment he decided to speak out against Perchinsky his days on Drug Squad were numbered. He just hadn't wanted to confront it. Now, he was forced to. He couldn't effectively protect the men who relied on him if his fellow officers weren't there when he needed them.

He knew that Knox was maybe in the minority, that perhaps there were a large percentage of men who felt he'd done the right thing, the only thing, but on the street, it was all or nothing. An undercover man's value was his knowledge, his contacts and his confidence in his buddies, the men who covered his back.

He'd been on Drug Squad for almost ten years now, exciting years, good years. He'd forgotten what it was like to wear a uniform. Maybe it was time to remember.

He'd testify against Perchinsky. But he'd also go to the OC—officer in charge—in the morning and request a transfer.

JUST BEFORE MIDNIGHT, Alex sat up in bed and switched on the bedside lamp. She heard Cam come in the front door of the apartment. She'd been waiting for him, needing him.

She listened to the familiar sounds he made, the clunk as he took his shoes off and dropped them by the door, the sound of water running as he washed his hands, the opening and closing of the refrigerator door, the whisper of his stockinged feet coming down the hall toward the bedroom. He stood in the doorway for several minutes, not moving or saying a word.

He'd taken off his jacket. The soft old gray T-shirt clung to his torso, exposing broad shoulders and muscular arms. His gaze was shuttered, as if he didn't really see her at all.

She finally said, "Evening, Sergeant. Come here often?" It was a silly ritual they had.

"Same old crowd." His answer was automatic, with none of the suggestive insinuation he usually managed to instill. Alex had the definite feeling he was thinking hard about something else.

At last he made a visible effort to smile at her, but it didn't quite come off. "You oughta be sleeping, babe." He sounded infinitely weary. He unfastened his leather pouch, removed gun and bullets and laid the gun on the dresser. Then he leaned once again on the door frame, a can of beer in one hand, and flipped the top. "You want some tea or something?"

She shook her head, wondering why he didn't come over and kiss her.

"I stopped in at the hospital. Your folks have gone home but Thea's still there. I sent her off to get something to eat—practically had to march her out at gunpoint, and she was back again in fifteen minutes. Wade's been awake off and on. He's still doing okay, according to the nurse."

Alex sensed the distance in his voice, and just as she had for several weeks now, she felt that he was holding an integral part of himself away from her. Her heart sank. At the hospital earlier, they'd been so close. Why this distance again, just a few short hours later?

"I called Intensive Care myself a while ago," she said. "He's pretty much out of danger now."

She remembered the court case. Maybe that's what was bothering him. "How'd you make out with David, Cam?"

He took a long swallow of beer. "David?"

For a moment, she actually had the feeling that he didn't remember who David even was.

"Oh, yeah, David. Fine. Well, not exactly fine, but at least he didn't pull jail time. Judge Raskins gave him a stern lecture, a five-hundred-dollar fine, a hundred hours of community service, probation."

He fell silent again. She waited and then she added with a note of impatience in her tone, "So? How did Dave react?"

Cam seemed unaware that she was irritated. He shrugged. "Oh, you know, typical Dave. Subdued in court, wisecracks when we got outside. He did indicate he's gonna make a real effort to clean up his act. I only hope he means it this time."

"And did your meeting go okay?" He hadn't said what it was about, and she knew from long experience that he wouldn't tell her if she asked. He'd explained many times why he couldn't, but she still had trouble understanding.

"Yeah." He sighed, blowing his breath out in a long whoosh. "Yeah, it went fine. Brought in a guy we've been looking for, I've been down at headquarters doing the paperwork on him."

Again the taut silence.

Alex hugged her knees beneath the light blanket, aware of exhaustion but unable to give in to it, wanting her husband to climb in beside her and comfort her.

"Are you coming to bed, Cam?" Tonight, of all nights, she needed to be held. She needed his arms, his body, wrapping her in a cocoon of warmth and pseudosafety, so that after a long while she might be able to forget the moment she'd looked down and recognized her brother's face.

But there was that distance in Cameron's voice, a kind of formality that both frightened her and prevented her from asking him to join her.

"I think I'll catch the late news." He walked over and bent to kiss her. He smelled of coffee and secondhand cigarette smoke, the odors she associated with a police office.

It was a perfunctory kiss.

"You get some sleep, love. You've been up a long time, and it was a rotten day."

"Yeah. Yeah, it really was." It wasn't improving, either.

She watched as he turned and walked out of the room. She heard the television go on, the volume muted.

Feeling bereft and angry, telling herself she was just overtired and imagining problems in her marriage where there weren't any, she tossed and turned and finally fell into an uneasy, dream-filled slumber.

She didn't wake completely when at last, sometime near dawn, he slid into bed beside her, but an enormous sense of relief and contentment filled her as his strong arms gathered her in, fitting her, spoon fashion, into the hard, familiar angles of his body.

She slept peacefully then, unaware that he didn't sleep at all.

"HI, WADE. How's it going?" Alex put a gentle hand on his shoulder and flopped into the chair beside his bed. "I've been trying to break loose all day, but it's worse than Bedlam down there. Must be a full moon."

His shoulder was one of the few places she could touch without encountering tubes or bandages or pulleys, and she let her hand rest on the well-defined muscles beneath the hospital gown. "How're you doing, little brother? How're the hands today? Pretty painful, I'll bet."

His room, overflowing with flowers, cards and balloons, was uncharacteristically empty of visitors this late afternoon, and Alex felt a guilty delight in having him to herself for the few moments she could spare from her duties in ER.

"I'm fine. My hands are sore, but the nurses keep me nicely drugged up." The words were slurred. Wade's face was grossly swollen. The reconstructive surgery had begun on his cheekbone, making speech difficult, but he was determinedly cheerful.

Twelve days had passed since his accident. Once Wade's condition had stabilized, he'd been transferred from ICU to the surgical ward on the hospital's fourth floor, and a steady stream of visitors had begun, chiefly rugby players, huge, awkward men clutching fistfuls of magazines, posters, cards, fruit, flowers.

Alex had been on hand when several of them visited the first time. She'd witnessed the shock and outright horror in their eyes when they first saw her brother, flat on his back on the special Stryker frame bed, totally immobilized, his head hooked to the skull tongs.

She gave them credit—they recovered fast, and their constant banter was wickedly funny and guaranteed to prevent any further show of real emotion, but Alex knew that although he couldn't turn his head to witness it, Wade was well aware of that first instinctive reaction. She could only guess what effect it had on him.

The reconstructive surgery on his hands had also begun two days before, and Alex knew from talking to the plastic surgeon, Ben Halsey, that Wade's left hand had suffered irreversible damage—the first and third fingers had been amputated the day after the accident, and it was still questionable that the thumb would ever be usable. Ben had assured Wade, however, that the right hand would be fully functional once the necessary surgery was completed. Ben was also reassuring as to the work he was doing on Wade's face.

"You're gonna be what the fan mags call rugged-looking when we get done," he'd predicted. "Which is pretty much what you were before this happened, am I right? This nose is definitely not the way God intended, and neither is your right ear, and that's not from the accident. So we'll straighten you out once and for all."

Broken noses and damaged ears were trademarks of rugby players, and Wade had worn the marks of his sport with pride.

Now, ironically, they would be eradicated. It would take numerous procedures, but when the surgery was finished, Ben was confident that Wade's face would bear little evidence of the damage it had sustained in either rugby or the accident.

The sight in Wade's left eye was still in doubt, although here, too, the ophthalmologist was optimistic. The dressing would come off in another two days.

Wade knew he'd lost his fingers. He also understood the full extent of his other injuries. Once he'd fully regained consciousness, he'd ordered Thea out of the room and demanded that Alex be brutally honest with him. It had been one of the worst moments of her medical career. In theory, she agreed with a patient's right to know every detail involving his body, but this was her brother. Every protective instinct urged her to avoid telling him the truth, to prevaricate, to soften the facts.

In the final analysis, though, she knew that if the situation was reversed, she'd want the unvarnished truth, just as Wade did. And so, feeling as though she was about to be sick, she quietly listed for him the staggering damage his beautiful young body had sustained, and to the best of her ability, she projected what the outcome of those injuries would likely be.

When there was nothing more for her to say, he'd been still and silent for a long time. "So," he said at last, "let's see if I've got this straight. The worst scenario is, I spend the rest of my life in a wheelchair, a half-blind gimp with limited use of my hands. But I'm gonna look like a real sex symbol doing it, thanks to the inspired work of the best plastic surgeon around."

"But that's not the way it's going to be." Alex was vehement. "I just told you, you've got a good chance at making a full recovery. Nobody can predict these things, and you've already regained some sensation in your legs. You have to concentrate on getting completely well."

He hadn't answered. Instead, he'd asked more difficult questions in an impersonal tone, as though they were discussing a stranger. The bandages half covering his face and the fact that he couldn't move his head made it impossible to read his expression, and when neither of them could think of anything more to say, he'd asked her to leave him alone. She'd refused. He'd insisted and then cursed her viciously, and at length, and when the curses finally became sobs, she'd held him as best she could and wept with him.

Since that time, Wade had said little about his injuries, either to Alex or to Thea, who still spent every spare moment at his bedside, although she wasn't here now.

"Where's Thea this afternoon?"

"She had a shoot." He sounded indifferent. "She'll be here later. She always is."

Alex was endlessly grateful to Thea for being so consistently there for Wade, but it was nice to have a chance to talk to him alone.

"So what's shakin' down in the ER? You said it was busy." The tongs made it impossible for him to move his head, but he rolled his good eye to the side in order to look at her.

"Is it ever busy! Phew! We had two drug overdoses right off the bat, and then they brought this other guy in. He seemed to have OD'd as well, but he had this distinctive smell, and I realized he was in a diabetic coma. I was still dealing with him when a woman staggered through the door and delivered right there on the floor—a good big baby, too, a boy. She said she ate burritos last night and couldn't make up her mind whether she was in labor or just had gas."

Wade laughed, just as she'd hoped he might. "Sounds as if she has as much trouble making decisions as you do, sis."

He'd always teased her about being indecisive, and it delighted her that he was doing it now. "Phooey. I make snap decisions all the time. Doctors have to."

"At work, maybe," Wade persisted. "But when we were kids at home you were hopeless. I remember you changing your clothes fifteen times before you'd leave for school in the morning. It used to drive me nuts, because I had to wait for you."

"Well, clothes, now that's different. I still have a few problems there. But you've got to admit when it comes to the big things, I make up my mind fast enough. Look how quick I got married once I met the right guy."

"I still figure Cam drugged you. Normally it would have taken you till you were forty-something to decide."

It was so good to hear some of Wade's old spark.

"Oh yeah? Well, I've got news for you, little brother. When I know exactly what I want, I move with the speed of light."

"I can't wait to hear Cam's take on that. Where is he, by the way? Don't you guys usually meet for lunch on his days off?"

Alex frowned. "I'm not sure where he's gotten to. I called the apartment, but he wasn't there. He's probably out for a run or something." Actually, she'd tried to call Cam numerous times that morning without success. He'd taken a few days off and he should have been home, but he wasn't. It was silly to feel so bereft just because she couldn't get hold of him when she wanted to, she told herself.

"I'd give a lot to join Cam for a run."

Wade's tone was wistful, and it brought sudden bitter tears to her eyes. His injuries would determine so much of Wade's life from now on. She turned away and pretended to rearrange a bouquet of roses on his bedside table, holding her eyes wide open until the tears dried.

"Dr. Ross to Emergency. Dr. Ross to Emergency." The disembodied voice brought Alex reluctantly to her feet. "Gotta go. See you when I get off shift," she promised. "Anything you need?"

"Nope. What the hell would I need that I don't already have in this five-star joint?" His good eye winked at her, and she bent to kiss his undamaged cheek before she hurried out.

She met Thea by the elevator, noting with amusement the lecherous glances the other woman was attracting from two male interns who stepped off the elevator right behind her. Alex would bet they had no real reason to be on surgical, apart from ogling Thea.

"Is he okay? The damned shoot ran longer than I figured. The photographer was a certifiable idiot." Thea cast an anxious glance down the corridor, in the direction of Wade's door. She was wearing tight, faded jeans and a skimpy red T-shirt, and Alex wondered a little jealously how anyone could look as stylish and outright sensual in such ordinary garb. There seemed to be an aura around Thea that telegraphed a sexual message to every male she encountered.

"He's fine. I just popped in to say hi while there was a quiet moment downstairs, but I'm being paged, so I guess it's over. Gotta run. See you later." She headed for the stairs, knowing they'd be faster than the elevator. As she hurried down the twisting stairwell, she pondered the relationship between her brother and his beautiful model.

She hated to be cynical, but it was more than likely Thea's visits would gradually become less frequent and then cease altogether as time passed. Her brother had been a celebrity of sorts, well-known and adored by millions of foreign fans, and even a fair number here in North America.

Thea had accompanied Wade on some of his tours, and he'd gone along on several of her exotic shoots, to Africa and once to Asia. Now, everything would change for them, and it wasn't going to be easy or fun or romantic at all. Wade was facing months of hospitalization, probably years of rehab, and Alex knew the depressing statistics on relationships in such situations. Very, very few of them survived.

"Statistics be damned," she muttered hotly as she burst through the doors on the main level and ran pell mell down the corridor toward the emergency room, dodging staff and visitors. Statistics didn't mean a thing. What were the stats, for instance, on marriages like her own, a doctor working three shifts and a cop doing the same, with schedules that never seemed to mesh? It had been three weeks now since she and Cam had even had days off together. Apart from the dreadful hours they'd spent when Wade was injured, she'd seen little of her husband recently.

She scowled because she couldn't help but feel that Cam wasn't trying as hard as he could to change that. In the past, they'd done their best to meet for lunch, at least. They'd kept each other posted on their schedules and stolen the odd half hour in which to be together, to share the small and large events of their days. She'd waited for him today, eager to spend even a few moments with him, but Cameron hadn't appeared, and there'd been no phone call, either.

So where the blazes was he?

Feeling a combination of anxiety and mounting annoyance, she burst through the doors and into the familiar chaos of the E R.

CHAPTER FOUR

"CAM? Cameron? You home?"

But Alex knew before she closed the apartment door behind her that he wasn't there. There was an emptiness and a silence to the rooms, apart from the yowling of her huge, cinnamon-colored cat.

Pavarotti did his best to tell her he was glad she was home at last. The distinctive, deep-throated yowl that had inspired his name reverberated throughout the small apartment.

She bent to stroke him as he twined around her ankles.

"Let's get you some food, you noisy old thing." She made her way to the kitchen. The message light on the answering machine blinked imperiously, and she punched the Play button.

Maybe Cam had called. Maybe there'd been an emergency and he'd had to go back to work early. Maybe—

But except for two, the messages were the ones she'd left herself, asking him to call her.

One of the other calls was from her mother, a reminder that the following Thursday was Wade's thirtieth birthday. Eleanor wanted the entire family to gather in his hospital room for a party.

Alex shook her head in exasperation. Eleanor should know by now that Wade hated having a fuss made over his birthday at the best of times—and these were anything but the best of times.

Alex was equally certain Eleanor hadn't asked her son's opinion—as usual, their mother was bulldozing along, doing what *she* wanted, regardless of her family's feelings.

For Wade's sake, Alex would do her best to convince Eleanor the party was a bad idea, but she was almost certain her mother wouldn't pay any attention.

The other call made Alex smile. It was from her mother-in-law, Verna Ross. If there could be an exact opposite to Eleanor, Verna was it, and Alex loved her for it.

"Alex, I've made up some casseroles for you and Cam. I figured you'd be spending every spare minute with your brother at the hospital and wouldn't have much time to cook."

Alex's smile grew wider. Verna was so tactful. She knew perfectly well that cooking was at the bottom of her daughter-in-law's list of priorities, so she regularly found some excuse for keeping the freezer equipped with her delicious vegetarian meals. The two women had had a discussion about it early in Alex's marriage.

"Cooking is something I love to do. It's creative and relaxing for me," Verna had explained in her usual forthright way. "I'd like it if you'd let me stock your freezer once in a while with my own version of TV dinners, but I don't ever want to make you feel as if I'm being an interfering mother-in-law. Would that bother you?"

"Just try me," Alex had told her. "In fact, if I mention it to the crew at work, you'll likely be able to start a good little business. They all talk a lot about how hard it is to get meals on the table."

"So talk away," Verna had said with the childlike enthusiasm that was so endearing. "Boy, I'd love to get something like that going. It would keep me from becoming Vancouver's oldest living waitress." Verna had worked for years at a restaurant renowned for its vegetarian fare. "Just make sure your friends know that if it has a mother or father, I don't cook it."

Alex spread the word at the hospital, and Verna now had a dozen customers who relied on her for healthy, tasty frozen meals.

Alex had loved Verna from the first moment she'd met her. Cameron's mother was an intriguing combination of aging hippie and modern feminist.

"Healing is a wonderful career for women—we're naturals at it. If I'd had the chance, I'd have studied medicine myself," she'd told Alex.

On impulse, Alex picked up the phone and dialed Verna's number.

"Alex, how super to hear from you." Verna always made it sound as if Alex were giving her a gift just by making a simple phone call. "How are you, and how's Wade doing?"

Alex filled Verna in on Wade's condition, adding, "It's such a relief to know he's going to live, but now there's the awful knowledge that he could be handicapped, that he might never walk again."

"Don't think about it that way, Alex." Verna's rich, warm voice was reassuring. "There's just as great a possibility that he'll regain all his strength with time. Think positive. I'm sure it's going to take a while, with lots of patience and perseverance on his part, but he'll come through with flying colors, you wait and see."

"God, I certainly hope you're right, Verna. I'll tell Wade exactly what you said the next time I see him." It was impossible not to be affected by Verna's optimism.

"If Cameron's there, could I speak to him for a moment, Alex? There's something wrong with my video machine. I accidentally pulled the wires out at the back, and now I can't figure out how they go." It was a standing joke in the Ross family that the boys' mechanical ability hadn't come from their mother.

"Sorry, Verna, he's not here just now. He's supposed to be on days off, so I thought he'd be home when I got here, but there's no sign of him."

"Probably has his head stuck in the motor of some machine somewhere, trying to figure out why it's not making the proper sounds. When they were teenagers, that's where both he and David always were when I needed them, up to their eyeballs in grease."

They laughed, and Alex promised to have Cam call as soon as he came home. She made arrangements to pick up the frozen meals on her way home from work the next afternoon. "I'd better go. Pavarotti is howling because he hasn't had his dinner." Alex turned to the cat. "Pavarotti, for heaven's sake, put a sock in it, okay? I can't hear with you doing that."

"I can sure hear him," Verna said. "I sometimes wonder where that awful voice came from. Give him my regards." Verna had found Pavarotti abandoned in the alley behind her apartment and given him to Alex the previous Christmas, a small, warm puff of fur with a voice that should have belonged to a lion. "I'd keep him myself," she'd said, "but it's such an awful cliché, a single woman my age with a cat."

Alex hung up the phone, opened a tin of cat food and put the kettle on, noting that the coffeemaker hadn't been used. Cam always made coffee, first thing. Where on earth was he?

She made tea and poured herself a cup, flicking on the television, then turning it off, putting on a CD and then pushing the Reject button, opening the vertical blinds and staring sightlessly out at the busy street below as she thought about her husband.

There was something wrong with Cameron. There had been for days—weeks? Weeks, she conceded. And whatever it was, he wasn't prepared to share it with his wife. That irritated her.

Granted, Wade had been the center of her concerns ever since the accident, and during those first few bad days, she just couldn't have handled any more stress. But this past week, things had stabilized. Surely Cam could have found an opportunity to talk to her about whatever it was that was on his mind.

It hurt, knowing that he wouldn't confide in her. She finished her tea and thought about making dinner. She hadn't eaten since noon, and it was now almost eight at night. Again, she wondered where Cam was. It wouldn't have killed him to thaw something out and have it ready, she thought peevishly.

She was standing staring into the refrigerator when she heard his key in the lock. Relief and irritation in equal measure coursed through her, but she plastered a wide, welcoming smile on her face and met him in the hallway. "Hello, love. I was beginning to wonder where you were."

Understatement of the century.

He returned her hug, but he didn't kiss her.

"I went to a movie. I guess I lost track of time."

A movie? Alex frowned at him. "I've never known you to go to a movie alone." She tried for a teasing tone. "Whatever happened to, 'It'll come out on video, and we can watch it right here in the living room'?" Realizing she was sounding accusatory, she tried for a smile. "So, what did you see? Anything interesting?"

He shrugged. "Some duster. I don't even remember the title."

He didn't remember? She hadn't a clue what was going on, and he sure wasn't helping her understand. Alex did her best to hold on to her temper. "I tried to reach you today, lots of times, Cam. When I couldn't get you, I got a bit worried. It's not like you to disappear on your days off. You must have left right after I did this morning—I called as soon as I got to work."

"Yeah, I did go out early. I went for a jog."

"I guess you didn't check for messages when you got back, then? I left half a dozen." She was doing her level best to stay reasonable, but it was getting more difficult by the second.

"I didn't get them because I didn't come back here. I went for a jog, and I was gone all day."

She gaped at him, and astonishment took the place of irritation. "You went for a jog this morning and didn't come back all day? What the heck did you do, join a twelve-hour marathon and then go to a movie to cool down?" Her voice was shrill. It was getting harder and harder to remain in control.

He shook his head. "Nope. I ended up at the rec center and played handball with some guy. I showered there, grabbed a burger, went for a walk and wandered into that movie. Time sort of got away on me." He shrugged and gave her a facsimile of a smile, moving past her down the hall to the bathroom. In a few moments he came out again. He went to the kitchen and opened the fridge, extracting a can of beer. He popped the top and drank.

Alex watched and waited. Surely he'd explain everything in a moment. He moved into the living room and she followed. He didn't sit down as he clicked on the television and flicked through the channels, up and down, up again.

His voice was distracted when he finally spoke. "How'd your day go, honey? How's Wade?"

She could feel the tension building inside her. "Wade's okay, I guess. As okay as it's possible to be in his condition." She snatched the remote Cam was still holding and turned the set off. She'd had about all she intended to take.

"That's it, Cameron, I'm running out of patience here. Now will you tell me, for pity's sake, what the *hell* is going on with you?" Exasperation and anger made Alex's voice tremble, and she scowled up at him. "Just what *is* this nonsense, anyhow? Since when is it perfectly natural for you to go for a jog at seven in the morning and not get back until eight at night?" Her voice rose and wobbled a little. "You could at least have called, left me a message, told me not to expect you for lunch. We always have lunch together when you're off, you know we do! I got worried about you, don't you see that?"

She was running out of steam. She'd never been able to stay angry long. Her tone was softer, more temperative, as she added, "I really wanted to be with you today, Cameron. It's just not fair to disappear on me like that."

He blew out a breath and lowered his long frame into an armchair. "I'm really sorry, love. I don't plan to be a jerk, it just comes naturally sometimes. Like I said, I forgot about the time. I didn't mean to worry you." He set the can of beer on the table beside him. "I've had a lot on my mind lately, work stuff." He leaned forward, reached out a hand and snared her wrist. "C'mere, Doc, come and talk to me now." He drew her down to his lap, enfolding her in his arms, holding her stiff body tight against him, stroking her hair.

She struggled for a moment, but slowly the last remnants of her anger seeped away and she relaxed. His warmth and strength worked like a tranquilizer. She pressed her nose into his neck, breathing in the familiar essence of his skin, soap and sweat and the good male smell that was peculiarly Cameron.

He trailed his lips along her jawbone, and his strong fingers searched out and found the painful knots in the muscles of her back, remnants of tension from the multiple car crash victims she'd worked over during the last few hours of her shift.

"Tough day at the office?" His deep voice tickled her ear and she shivered.

"Mmm. Same old gory stuff."

His hand cupped her chin, tilting her mouth up. He kissed her, tenderly at first and then with increasing intensity. His hand slid under her blouse, cradling her breast, his thumbnail flicking across the nipple and starting a familiar ache deep in her groin.

She could feel his erection pressing against her bottom, and as always, knowing how much he wanted her acted like a spark on gasoline. Need welled up inside her, impatient need that demanded fulfillment.

"Love me, Cam." It had been too long. Her whisper was choked and breathless. "Make love to me? Please, now."

"My pleasure, madam." He made a sound deep in his throat, an animal growl of approval. He kissed her throat and then captured her lips again, his mouth hungry.

His clever long fingers undid the buttons of her blouse and slid it off her shoulders. He unhooked the fastening of her white lace bra, cupping each bare breast and using his tongue to stroke the sensitive tips until she gasped and writhed with the tension building within her.

She arched against him and tugged at his T-shirt, struggling to draw it up and over his head. At last, his hair-roughened skin was bare to her touch. Greedy, she stroked him, kissed him, bending her head to taste his saltiness, teasing his male nipples with gentle nips and tugs of teeth and lips. Her fingers reached to the back of his neck, expertly untying the lace that held his hair back. She buried her fingers in the silky mass, drawing it loose around his skull.

"My beautiful woman." His voice was uneven, labored. "I need you, Alex, more than you know."

Urgency deepened. His heart hammered against her cheek and a pulse deep in her abdomen matched its rhythm, beat for beat. She squirmed on his lap, aching for him, and their mouths met in a blind, frenzied kiss.

"Hang on to my neck."

She clung, and he tumbled them down to the carpet, skimming off her cotton slacks and bikini panties, efficiently ridding himself of shorts and jock strap. Their naked bodies were sheened with sweat, and lust and anticipation heightened.

He knelt over her, his face intense, running his hands slowly down her body, exploring every inch, and she thought he looked like some wild pirate from another time, lean and brown and hungry, his long, thick midnight hair framing his dark, dangerous face.

"The only thing that makes any sense is this, my darling." The words were passionate, almost angry. "The rest of it doesn't matter a damn."

She had no idea what he meant. She wanted to ask, but he bent over her, touching her with his hands and tongue until she arched and cried out, reaching up shakily to pull him down, wordlessly begging him to enter her.

He did at last, excruciatingly slowly, his face beaded with sweat, his strong arms trembling with the effort it cost him to hold back, to tease, to entice, to lead the way.

Sensation rose from her toes and arrowed down from her breasts, joining at the apex of her thighs and growing until the last remnant of her reason was gone and nothing but urgency and primeval instinct remained.

He knew her so well. He knew the exact moment when she poised at the brink, wordless, her eyes wide, silently begging him to join her, unable even to speak with the delirious craving that racked her.

And at that precise moment, he abandoned control. Untamed, frenzied, he drove deep, and she rose to meet him until the pleasure became unbearable and waves of sensation undulated through her. She cried out, and the sound filled the room, followed in an instant by his own guttural song of ecstasy.

Gasping for breath, he collapsed beside her, their damp bodies still joined. Slowly, their breathing became normal again. He rubbed his forehead against hers and kissed her tenderly, passionless and spent.

"How I love you, Alexandra Ross." He usually joked at a time like this, but this time his voice was somber.

"I love you, too, Cameron Ross." She sighed, long and deep and blissful. "But I also love food, and right about now I'm starving."

"Greedy woman." He kissed her shoulder and she wrapped herself a little tighter around him. "If you could wait just a couple of minutes, maybe I could take your mind off food."

"Not a chance," she declared, but for a while they lay in the twilight on the rug. Alex imagined that happiness rose from them like steam and filled the room, shadowy now in the growing dusk.

Eventually her stomach rumbled, reminding her again that she hadn't eaten. "Aren't you hungry at all, Cam?"

His eyes were shut, and he rolled his head from side to side, pretending to imprison her even tighter in his arms. She wriggled away and knelt beside him.

"C'mon, lazybones. You can help me microwave a couple of those frozen dinners your mom makes. I talked to her tonight, just before you got home. She's making us a whole new batch, and you're supposed to call her. There's something wrong with her video and she needs your advice. Get up and I'll tell you all about my harrowing day. Then you get to tell me what's going on that has you acting so weird, okay?"

His face tightened, and a flicker of anxiety went through her. "Is it just something at work, Cam? Or—or is it something else, something—some problem between us? That I'm not aware of?"

He opened his eyes and looked up at her. In one lithe movement, he sat up, reaching for his shorts. He got to his feet and tugged them on.

"It's not us," he said with vehemence. "It's work. I've meant to talk to you before this, but the time never seemed right." His voice was suddenly edgy, and it made Alex uneasy for some strange reason. She tugged her panties on and stood up again, facing him.

He was staring past her with an expression in his eyes she couldn't interpret. He looked tired and older. There were lines on his forehead, weariness and a kind of desperation in his eyes that she hadn't noticed before, and something tightened in her chest.

"Cam? Cameron, what on earth is it?" She knew she sounded nervous, unsure of herself again. "Just tell me and we can talk it over. It can't be that bad."

He seemed to come back from a distant place. He looked at her and his brown eyes were shuttered, his face grim. His voice was low and even. "I'm afraid it is that bad." The muscles around his mouth tightened. "Alex, I've asked for a transfer out of Drug Squad. I've accepted a posting to Korbin Lake, that little coal-mining town in the East Kootenays. I'll be back in uniform, the senior officer in a two-man detachment, and I start work there July second." She looked at him, certain he was joking.

He had to be joking, didn't he?

CHAPTER FIVE

FOR AN INSTANT, Alex clung to the desperate hope that he was kidding, but when she met his eyes and saw the bleakness there, she knew he wasn't. For a long moment, she simply stared at him, her heart thudding inside her chest. Her mouth felt parched, and it was difficult to form words.

"You—you asked for a transfer? With—without even, even telling me?" Her voice was shaking. "How could you do a thing like that, Cam?" She stared at him. He looked the same, but she suddenly felt as if he were a stranger. It struck her that she was naked except for her panties, and she suddenly needed the protection of clothing. She snatched up her blouse and thrust her arms into the sleeves, grabbed her slacks and yanked them on, her mind grappling with this bombshell.

He watched her in silence. The angles of his face hardened, his expression became still more remote and several more charged moments passed before he answered. His words were clipped, his tone without inflection.

"You met Perchinsky at the Christmas party, remember?"

She frowned and dredged up an image of a loud, insensitive man she'd disliked intensely. *Cam's boss.* She nodded, wondering what the connection was.

"Well, Perchinsky's been an addict for well over a year, stealing from the exhibit locker to satisfy his habit."

Alex was surprised and shocked, but she knew such things happened. She knew of too many doctors who'd succumbed to the lure of drugs. She waited expectantly for Cam to go on.

"A situation came up, he shot off his mouth to a reporter and he put one of my guys in jeopardy. I blew the whistle on him. Last Monday I testified at orderly room proceedings. Perchinsky was discharged and he's facing jail time. Anyway, my coming forward changed everything, and now I can't stay on Drug Squad. I have to get out, get far away."

She shook her head, frowning in confusion. "But I don't understand, Cam. You did the right thing, why should you have to leave? You love your job. You've always said you thrive on the challenge."

"Yeah, well, that's all changed now."

She waited expectantly for him to go on, but he didn't.

"That's it?" Her voice squeaked into the upper registers and she made an effort to control it. "Perchinsky turns into an addict, and because you do something about it, you have to give up your job?"

"Turning in a fellow member isn't the way to win a popularity contest in the force, Alex."

"But I still don't get this, Cam. You went through the whole thing without saying a word to me. You—you applied for a posting to some town I've barely heard of. You start work there the second of July, and you only get around to mentioning it now?" Her head felt as though it were swelling. She felt worse and worse as all the ramifications sunk in. "This is— My God, Cam, it's already the middle of June. You'll be leaving in—in what, a week? Two?"

He nodded. "I put the request in a couple of weeks ago, but I just found out this morning that my transfer came through."

And she hadn't even known he'd asked for one. A new, inconceivable thought came to her. "Were you—are you—planning to . . . to—just leave me, Cameron? Walk out on our marriage?" The emptiness in her stomach extended into her chest, and an awful abyss yawned before her.

From the moment they'd met, she'd known she wanted to spend her life with this man. He'd said it was the same with him. God, had that changed when she wasn't looking? Had she been so self-absorbed she'd missed all the warning signs?

"Is that it, Cam? I—I know things have been less than ideal lately. We're both so busy—" Her voice quavered, and he swore viciously. He moved toward her and caught her in his arms, a brutal embrace that was like balm to her soul.

"I'd never, never do that." His voice was raw and shaking. "You must know I'd never leave you. How can you even think that? You're my wife! I love you with all my heart, Alex."

For an instant, it was enough. But then the other words he'd said came back to her, and she stiffened in his embrace, icy cold, unbending. "But you've taken this other job, without even asking me. And that affects my job as well as our life together."

His voice was harsh again. "I explained why. My reasons for that have nothing to do with you and I."

She pulled away enough to look up into his face. "But—but they have *everything* to do with us, Cameron. If I want to live with you, I'll have to move to this—this place, this Korbin Lake."

She felt him draw in a breath. "I'm afraid so. I'm really sorry, Alex. What more can I say? I know it's unfair." She could feel the sigh shudder through him. She could still smell the musk of their loving on his skin.

The muscles in his arms were locked tight against her sides and back. She was pressed hard against his chest. His shoulder bore the scar of her scalpel, and she knew without looking exactly how many moles he had on his back and what the nape of his neck looked like under his clump of silky hair.

She'd thought she knew him, inside as well as out, but obviously she'd been wrong.

"I can't turn the clock back and undo what's been done." He sounded as if his throat were raw, and the words hurt him. "All I can tell you is that I love you and I want you with me."

She started to shiver, even though it was warm in the room. She pushed against his arms until he released her. She stepped back and gave him a level look, and this time her voice was steady. "You love me, but not enough to discuss a major decision with me, a move away from Vancouver, a transfer that means I'll have to leave my job and my family. With Wade the way he is—"

It felt as if a stone was lodged just behind her breastbone. Her voice dropped to a whisper. "How could you do this without even asking me?"

His shoulders lifted and dropped. His eyes gave nothing away. "I apologize. I should have told you, but I didn't. I can't change this. I can't reverse my decision now."

"Can't?" She drew in a shaky breath and released it. "Or won't? Cameron?

"What's the difference, for God's sake?" For the first time, his temper flared, but in an instant all traces of it were gone. Part of her marveled, as always, at his extreme self-control.

"The transfer's been approved, I have to go. I explained to you a long time ago that the RCMP moves its members around, that there was always a chance that we'd have to move out of the lower mainland. You said you understood that. You seemed to accept it."

She shook her head. "C'mon, Cameron. Being transferred is one thing. Asking to be transferred is another."

He nodded, and again he was silent.

She put every ounce of entreaty she could muster into her voice, into her expression. "Can't you change your mind, Cam? Can't you go to your OC or—or CO, or whoever, and just tell them we need to stay here? Surely they'd understand if you explained about Wade. Please, Cam?"

But he shook his head slowly. "I can't." Beneath the tan, his face was chalky, and now she could see the lines of strain, the tautness of the muscles around his narrow mouth, the weariness in his eyes. He looked older, as if he hadn't been sleeping or eating well, and she felt a quick stab of guilt.

Was this new, or had he looked like this for weeks and she just hadn't noticed? Her every waking thought for so long now had been for and about Wade. She hadn't really paid much attention at all to Cameron. Her emotions hopelessly tangled, she asked, "Exactly how long ago did you ask for a transfer?" She knew nothing happened overnight.

He shrugged. "Like I told you, a couple of weeks. Around the time Wade got hurt." He made a sad attempt at a smile. "I'm truly sorry, Alex, if that means anything. I seem to remember something about better and worse when we got married. I guess this is definitely worse." His deep brown gaze met and held hers, and now there was fear there, stark and open. "So what do you think you'll do? Will you come with me, Alex?"

It was totally unfair. It was outrageous of him to expect her to quit her job, abandon her injured brother, leave her friends and family, pack up everything she owned and follow him to some hole-in-the-wall place when he wouldn't even explain why it was necessary. She told herself she really wasn't sure what she'd decide to do. It gave her an illusion of control to pretend she had any choice.

"I don't know, Cam. It's a major decision. There's my career to consider. I'll have to think about it." She was terribly hurt. She felt betrayed. She wanted in some childish fashion to hurt him as much as she'd been hurt, to make him suffer the way she was suffering at this moment.

FOR THE NEXT FEW DAYS, Alex felt as if she were split in half. One part of her went about her usual routine at work, doing her job, gossiping with her co-workers, dealing with her family, acting as if nothing had changed.

The other part went over and over the scene with Cameron, reviewing each little detail, every single word he'd said, searching for the part she must have missed. There had to be more to their conversation than she remembered. He must have explained it more clearly than she thought.

Twice, she tried to talk to him about it. Both times he repeated what he'd already said. He loved her, he wanted her with him, but he couldn't change his decision. He was going and that was that.

Thursday came, Wade's birthday. He'd insisted he didn't want this fuss made over his birthday, and Alex had relayed the message to her mother, but Eleanor was adamant. She had this thing about family birthdays, she repeated, and this birthday in particular should be celebrated—after all, she'd said, her eyes filling up with tears, she'd come so close to losing her baby. There was so much to celebrate.

"But maybe Wade doesn't feel that way, Mom," Alex had persisted. As usual, her mother overrode her.

For a psychotherapist in high demand for her ability to solve other people's problems, Alex often marveled at how blind Eleanor was to the real needs of her own family.

The party was to begin at five o'clock. Alex was on afternoon shift, and a man with a severe gunshot wound was admitted at 4:37, so she was half an hour late by the time she hurried off the elevator on Wade's floor. She could hear loud voices and laughter coming from her brother's room, and when she rounded a corner she saw that Cameron was lounging against the wall outside Wade's door.

He straightened when he saw her, and she noted that he'd dressed for this occasion. He was heart-stoppingly handsome, wearing tailored gray slacks and a patterned gray silk shirt she'd bought him. It was obvious he'd been waiting for her.

"Wow, look at you. I'm feeling seriously underdressed here." She'd taken off her lab coat, but the simple shirtwaist she'd worn beneath had gotten stained and crumpled during the hectic morning.

"You're gorgeous, Alex." He fell into step beside her and their eyes met, but he didn't automatically take her hand the way he always had. The strain of the past few days was a huge wall between them.

In Wade's room, Eleanor had strung ribbons from the light fixture, and there were dozens of helium balloons floating near the ceiling. An immense square cake on a tea trolley stood near the bed, and a stack of gaily wrapped gifts were heaped on a table.

Alex's parents and Thea were grouped around Wade's bed, holding glasses of champagne. There was music, Wade's favorite recording of Rod Stewart, coming from a portable stereo.

Alex looked at her brother. He lay unmoving at the epicenter of the scene, and he wasn't smiling. Alex wished again she'd been able to convince her mother this party wasn't a good idea.

"Well, here she is at last. Hello there, dear." Eleanor came over and kissed Alex's cheek. Perfectly groomed, wearing a flame-colored silk tunic with matching slacks, she was petite, slender, very blond, very beautiful, and as usual, Alex felt large, awkward and dowdy beside her.

Eleanor looked years younger than fifty-nine, and she never tired of having everyone tell her so. She was delighted that people often thought she was Alex's sister instead of her mother, and she never seemed to realize how uncomfortable that made her daughter feel.

"Hi, Mom. Sorry I'm late. Hello, Dad." She held up a cheek for a perfunctory kiss. Bruce Keenan was tall and distinguished-looking, with a thick head of silver hair and tanned skin. As always at family gatherings, he stayed in the background, letting Eleanor run the show. Her father's docility in domestic situations always amazed Alex, because Doctor Keenan had earned a well-deserved reputation as a tyrant amongst the staff at St. Joe's before he'd retired.

"Hiya, Thea." Alex smiled warmly and gave the other woman a quick hug as she slid past to her brother's bedside, bending to kiss him. "Happy birthday, kid."

"Yeah. Thanks." Wade's voice was tense, but Eleanor joined them, oblivious to his despondency.

"I suppose you can't have champagne, dear? You have to go back to work?" Eleanor was handing Cameron a stemmed glassful, and she raised a well-plucked eyebrow at Alex.

"Yup, I sure do, and I can't head back down there smelling like a souse."

"You'll have a glass, though, won't you, Cameron? Are you on days off? I can't keep track of you two. Your schedules are so confusing. I suppose as usual you'll start back just when Alex gets *her* days off?"

Cam didn't reply, and it seemed that everyone stopped talking at that exact moment. To Alex, the silence stretched on and on. Cameron was looking at her instead of at Eleanor, and Alex suddenly couldn't bear the strain any longer.

"Actually, Cam and I have something to tell you all." Her voice was too loud, falsely cheerful. Her hands curled into fists at her sides, and she tried to draw a deep breath, but found that her chest felt paralyzed.

Her eyes fixed on the unbandaged portion of Wade's face. He couldn't look at her, she knew that, and yet at this instant she longed for the comfort of his glance. But he was staring expressionlessly up at the ceiling, and his indifference somehow made it harder for her to say what had to be said.

"We're moving," she blurted out in a phony, chirpy voice that appalled her. "It's all quite sudden. Cam's been transferred to the town of Korbin Lake, in the East

Kootenays. He's leaving next weekend, and I'll follow as soon as I can."

Again, there was silence, this time a charged, breathless silence.

"What's going on, sis? You didn't say anything about moving." Wade's voice was puzzled. She wished she'd found a moment to prepare him for this, but she just hadn't been able to talk about it. The hurt and confusion were too new, too raw.

She looked from Wade to her father. Bruce was staring at her, his brow furrowed, his displeasure evident. It wasn't the fact of her leaving Vancouver that would bother him most, Alex knew. It was leaving St. Joe's that he'd see as a monumental betrayal—he'd spent most of his career here, and he'd always made it plain he wanted her to do so as well.

"Korbin Lake?" Eleanor recovered first, and she made the name sound preposterous. "Korbin Lake, for heaven's sake, Alex. Isn't that some godforsaken little coalmining town up in the Rockies? Why on earth would anyone go to Korbin Lake?" She was frowning, building steam. "Cameron, didn't you say that being on the drug squad at least guaranteed that you'd stay in Vancouver?"

"I'm not on Drug Squad anymore, Eleanor. I'll be in uniform again. It's time for a change." Cam sounded easy and relaxed, and Alex could only admire his acting ability.

"Is there even a hospital in Korbin Lake, Alexandra? Will you be going into private practice there? Have you already given notice here at St. Joe's?" Bruce's questions were rapid-fire. He set his glass down and studied his daughter, disapproval evident in his stern expression.

"We only found out ourselves about the move, so I haven't looked into anything yet, Dad." Her father could still make her feel like an irresponsible child—a child who was a disappointment to him, no matter how hard she tried. "I'll be handing in my resignation tomorrow." Alex was aware that Cameron had moved to her side, and his physical presence was comforting, because now her mother took over the interrogation, her tone deceptively warm and affectionate.

"Surely you must have had some forewarning of this, Cameron? It would have made it easier on all of us if you'd mentioned that moving was a possibility, dear." Gently spoken, but the reprimand was clear. "You'll have to forgive us for being distressed by this. We've all been under enormous strain lately. It does lower one's ability to cope with change. Perhaps you should have explained the circumstances to management, Cameron? Even an organization as—" she waved a hand as if searching for a word "—as antediluvian as the RCMP must have allowances for family crisis?"

Alex knew her mother was seething, in spite of her calm, reasonable tone. It showed in the glitter in Eleanor's hazel eyes, the set of her carefully made-up mouth, the way the tendons stood out in her neck.

Cameron knew it, too. He took Alex's icy hand in his, sliding his fingers between hers and cupping their palms, squeezing reassuringly. "Ideally, that would work. In this particular instance, it wasn't an option." His tone made it plain he wasn't about to elaborate.

Thea had been silent until now, sitting close to Wade, one graceful, beringed hand always touching him. "It's sort of exciting, though, isn't it?" Her husky voice was like a deep-toned bell in the strained silence. She shook her mane of hair back over her shoulders. "Making a new start in a strange place is an adventure. And I've always thought Drug Squad wouldn't be the most pleasant place to work.''

Bruce and Eleanor both turned to glare at her, outrage evident on their faces. Alex knew they considered Thea an outsider who had no business voicing an opinion when it came to family business.

''That's certainly a commendable way of looking at it, Thea,'' Eleanor said, making it sound as though she were addressing a child who required humoring. ''However, I would suppose Alex feels as I do—that her place, at least for the time being, ought to be here with her brother.''

''Bull.'' For the first time, Wade sounded the way he always had, strong and decisive . . . and furious. ''That's utter bull, Mom, so can it, okay?''

Eleanor gasped and moved closer to the bed.

''Wade, you mustn't let yourself become agitated.'' She reached out a restraining hand and put it on his arm, but he shook it off.

''You're not going to use what's happened to me as a tool to help you make Alex feel rotten, Mom, so forget it. The truth is, I'm sick of having all of you hovering over me anyway. It's about time you got on with your own lives and let me alone for a while.'' He was breathing hard, and the visible portion of his face was scarlet. ''Thea's right. This is a good move for Cam and Alex. He's been chasing drugged-up maniacs long enough, and Alex needs a break from the ER.''

He coughed and recovered, his voice husky now. ''Lay off them, Mom. And lay off me, too. Get these stupid bloody balloons and that cake and stuff out of here. I always hated birthday parties, and being trapped flat on my back doesn't change that.'' His voice became still more agitated. ''I need some privacy, I'm sick of having you all hanging around me all the time like this. I need to be by myself. I need to get out of this damn bed—''

He reached up with his bandaged hands and tried to grip the tongs attached to his head, struggling to free himself.

Eleanor screamed, and Bruce and Cameron moved swiftly to restrain Wade's arms. A dreadful, forlorn cry escaped from his throat, and after a moment of struggling, he collapsed and began to cough, deep, shuddering coughs that racked his body.

"Damn it! Trapped. I'm trapped!" he gasped, teeth gritted against the pain. It was evident that the outburst had taken all his energy. He was panting, and there was a sheen of sweat on his skin. He was also having trouble breathing.

Alex moved swiftly, pushing the button to summon the nurse, hurrying everyone out of the room. Bruce refused to go, and there was chaos at first as nurses hurried in and he issued peremptory orders. Following Alex's lead, however, they quietly ignored Bruce and worked around him, clearing Wade's breathing passages and administering the pain medication ordered by Wade's own doctor. When he realized no one was paying the slightest attention to him, Bruce finally stormed out the door.

In a few moments Wade was quiet once again. Alex smoothed a hand down her brother's cheek. "You okay now, kid?"

His good eye was trickling tears, and she wiped it with a swab.

"No," he said softly. "I don't really think I'll ever be okay again."

The quiet words seemed to lacerate Alex's heart.

"You will be, though. You just have to be patient."

"I'm running on empty as far as patience goes." His eye was shut now, and he was lying absolutely still. The medication was taking effect. His words were slow and slurred, but there was no doubt as to their sincerity. "I meant what I said, Alex. I don't want anybody around, not Mom, not Dad, not Thea, either. Tell them all not to come back in here tonight, and when my doctor turns up I'm gonna beg him to put me in solitary confinement. A note on the door, an order at the desk, whatever it takes. Absolutely no visitors. He can claim I have the bubonic plague or something else contagious. Anything."

"That apply to me as well?" Alex kept her voice light. She felt terribly responsible for the scene that had just occurred, and she longed to apologize, but she knew it wasn't the time.

"Yeah, it does." He sighed. "Why the hell didn't you just let me die, Alex? Why did you have to save me? It sure as hell wasn't any favor to me." His tone was ironic, his voice infinitely weary, and she felt as if he were tearing out her heart.

"I need to do some heavy thinking. All on my own. Surely I deserve privacy. God knows there's not much else I can have."

Tears prickled behind her eyes, and she had to clear her throat before she could speak. "You got it. I'll talk to your doctor if you like. I saw him downstairs a while ago, and the nurses put in a call for him to drop by just now, but I'll probably see him before you do."

"Yeah. Please." His words were barely discernible, his good eye still closed. "Do that for me, sis, okay?" His voice faded and his breathing regulated. He'd fallen asleep.

Alex wrapped her arms around herself, shaking with the impact of Wade's words. She had to get control of herself. She had to get back to work. She had to carry out her brother's wishes. Steeling herself not just from her own pain, but also against the inevitable outrage and hurt of her family, she hurried along the corridor to the visitors' lounge.

The resulting scene with Eleanor and Bruce was terrible, every bit as bad as she'd anticipated. Hearing that Wade didn't want to see them, not now, and not in the days ahead, shocked and angered them. Alex listened patiently to their comments, telling herself this was painful and hard for them to accept, that they were hurting the way she was herself.

Eleanor insisted Wade needed therapy instead of privacy. Bruce, furious that Wade was behaving in a way he considered reprehensible for a son of his, finally took his wife's arm and marched her off, insisting he'd find Wade's doctor, Mike Parsons, and have a word with him.

Thea didn't say anything at all. Her emerald eyes widened and darkened with hurt when Alex quietly related Wade's wishes, and then she shrugged, nodded, shouldered her leather backpack and strode off down the hallway in the direction of the stairs.

Cam had been sitting apart from the rest of them, and he got to his feet when everyone was gone, putting an arm across Alex's shoulders.

"God, I'm sorry about all that," he said quietly. "I sure as hell didn't intend to start a riot."

"You didn't start it, I did." Alex felt bone-weary and totally exhausted, and she had another four hours of work before she was done for the day. And in spite of her words, she realized that she felt deeply and irrationally angry with Cam.

She shrugged off his arm and moved away. "They had to know sooner or later about the move, but I should've waited, instead of getting Wade involved in a family brawl,'' she snapped. ''That's about the last thing he needed right now. No wonder he's decided he doesn't want any of us around.'' She swiped at the sudden tears that trickled down her cheeks and added fervently, ''I don't blame him one bit. My parents are enough to make anybody crazy. Why can't they consider Wade for once, instead of themselves?''

Cameron stood beside her, but he didn't touch her again, and she was glad. She didn't want his arms around her right now, she thought rebelliously. She didn't even want to be around him until she cooled down a little.

''I've got to get back to work. See you later, Cam.''

Her voice was brittle. She didn't kiss him or suggest he accompany her back to the ER, the way she normally would have done. She wasn't certain she could contain the pent-up anger and sense of betrayal that had simmered inside her ever since he'd told her of the transfer. She was afraid if she was with him alone right now, she'd explode. She'd say things that would damage their relationship even more than it was damaged already.

He spoke to her as she hurried away, but she didn't turn around.

CHAPTER SIX

CAMERON WATCHED her walk away.

"I'll be home when you get there, Alex," he called after her, but she didn't indicate she'd even heard him.

He swore viciously, earning a reproving glare from a heavyset woman walking slowly down the hall dragging her IV pole.

Cam glared right back, too frustrated for social niceties. He knew by Alex's body language, by the expression in her eyes, that she was deeply angry with him. Her lovely face was an open book. Every emotion showed clearly on her mobile features. He'd often teased her about it, saying that she'd missed her calling. She should have been an actress—she'd sure never have made it as a poker player.

He blew out an exasperated breath and tossed the paper cup with its dregs of awful coffee into the garbage, aware that his hand was trembling slightly. Until he'd heard her tell her family she was moving with him, he'd resigned himself to the possibility that Alex might let him go to Korbin Lake alone. In spite of their differences, her ties to her family were strong, and her sense of duty to them powerful.

Her announcement at the party had made him half sick with relief. The alternative would have meant the end of their marriage. Hell, they had to struggle now to snatch a few hours together. How would they ever get together living at opposite ends of the province?

He sank into a flimsy orange plastic chair and let his head flop forward on his chest. He was such a damn failure when it came right down to it. He'd messed up his career and he felt as if he'd deserted the young guys he was responsible for, guys who relied on him. Sure, they'd be assigned another trainer, but who knew whether his replacement would be an all-right guy or an idiot?

Cameron shuddered. For the first time in his life he was choosing to run away from a situation rather than stand and fight. Somehow, he'd learn to live with that. He'd go to Korbin Lake and do his job the best way he knew how, and sooner or later, if he was lucky, the nightmares would go away and this tight, nagging ache in his chest would ease. The thing he'd been most afraid of, the thing he couldn't have lived with, was losing Alex. On impulse, he pulled his wallet out and flipped it open to a favorite snapshot of her, one he'd taken last summer.

She was sitting on a log at the beach, wearing shorts and a halter top, her arms balanced on the log, her long, shapely legs stretched out, bare toes digging into the warm sand. She was grinning at him, a roguish, sexy grin. Her nose was sunburned, her curly hair a golden nimbus around her delicate, expressive face. She'd had a navy bikini on under her clothes, and he'd marveled that day at the lushness and lithe strength of her body as she tumbled playfully with him in the waves.

He was so proud of his wife, of her beauty, of her efficiency and compassion as a doctor. He loved her so much. He shook his head, and his mouth twisted in a parody of a grin as he remembered how she'd stood just an hour ago in front of her family, hurting and furious with him, but loyal as could be, sticking her chin out and acting as if everything were just great between the two of them.

He didn't deserve her. He didn't have much use for Eleanor Keenan, but she was right about one thing—he, Cameron Ross, wasn't half-good enough for her daughter.

He tucked the wallet back into his hip pocket, and the steely control he maintained on his emotions slipped a little more, horrifying him. Tears burned at the back of his eyelids, and he clenched his fists and fought them away.

He'd make it up to his wife. He had no idea how, but he'd do his damnedest to make it up to her. Not now, though. There was nothing he could think of to do right now to ease away her anger. It would have to run its course, and if it made his life tough for the next while, well, he richly deserved that, didn't he?

He had ten days before he left, ten days to make some sort of peace with Alex, and he'd do his best to accomplish that.

Making peace with himself was another story altogether.

NINE OF THOSE ten days passed in a flurry of things to be done. The day before he was to leave, Cameron's mother invited him and Alex over for a farewell family dinner.

"More lasagna, Alex?" Verna didn't bother asking Cameron or David if they wanted more—she simply ladled generous second helpings onto their plates.

Alex shook her head. "Thanks, but I can't eat another bite."

"There's chocolate cheesecake for dessert. Make sure you save some room for that." Verna gathered up several plates and dumped them in the already littered sink. She picked up the half-full wine bottle on the counter and poured more wine all round, then held up her glass in a toast.

"To new beginnings," she said softly. "May Korbin Lake bring you both prosperity and happiness." Her exotic face creased in a loving smile, but there was more than a hint of tears in her dark eyes.

"Hey, now don't go all weepy on us, Mom," David warned, raising his glass to acknowledge the toast. "Alex, Cam, hope this move is a good one." He smiled at them, his infectious, open smile, and Alex smiled back, sipping her wine and musing on the physical differences between the two Ross brothers.

Cam looked like his mother, tall, slender, graceful. He'd inherited a male version of her dark gypsy beauty, his face a more rugged version of hers but just as dramatically drawn with its high cheekbones and strong jawline. Even when they smiled, Cameron and his mother retained an aura of somber mystery.

David, just as handsome in an entirely different way, looked nothing like his mother and brother. He, too, was tall—well over six feet—naturally muscular, with well-defined biceps, a wide, sturdy body, broad hands and feet. He was fair skinned, with sun-streaked light brown hair that curled in an unruly mass around his shoulders. His eyes were green—strange, clear eyes that gave the mistaken impression David was a simple man with no hidden depths.

Alex knew it was an illusion; her brother-in-law was anything but uncomplicated. He was a restless rogue, flitting from one job to the next. He was also what Verna despairingly called a ladies' man. She often told Alex her younger son was like her and would probably never marry.

Cam and David had different fathers, and although Verna's apartment was littered with pictures of her sons, there were no photos at all of the men who'd fathered them.

Early in their relationship, Alex had asked Cam whether he was curious about his father.

"Not anymore. I was really curious when I was a kid," he'd confessed. "I used to ask Mom where he was, whether he'd ever come to see me, and like always, she was bone honest. She sat me down one day and told me everything she knew about him, which actually wasn't that much. His name was Martin Lathrop, he was in the U.S. Army, an intelligence officer of some kind, in Vancouver investigating draft dodgers. It was during the Vietnam war. Mom was waitressing at the restaurant in the hotel he was staying in, and he used to come in there for dinner every day. She said he was up front with her from the start, told her he was married and had four kids and that he'd be going back to them. She said they could talk to each other, that they'd fallen in love during the time he spent in Vancouver, which wasn't much, two months or so. He went back to his wife and four kids in Maryland, and she never heard from him again, never even told him she was pregnant with me."

"Have you ever thought of finding him?"

Cam shook his head. "He'd be a stranger. I'd upset his life, and for what?" His voice hardened. "Donating his sperm doesn't make him my father."

"And what about Dave's father?"

Cameron shrugged. "Dave's dad was a different story. His name was Michael O'Reilly. He was a contractor with a small business. I was eight at the time Mom was going out with him, so I remember him pretty well. I hated him, but at that age I hated every guy she dated. I don't remember much about him, but looking back, I think he was probably a pretty nice guy, big and blond and strong. Dave looks like him. I remember hearing him and Mom laugh a lot. He used to try to make friends with me, and he bought me a bike, the first and only new bike I ever had. He was killed in a construction accident a few months before Dave was born. Mom was pretty wrecked over it for a long time, and after that she never got seriously involved with anybody again."

"Do you think they'd have gotten married?"

Cam shook his head. "I asked her that just after I met you, and she said she decided early on that she wanted kids, but she never wanted to get married."

Alex looked across the table now at Verna, relaxed and seemingly happy with her life, but also very alone as she grew older. Alex wondered if her mother-in-law ever regretted any of the decisions she'd made in her life.

Life hadn't been easy for Verna Ross. She'd had minimal education and financially, she'd always lived a hand-to-mouth existence, holding down two jobs during the years the boys were growing up. Alex knew from talking to her that Cam had felt responsible for his mother and done his best to help from the time he was a small boy, first with paper routes and then with jobs in supermarkets and gas stations. As soon as he finished his RCMP training and started earning a decent wage, he'd taken over financial responsibility for his brother and tried to give Verna a generous monthly allowance. She refused the money, insisting that she was quite capable of supporting herself the way she'd always done. Alex respected and admired the other woman for that determined independence.

At sixty-two, Verna was a singularly unusual and attractive woman, Alex mused. She shopped exclusively at secondhand stores, and she was dressed tonight in a worn burgundy velvet skirt and a man's white dress shirt. As usual, she looked elegant and rather bohemian. She had an enviable body still, tall, long limbed and slender. Only the white at her temples and the deep lines that bracketed the corners of her mouth and the similar ones etched around her dark brown eyes indicated her years.

At the moment, she was smiling a little but obviously not really listening to the good-natured banter going on between Cam and David—they were arguing the merits of some linebacker the Vancouver football team had just traded.

Verna looked over and caught Alex's eye. She rolled her eyes in the men's direction and got to her feet, extending a hand to grasp her daughter-in-law's in a firm, affectionate grip.

"C'mon. Let's go into the other room and have some tea and talk intelligent woman talk. A person can't hear themselves think around these two. I'll serve the cheesecake later. You boys can clear the table and do the washing up."

Mock howls of protest from Cam and David followed the women into the small sitting room.

Verna's apartment was old, cramped and more than a little messy, but it was also warm and welcoming. She drew Alex over to a comfortably worn armchair and sat down across from her on the sagging sofa. "I'll get us tea in a moment, but first tell me about this job you've got in Korbin Lake."

"Well, it was my father who found out about it. Apparently he knows the hospital administrator from years ago. Dad talked to him and learned that one of the doctors at the local clinic had just left and they were anxious to fill the vacancy."

Alex felt a surge of excitement just thinking about it. "It seemed such a coincidence I could hardly believe it, but apparently the doctor who left didn't give them much notice—he had a chance to buy a practice up in the Yukon or something. So I faxed them my résumé, and the administrator called almost immediately and interviewed me by telephone, and bingo, I was hired. I guess they didn't get a ton of applicants, and one of the deciding factors with me was the fact that early on I thought I'd go into anesthesia as a specialty.

"Dad used to push me. He'd go on about regular hours and how exciting it was to be in the operating room—even though we both knew I didn't have the makings of a surgeon. Anyhow, I did a year and changed my mind. They were doing lots of studies just then on the bad effects all the chemicals an anesthetist uses might have on offspring. I want kids someday, and I sure didn't want to endanger them that way. And I also realized I wanted more personal contact with people. But I guess that year tipped the scales with this job—they need someone who can give anesthetic for the odd minor emergency procedure. The serious surgical cases are sent out, to Vancouver or Calgary, so giving anesthesia would only be an occasional thing. Mostly, I'd be doing family practice."

"And how many doctors are there in the town?"

"Only two, me and an older man named Hollister King, who's been there for years. It's a really small place, Verna. The only reason there's even a hospital is because of the coal mine. Years ago, the mine put up the money to build and equip a hospital and clinic, and they still help maintain it."

"Well, they couldn't do better than to hire you, Alex. I hope they appreciate what they're getting."

Alex jumped to her feet and gave Verna an impulsive hug. "My fan club. You don't think maybe you're just a trifle prejudiced?'

Verna smiled and hugged Alex back. "Nope. If I ever need a doctor, God forbid, I'm coming to you, even if I have to take a bus to Korbin Lake."

"With a broken bone, a bus trip could be a problem."

They both giggled. It was a joke between them that the last time Verna had been to a medical doctor was ten years before, when she fell and broke her ankle. She had a deep-rooted distrust of both doctors and hospitals, dating from the death of her mother when she was a child.

David walked in just then, balancing mugs and a cake on the old cookie sheet Verna used as a tray, a white tea towel folded across his arm.

"Evening, ladies. May I tell you about our dessert choices?" He smirked in a wicked parody of an overzealous waiter. "There's chocolate cheesecake that's to *die* for, and I strongly suggest you order it, seeing it's all we have."

Cameron followed him with plates and the teapot, and with much buffoonery, the two men served the women and themselves cake and tea.

As usual when Verna and her sons were together, the conversation veered to the past, when Cam and David were youngsters, and soon everyone was laughing over the time Verna, concerned about their diet, mixed up some vile concoction called moose milk, heavy on nutritional yeast and soy yogurt and lecithin, and insisted the boys drink it each morning before they left the house.

"God, I despised that stuff. Remember, Cam, the minute her back was turned, you used to drink mine for me?"

"Ahh, but look how I grew. No wonder you ended up such a runt, kid." Cam landed an affectionate punch on his brother's arm.

Alex laughed with them, but part of her was envious of the tight cocoon of affection and mutual respect that bound the Ross family into a unit. She thought of Wade in his hospital bed, and of her parents, rigid, judgmental, unable to laugh or tease or even relax the way these three did so easily. Dinners at her parents' house had all the right china and silverware but totally lacked warmth.

Cameron sat down close beside her, an arm circling her shoulders, and she watched him as he talked and laughed. This afternoon he was seemingly free from whatever demons haunted him. Since she'd gotten the job in Korbin Lake, some of the anger and resentment she felt toward him had dissipated, and things were easier between them, at least on the surface.

He'd taken on all the responsibility for the actual move, packing their belongings into boxes, labeling them, arranging for a moving company to transport the furniture, making certain that when she followed him, everything would be taken care of.

Cameron had always taken care of her, Alex reflected. It was one of the things about him that was so endearing, his concern and thoughtfulness for those he loved, his willingness to solve their problems and protect them. It was one of the things that had made her fall head over heels in love with him, because she'd never experienced it before.

Which was why she still didn't begin to understand the arbitrary, uncharacteristic way he'd acted during the matter of his transfer and their forthcoming move to Korbin Lake.

He was leaving before dawn the following morning, and she wouldn't see him again for two weeks, when her resignation took effect at St. Joe's and she was free to follow him.

Maybe the two weeks apart would be good for them, she mused. Maybe she needed time away from Cam, time to miss him, time to put her feelings into perspective again.

She loved him, that was certain. And she would miss him.

She reached out impulsively and touched his long silky hair, tied back as usual, and he turned his head and planted a kiss in her palm.

His long hair would be gone when she saw him next. Going back into uniform meant he'd have to have a haircut. She'd never seen him with short hair.

So many changes, big and small.

Change frightened her.

KORBIN LAKE BARBER SHOPPE. The red letters were emblazoned across the front window of the small building, and Cam looked past them before he opened the door and went inside, taking in the single chair and the middle-aged barber leisurely snipping away at a customer's hair.

He'd arrived in Korbin Lake the night before, and he had to report for work early tomorrow morning, in uniform. Why the hell hadn't he had his hair cut to the regulation earlobe length before he left Vancouver?

The truth was, he'd put it off as long as possible. There was something symbolic about his haircut. It was a ritual that would visibly mark the end of one phase of his career and the beginning of another.

He sat down on a battered wooden chair and picked up an equally battered copy of *Outdoor Life,* praying that the barber wouldn't make it necessary for him to wear his regulation cap day and night for the next six weeks.

"Afternoon, sir. Be with you in jiffy." The barber nodded courteously and went back to rubbing something from a large blue bottle on his customer's head. He then meticulously combed and arranged a fringe of long hair across the man's large bald spot, and a few moments later, Cam found himself in the chair.

"I'm Steve. Haven't seen you before. You new in Korbin Lake?" One shake of the hairy cape and it was around Cam's shoulders.

Thinking it might prevent reckless abandon with the scissors, Cam explained that he was starting work the following morning at the RCMP detachment.

Steve raised his bushy eyebrows and loosened the leather thong that held back Cam's hair. "Heard they were getting a new boss over there. You're him, huh?"

"Guess so."

"Then I reckon you want this—" Steve made a chopping motion and Cam swallowed hard and nodded.

"Right. I cut all the guys' from the detachment. Short back and sides coming right up." One gigantic snip and a large portion of Cam's past lay at his feet. "You're from the coast, right?" *Snip, snip.*

Cam, shocked at how unprotected his neck and ears felt, nodded once again, mesmerized by the emerging image of a stranger in the mirror.

"Guess you was one of those undercover cops, huh?" Steve's scissors moved with the speed of light.

Cam conceded that he had been, and Steve responded with a barrage of questions that Cam answered automatically as most of his hair disappeared and an electric trimmer buzzed up his neck.

Twenty minutes after he'd walked in, Cam was once again out on the sidewalk. He felt naked and strangely vulnerable. He thought of Alex, of how she used to bury her hands in his hair and hold him to her when they made love, and a combination of anger and unbearable sadness filled him.

A haircut was a small thing, but to Cam at that moment it seemed to symbolize all the losses he'd experienced over the past month. He hurried down the small-town street to where he'd parked, feeling totally alone and horribly conspicuous, an unwilling stranger in a very strange land.

That feeling of alienation became even more acute the following morning when, dressed in regulation uniform, he stopped for breakfast at the small café where he'd eaten all his meals since arriving in Korbin Lake.

He ordered bacon and eggs, toast and coffee, uncomfortably aware of the attention he attracted from both the proprietor and the other customers. On Drug Squad, anonymity was an important part of the job; in this uniform, he was all too visible, his every move scrutinized, his occupation obvious.

When it came time to pay the bill, it was half what it should have been. "Always a special price for police," the owner insisted when Cam questioned it. Wishing with all his heart that he was just one of the crowd again, Cam put down the money and hurried out.

At the police office, Corporal Ken Barnes, the man Cam was replacing, was already waiting to begin the tedious task of inventory. He introduced Cam to the clerk-steno, Lorna Berringer, and to the constable, Greg Townsend. Both were friendly and welcoming, but it was obvious Ken was in a hurry to turn over command and be on his way; he was going to Kelowna as a shift NCO and wanted to leave that afternoon.

As the morning progressed, Cam became aware that the transition from the drug squad to general duty policing was going to be much tougher than he'd imagined.

The inventory was easy; he signed for every last thing the detachment owned, from cars and desks and computers right down to mops and buckets and pencils. Ken explained that Lorna did the simpler administrative tasks, like preparing the individual expense accounts, but Cam was expected to look after the contingency accounts.

"You'll have about eight hours' reading to do on the files to familiarize yourself with where things are at here," Ken commented. "Coming from Drug Squad, I'd guess it's the operational part of the job that's going to give you the most headaches."

Cam knew it. He'd heard it said often enough that general duty policemen were considered the backbone of law enforcement because of their familiarity with every aspect of policing, and in that department, he was sadly lacking. On Drug Squad, he'd had to be familiar with only two statutes—the Criminal Code of Canada and the Narcotic Control Act. As the noncommissioned officer in charge of Korbin Lake Detachment, he'd be dealing with everything from the bylaws governing dog control to the statutes covering murder.

Every moment he had to spare for the first few weeks would have to be spent familiarizing himself with the Motor Vehicle Act and the regulations, a formidable task.

At least he had plenty of work to fill in the lonely two weeks until Alex arrived, he thought with a sinking sensation in his gut.

"When we're done here we'll head over to the café so you can meet George Evans, the magistrate," Ken said.

"He's a good man, but he's a stickler on search warrants. Feels a man's home is his castle, so you need really strong grounds before you go to George for one. After that, Greg'll take you out and familiarize you with the town."

As the day progressed, Cam felt more and more overwhelmed with new faces, new places, new systems, and he began to wonder if he'd ever master all of it. He stayed late at the office that night, reading files and familiarizing himself with the computer system, until at last his growling stomach told him it was long past dinnertime.

He went back to the motel and changed into jeans and a sweatshirt before heading into the café, but he attracted just as much attention as he would have if he'd stayed in uniform.

They'd made him, he thought with a wry grin. As he ate, he fielded a barrage of questions from other patrons, everything from whether he had children to his opinions on the political situation in British Columbia. He was the new cop, and he was public property.

In the deep of night, unable to sleep, he walked up one quiet street and down another, his brain frantically going over everything he had to do and learn.

One of the most important things was finding a place for him and Alex to live—he was entitled to the housing the RCMP provided, next door to the police office, but Greg Townsend and his wife had been living there for the past year, since the previous officer in charge had been a single man, and Cam wouldn't dream of evicting them. He wanted to find something special for Alex, a house that might make up to her in some small way for the move.

Alex. The very thought of her caused a tightness in his chest, an ache deep inside. He missed her desperately.

He'd called her earlier, but she was getting ready for her first night shift and was obviously in a hurry and distracted, and his day had been so busy he couldn't even sort out what he wanted to tell her when she asked about it.

It hadn't been a satisfactory conversation, but none of their conversations had been since he'd told her about Korbin Lake, he admitted. It seemed to him as if a vital connection had come undone between them that day, like an electrical plug pulled from its socket, and for the life of him, he couldn't connect it again.

It would be better when she got here and things were back to normal for them, he assured himself. He'd stop having nightmares about narrow hallways and men with guns instead of hands. The feeling of deep anxiety that plagued him, the sense of being out of his depth and incompetent would surely have disappeared by the time she arrived.

Two weeks to get through...

The streetlights suddenly switched off and he realized that dawn had come. There were only a few scant hours left until he had to put on his uniform and go to the office and pretend to be the boss.

Alex, I love you. Stay safe and well, my dearest one. And please forgive me for what I've done to you... to us....

He turned and retraced his steps to the motel, wishing with all his heart that Alex was arriving that very day.

CHAPTER SEVEN

"PAVAROTTI, WOULD YOU kindly stop that infernal screeching?" Alex scowled at the wailing cat locked in the special carrier on the seat beside her. "We're almost there, I promise you'll be free of that cage soon."

She steered her way down the last long, twisting hill to Korbin Lake, gazing with excitement and curiosity at the mountain valley that would be her new home.

Cameron had already been here two full weeks, and in their daily phone conversations he'd done his best to describe the place, but obviously he'd forgotten to tell her that in spite of the coal mining that was the major industry here, the setting was breathtakingly beautiful.

Below and to the right, snugged against the foot of the majestic Rocky Mountains, the long green lake that gave the town its name shone like an emerald in the mid-July afternoon. The valley that cradled it was wide, bracketed by range after range of craggy mountains, several of whose tops were curiously flat. Their surface was inky black and devoid of evergreens, evidence of the massive strip-mining operations that harvested the valley's rich caches of coal.

The highway wound sharply down in a series of hairpin curves, and as she reached the bottom, Alex lost sight of the lake. The valley floor was rich with evergreens and poplars, and the town was actually some distance away

in. They even let me choose the colors. Thanks
much for letting us stay."

had explained that he'd rented a house some-
out of town instead, he'd told her, a house Alex was
to see. They'd never had a whole house before.
re more than welcome." Alex wanted to add that it
generosity at all. Having to live next to the police
day and night seemed more of a penalty than an
tage to her, although it was evident Nancy didn't
at way at all.

reg told me you're a doctor," Nancy went on. "Will
working at the clinic?" She looked up and flashed
arming smile. "Oh, thanks, Lorna."

na handed them each a tall, ice-filled glass of cold

x took a long, refreshing drink before she an-
d.

will be, yes. I'll be starting in two weeks."

t must be really satisfying, being a doctor," Nancy
nented with a trace of envy in her tone. "Did you
your own practice in Vancouver?"

x shook her head. "I worked at St. Joseph's, in
gency." She thought of all her friends there and the
ap farewell party they'd given her, and she had to
ow back the tears. It had been painful, leaving them
he pushed the emptiness inside her away and changed
ubject.

Cam mentioned on the phone that you've got a beau-
new son, Nancy."

ancy's round face lit up like a signboard. "We sure
He's six weeks today, in fact. You want to come over
meet him? He's sleeping in the kitchen, right where I
ear him."

from the water. She tapped the brakes, slowing the car to
the fifty kilometers the large wooden sign demanded.

Korbin Lake, population 2,640, it proclaimed. Home
of Silver Mountain Mines. Alex slowed to a crawl, trying
to get an impression of the town which would be her home
for the next few years at least. It seemed to doze, drugged
by the afternoon heat. Storefronts flickered past the car
like images on a silent movie screen. The people she
passed moved at a leisurely pace, unlike the frenzied bustle of pedestrians on the city streets she was used to.

She drove past the Shady View Motel and Trailer Park,
Tastee-Freez, The Laundry Mat, Korbin Mercantile, Ella's
Beauty Salon, Marvin's Hardware and Home Supply,
Edna's Tea Shoppe and Bakery, then slowed at the first set
of lights. There were only two in the entire town, Cam had
explained. She turned right as he'd instructed. The RCMP
office was halfway down the street on the right, a neat
redbrick building, half office, half living quarters, fronted
by a green lawn and a sidewalk bordered by red and yellow flowers. A flagpole sprouted from the middle of the
lawn, and the red-and-white Canadian flag hung limp in
the airless heat.

Alex pulled to the curb behind a white police car
marked with the RCMP crest. She opened the door, and
the blast of dry, hot air after the air-conditioned coolness
almost choked her.

Her body felt stiff and sore after the long drive—it had
taken her two days, fourteen hours in all—and she took a
moment to try to straighten her wrinkled khaki shorts and
tuck in her red V-necked T-shirt. She stretched to get the
kinks out of her arms and legs, wondering with a feeling
of glad anticipation whether Cameron was inside, whether
he'd seen her drive up and would come hurrying out to
greet her at any moment.

Inside the car Pavarotti's yowling redoubled in volume. She grumbled at him under her breath and rolled the windows down so the cat would have fresh air. Then she closed the car door with a bang, disappointed that there was no sign of Cameron. She made her way up the sidewalk and into the office, feeling a little shy and awkward.

"Can I help you?" The pretty, dark-haired woman behind the desk was probably in her early forties, although her flowing hairstyle and dramatic makeup belied it. She wore a narrow flowered skirt and a tight-fitting top with a see-through red shirt over it. She was just overweight enough to be sensual, and with her scarlet lipstick and long matching nails, Alex thought she looked as if she should be serving drinks in the Tiki Lounge instead of working in a police office.

"I'm Alex Ross. My husband's—"

"Sergeant Ross, of course." The woman grinned and stuck out a soft, beringed hand. "Hey, glad you made it. We've all been waiting for you to arrive. I'm Lorna Berringer."

Words tumbled out of her like nickels from a slot machine. "The sergeant said you'd be arriving this afternoon. I'll just give him a call and tell him you got here safely. He was in the office till about fifteen minutes ago, and then Greg came and picked him up. Wouldn't you know you'd arrive just when he stepped out for a minute?" She moved to the switchboard, hips gyrating like pistons, but her voice was all business as she spoke into the mike.

"Korbin Lake, 851."

Alex heard Cam's distinctive voice respond almost instantly. "851."

"Your wife's arrived, Sergeant."

"851 copy. Tell her to sit tight. My [...] moved utes."   ever s

"You catch that, Mrs. Ross? Or shou[...] Ca tor?"   where

"I heard, and please just call me Alex[...] eager

"Sure thing. You want some coffee? [...] "You iced tea in the fridge back here. It's mor[...] wasn' day like this. Hot as Hades, eh?"   office

"Tea sounds great." Alex could al[...] adva trickling down her back. The offi[...] feel t conditioned, and the single forlorn fan [...] corner just wasn't doing the job.   "C

"You can sit in the lunchroom and wait [...] you cooler than out front." Lorna opened a [...] L counter and let Alex through, then led th[...] tea. back of the building to a room with a tabl[...] A microwave and fridge. There was a door th[...] swer wide expanse of lawn, where a very heavy [...] " in a loose blue dress was hanging baby [...] " clothesline.   com

Lorna went to the door and called to her. [...] have come and meet the sergeant's wife."   A

Alex smiled and held out her hand whe[...] Eme in the door. The other woman was probab[...] mad thirties, and her smile was warm and welcc[...] swai tle bashful.   all. the

"Hi, I'm Alex."   "

"Nancy Townsend. My husband's Greg[...] tifu boiling out there." Her face was flushed a[...] N tissue to blot her forehead and neck, addin[...] do. tone, "It's really kind of you and Sergea[...] and Greg and I keep the living quarters. I love t[...] can big and cool and it was all freshly painted j[...]

The telephone in the office rang. "Damn, wouldn't you know it, just when I wanna stay and talk?" Lorna waggled her fingers at them and hurried away, and Alex followed Nancy out one door and into the next. A wicker bassinet sat on a table in a gleaming kitchen, and Alex smiled at the tiny, dark-haired baby sleeping on his side.

"He's a fine-looking fellow," she said, reaching out a finger to stroke the baby's minute hand. "What's his name?"

"Jason. Jason Edward, actually. I'm glad he's sleeping like this—he was up most of the night." Nancy hesitated, and then blurted out, "He cries an awful lot. The doctor says it's colic, and I worry too much, I guess. But I— Well, I had three miscarriages before this pregnancy. Greg and I thought I'd never be able to carry a baby to term, and then Jason came." She gave Alex an apologetic glance. "I know I'm silly, but he really throws up a lot—it sort of explodes out of him about ten minutes after he eats, and there seems to be so much of it." Her face reflected her anxiety. "I've asked Dr. King about it time after time, and he says I'm just an overcautious mother."

Excessive vomiting could be a signal that something was amiss with the baby's digestive tract, but Alex knew that the utmost diplomacy was called for. The last thing she wanted to do was alienate the man she'd be working with by questioning his diagnosis—especially before she even had a chance to meet him.

"Babies do spit up, sometimes a great deal," she temporized. "Are you nursing him?"

Nancy nodded. "For sure. I read all about the advantages breast feeding has, how it's the best for the baby."

"It really is. And is he gaining weight normally?'

Nancy hesitated. "Dr. King says he is, but according to the books I've read, I don't think so. He took forever to regain his birth weight, and he's only gained a pound since."

Nancy was right, a pound wasn't within the normal range for a six-week-old baby. Alex wasn't sure what to suggest. Nancy's concerns seemed legitimate, but if Dr. King had examined the baby and found everything normal... But then, there was nothing wrong with getting a second opinion, she reasoned. Probably King would appreciate having her confirm his diagnosis.

"Alex? Hey, where are you?" It was Cameron's voice, and she felt a surge of joy. Two weeks was the longest they'd been apart in the entire two years they'd been married, and she'd missed him terribly. It had seemed an eternity.

"Over here, Cam," she called, adding hurriedly to Nancy, "Look, I'd be happy to have a look at Jason if you want me to. Give me a call in the next couple of days, and I'll come over if you like."

"Oh, thanks, I'd so appreciate—"

"Alex?" Cameron stood at the open door, smiling a welcome that made her heart pound. On his lean, dark features Alex recognized the same relief and outright happiness she felt, but for a moment she simply stared, trying to get used to the sight of her husband in uniform and with a short haircut.

The uniform suited him, she decided, although with his tall, long-limbed frame, almost any type of clothing would look good on him. It was just such a change from the faded jeans, gray sweatshirt and worn brown leather jacket that had been his chosen uniform for as long as she'd known him. And his hair—

He almost seemed a stranger until he smiled at her, his signature smile, closed-lipped and crooked, and her heart lifted.

"Oh, Cameron, I've missed you so." She threw herself into his arms, oblivious to the wide grin on the face of the policeman standing just behind him.

Their kiss was passionate but short. With his arm tight around her shoulders, Cam turned to introduce her to his fellow Mountie, such blatant pride in his voice that Alex had to smile.

"Alex, this is Constable Greg Townsend. Greg, my wife, Alex."

Greg was stocky, with a broad, friendly face, a wide grin and a firm handshake. "Really pleased to meet you at last, Mrs. Ross." He shot Cam a mischievous look. "I'll bet the sarge's gonna be a lot easier to get along with now that you're here. He's been like a bear with a sore tooth, waiting for you to arrive."

"Don't you bet on it, I'm just snarly by nature," Cam growled, but he couldn't quite suppress his smile.

There was a good feeling between the two men Alex decided.

Cam kept his arm tight around her shoulders as she acknowledged the introduction, adding, "I've just met your son, Greg. Congratulations. He's a beautiful boy."

Greg swelled with pride. "*We* sure like him. We waited a long time for him, which I guess makes us appreciate him all the more."

"I'm sure it does," Alex agreed, really liking the young man.

"I'm taking Alex over to the house now," Cameron said. "I probably won't be back today unless something urgent comes up. If you need me, Lorna has the number."

"If we can help you at all with getting settled, just holler," Nancy offered.

"Thanks. That's very kind." Alex smiled at the other woman and followed Cameron back into the office. After a few words with Lorna and a repetition of the offer of help, they made their way out to Alex's car, where Pavarotti was still in full voice. His complaints increased in volume when Alex shoved boxes and several plants to one side in order to move him to the back seat so she could sit beside Cam.

Cameron scowled at the cat. "God, what a racket. Has he been doing that long?"

"Almost the entire way from Vancouver. I stopped at nearly every rest stop to let him out. The first time, he was hard to catch, so I hooked him to a leash after that, and he got insulted. After fighting him into it and then listening to him all day yesterday and today, he's lucky I didn't just abandon him somewhere. He obviously doesn't like moving."

Neither do I, she nearly added, but she stopped herself just in time. She'd already made her feelings on the matter all too clear, and she didn't want to spoil this reunion in any way.

"Apart from Pavarotti, did you have any problems on the trip?" Cameron slid behind the wheel.

"None at all. After the movers were done last week, there wasn't much left to pack except the last of my clothes and things. You did all the rest before you left."

"We didn't have a lot," Cam said. "Everything we owned didn't come anywhere near to filling the mover's van."

"Guess we've been too busy to think much about furniture. We'll have more time here. Things seem a lot more laid back than in Vancouver. Did the stuff get here okay?"

"It all arrived two days ago," Cam confirmed. "Greg helped me move it in. God, I'm so glad you're finally here, sweetheart. It's seemed a lot longer than two weeks." He didn't start the car immediately. Instead, he reached over and drew her into his embrace, threading his fingers through her hair and smoothing it back, trailing hungry kisses down her forehead, across her nose, on her cheeks, ending finally at her mouth. He kissed her with leisurely thoroughness this time, his mouth intent.

She rested a hand on his chest, feeling his heart hammer against her palm, feeling, too, the fever of pure sensation he set off inside of her.

A low, tortured sound came from his throat. "I'm not certain, but I think there's a bylaw against making out in front of the police office in broad daylight, particularly in uniform. Let's go home." With a long, shaky sigh, he reached for the key to start the motor. He turned the car around and drove swiftly out of town, one hand on the wheel, the other covering Alex's hand where it rested on his thigh.

"Everyone's friendly around here. Lorna and Nancy made me feel welcome," Alex commented as they angled off the main road.

Cameron nodded. "Yeah, they're good people. I've had invitations to dinner almost every single night from Greg and Nancy. I accepted a couple of times, but I didn't want to impose on them. She's got enough to do with the new baby. God, I'm glad you're here, honey. I was running out of excuses. I guess it's just the custom in a small town, but for a city boy, it takes some getting used to."

They chatted as well as they could over the constant wailing of the cat. She told him about the party at the hospital, about Wade's small physical gains and his continuing insistence that everyone leave him alone, but Alex was distracted. She kept glancing over at Cam, trying to get used to his new image.

He caught her staring and raised an eyebrow. "If it looks weird to you, sweetheart, think how I feel in this rig," he said dryly.

"It's just so different. Your hair, all the rest of this—" She gestured at him, still staring.

His arms were muscular and tanned beneath the crisp short-sleeved gray shirt, open at the neck. He wore a black leather belt with holster, leather bullet pouch and handcuff holder, and sharply creased navy blue trousers with the distinctive yellow stripe down the outside of each leg. On his feet were highly polished black ankle boots, and beside her on the seat of the car was his hat, the navy blue and yellow-crested forage cap.

"You look so—so official. I feel as if I've been arrested for something."

He shot her a frankly lecherous look. "Think of it more as an abduction, honey. I can't wait to get you home." He turned her hand over, placing his palm against hers, and the intimate warmth of his touch and the sexual intensity in his tone set off a purely physical surge of lust that made her heart beat faster and blood pool heavily in her abdomen. All of a sudden, a sense of optimism and joy overcame her.

Maybe the strain that had been between them would disappear now that this move was accomplished. Maybe the chaos it had created in their lives would subside. Maybe such enormous change would actually be a positive thing for their marriage. Lordy, she hoped so. And surely now there'd be time to talk, to share their feelings about this transition in their lives.

"I can't wait to see the house you rented!" she exclaimed. "Oh, Cam, is this our street?" They were driving along a gravel road, thickly lined with evergreens, and he turned beside a large red mailbox and wound down a long, treelined driveway. She caught glimpses of a gray-shingled roof and weathered wood siding, interspersed with dazzling flashes of sun-drenched lake.

"This is it, love." There was a touch of uncertainty in his voice. He'd told her about the house he'd rented for them. He'd said it was large and old and out of town, partially furnished, close to the lake. He'd said he liked it, but if she hated it they'd find something else. It belonged to an old woman who now lived in a nursing home. Her husband had been a Mountie, and she was grateful to have another member of the RCMP living in her home. The rent was ridiculously low by Vancouver standards.

Alex had barely listened when he described it over the phone; what did she care about a house, when her entire life was being torn apart? But the reality of it now took her breath away. Big and rambling, with deep porches that held comfortable old wooden chairs and an antiquated glider, the house seemed to have grown naturally out of the surrounding foliage. And best of all, it was right on the lakeshore. Alex could see a stone pathway winding past the separate garage, down to the water's edge.

Pavarotti abruptly stopped complaining as Cam pulled the car to a halt under an immense pine tree and shut off the motor.

Trembling with excitement, Alex opened her door and stepped out. The only sound was birdsong and the sighing of the trees as a gentle breeze rippled through them. "Oh, Cam, it's so quiet here." Her voice sounded muted by the open spaces all around.

She lifted Pavarotti's cage out and turned him loose. He arched his back and let out one last, relieved yowl, stretched like a ballet dancer and then set off to explore, tail swishing.

"Think he'll get lost?" She frowned anxiously as the cat disappeared into the bushes.

"We can only hope," Cam said dryly.

She grinned at him. "I want to see the lake first." She walked down to the pebbly beach, enchanted at the thought of having a lake for a front yard. The water was clear and green, inviting in the heat. "You forgot to mention the size of the swimming pool," she teased when she heard Cameron behind her. "It *is* good for swimming, I hope?"

"I've been in every day after work." He looped his arms around her midriff, and she turned toward him and took his hand, lifting it to her lips and kissing his knuckles.

"You approve, then?"

"Cam, it's absolutely beautiful here. I love it already." She smiled at him, and she saw some of the tension disappear from his face. "And I love you, too, Sergeant Ross."

"I was afraid you might not like being this secluded. It's actually only a couple of miles from town, but it feels pretty isolated, since there aren't any close neighbors," he admitted. "You've never lived in the country and neither have I, so it'll probably take some getting used to. And we might hate it when winter comes. I've imagined that driveway under a couple of feet of snow. We'd never get your car up."

"So we'll buy another Jeep," she said recklessly. "Where's yours, anyway?"

"In the garage." He pointed at the roomy structure. "I had Greg pick me up this morning so I could drive you back."

"Thoughtful man. C'mon, I want to see the house." She ran back up the sloping shore to the front of the house and hurried up the wide stairs. Cam was right behind her. He used a key to open the heavy front door, and then he slipped it from the ring and handed it to her with a bow, a smacking kiss and a grin. "Your palace awaits, madam."

She walked in, finding herself in a huge room that stretched from the front of the building to the back. "Wow. This is immense. Good thing there was furniture here already. Ours would have looked ridiculous in all this space."

A rock fireplace formed one interior wall, and at right angles to it was a bank of windows with sliding glass doors that opened to the wraparound porch and a panoramic view of the lake, sparkling like quartz in the late-afternoon sunshine.

Couches, low tables, chairs and a big old rocker with a faded velvet cushion were scattered around, interspersed with Alex's own love seat and two easy chairs. The furniture in the house was old and much of it was shabby, but all the same, the rooms breathed comfort and hominess.

"Come see the kitchen." Cameron took her hand and tugged her into a large, outdated room with shallow cupboards and the oldest gas range Alex had ever seen. The fridge rattled alarmingly as the motor started up, but here, too, there were sliding glass doors that led to the outdoors.

A round wooden picnic table and curved benches sat just outside the door on a wide porch, and Alex could imagine cozy early-morning breakfasts and romantic dinners out in the open air.

Time. They'd have so much more time here.

There was a pantry off the kitchen with row upon row of built-in shelves for cans and a long, narrow shelf that Cam insisted was built to hold pies.

"You put them there to cool when they come out of the oven," he said in a reverent tone.

"In your dreams." Alex hadn't made a pie in her life, and she didn't think she was about to start. Delighted by the pantry in spite of her lack of cooking skills, Alex peered into wooden bins that held flour and sugar. There were canisters marked Coffee and Tea and a huge, ventilated bin for storing fresh loaves of bread.

She laughed with delight. "I love this! I've never seen a real pantry before. Your mother's going to adore it here. We're going to have to invite her up here for a visit after we get settled, Cam."

"We'll do that. Come and see the TV room." It was a small cedar-paneled room under the stairwell with worn couches and seat-sprung chairs, and Cam had already hooked up their television.

Alex marveled at the size of the house. There was a large bedroom with an iron bedstead on the main floor, and a small bathroom with a shower but no tub. That was up the winding stairs, with toilet and sink in one small room and claw-footed tub in another, larger space.

There were four more bedrooms off a wide corridor, two with lake views. Cam had installed their bedroom furniture in the largest, brightest room, but Alex discovered there were already beds and dressers in the other rooms, as well.

"Lord, look at all these beds. We could run a bed-and-breakfast. Everyone at work threatened to come and—and visit us." She swallowed hard, trying to keep her voice even as sudden homesickness assailed her. "I'll—have to, umm, write and tell them we've got enough room for them to shut the ER down and all come at once." Her voice quavered no matter how she tried to steady it. The ER staff had been her extended family.

Cameron was watching her, an unreadable expression in his eyes. "You miss them already, huh?"

"Yeah. Yeah, I do," she confessed. "I—I know them all so well. I know about their lives, their families, their problems. It's sort of—scary, thinking about meeting all these new people here, starting a different job, making new friends. And family practice is a far cry from the ER."

He didn't answer. He moved to the window, his back to her, and stood looking out, his arms folded across his chest.

She hated the tension that had suddenly sprung up between them. She shouldn't have brought up the way she felt just now.

But if not now, then when?

Suddenly she needed to be by herself. "I'm going out to see what's become of Pavarotti, Cam."

"Yeah." His voice was flat. "Yeah, I guess I'll change and start bringing in the stuff from the car."

He walked across the hall to their bedroom and unbuckled his gun belt and set it on the dresser. For a moment she was tempted to go in to him, unbutton the gray shirt, ease it off his broad shoulders and lift her mouth for the kiss that would lead to the lovemaking that might heal the awkwardness that had appeared like a sudden virus in their relationship.

But some remnant of resentment inhibited her, and instead she shot him a rueful smile and raced down the stairs and out into the sunshine.

CHAPTER EIGHT

THE REMAINDER OF the day was spent getting settled in, arranging furniture and, just before the stores closed, driving into town for groceries to augment the scant necessities Cameron had stocked.

When they were hungry, he lit the barbecue on the deck and grilled burgers and vegetables for dinner. It was after sunset when at last Alex slipped into her bathing suit and headed down to the lakeshore for the swim she'd been promising herself.

The air was balmy, the water refreshingly cool. Cam was already in, and Alex swam out to him. He saw her coming and dove, grabbing her ankles and tugging her under. The awkwardness between them gradually disappeared as they splashed and played like otters, and she was aware of the desire that smoldered in his eyes as their slippery bodies touched in the cool water. It was growing dark by the time they made their way to shore and toweled off.

"Alex." He was drying her back with long, gentle strokes that lingered just where her abbreviated black bikini bottoms began. He put his hands on her shoulders and turned her toward him, tipping up her chin with a finger so he could look into her eyes.

His gaze was troubled, his tone somber. "Alex, I've been so damned lonely without you. I'm glad you're here with me now. I know how tough this move has been for you, and I'm grateful. I'll try to make it up to you."

The reserve inside her melted like wax in a flame. "Oh, Cam, just love me. Love me and I know everything'll be all right."

"That's the easy part." His voice was husky as he dragged her close against his bare chest.

She moved back enough so that she could look up into his face.

"Are you going to be happy working here, Cam? It's such a drastic change for you. I always thought that even with all its problems, you loved your undercover job, the tension and excitement, the challenge, the fast pace of the city." She frowned up at him and slid her hands around his neck, missing the silkiness of his long hair. "Being in uniform, working in a small town—aren't you going to get awfully bored, Sergeant?"

It was a beginning, a lead in to the dozens of questions she needed to ask him.

"Far from being bored, I'm almost snowed under with all the things I have to learn about small-town policing. I've worked late every single night since I got here."

He pushed back her curly wet hair, looping it behind her ear as he leaned closer, taking her earlobe gently in his teeth, biting a little, making her shudder and press tight against him.

"Have I told you you've got sexy ears?" His thumb outlined her lips, and she opened her mouth and drew it in, relishing the low sound that came from his throat.

"I think we can find plenty to do to keep either of us from getting bored," he murmured hoarsely, running his hands in slow motion down her nearly naked body. "God, Alex, you're making me crazy with wanting you. Let's go in and start trying out some of those beds, sweetheart."

He drew in a shaky breath and folded her into his embrace. "We really ought to make sure they're all in working order before we have guests, right?"

"Right."

They drifted up to the house in the twilight, his arm tight around her shoulder, hers around his narrow hips, stopping often to kiss and hold each other close, their breathing ragged long before they reached the door. On the porch, his kisses became urgent, and he opened the door and hurried her through, kicking it shut behind them.

He turned her toward him and kissed her, scalding and deep, lifting her so that her hips rested against him, making her forcefully aware of how much he wanted her.

Sudden frantic need leaped from one to the other. He untied the string that held her bikini top in place, and her breasts spilled free. He cupped them in his palms, then dipped his head to draw first one aching nipple and then the other into his mouth, and she tugged at his trunks, sliding them down, dropping her own bikini bottoms to the floor along with them.

"Upstairs? Our bedroom?" He was short of breath. He trailed kisses along her jaw, his hands touching her breasts, her belly, sliding between her legs.

Hardly able to think, she shook her head, clinging to him, drowning in the deep, hot kisses that unleashed a storm of wanting. "I don't care where. Just hurry, Cam. Please hurry."

He moved his pelvis against her, and sensation jolted through her like a bolt of lightning. Frantic now, she tightened her grasp on his neck and wrapped her legs around him, desperate to have him inside her.

Dragging in a shaky breath, he cupped her bottom.

"Hold on tight, love. We'll never make it up the stairs."

Supporting her, his body trembling, he made his way to the main-floor bedroom.

The springs on the old bed creaked alarmingly when he set her down, and from the direction of the kitchen, Pavarotti answered. Alex giggled, her voice wobbly. "He thinks it's another cat. He'll be in here in a minute—"

Cameron swore and kicked the door shut, and her laughter faded as he settled himself over her, his strong thighs cradling hers, his mouth plundering hers in a kiss that brought a low moan from deep inside her throat.

"My beautiful lady—"

Hungry, wild with wanting, she writhed beneath him, need throbbing. He moved his legs, separating hers, and at last, she was filled with him. Sensation, hot and delicious, gathered intensity as he rocked against her, and she moved in counterpoint rhythm, reality fading.

From somewhere far away, she was aware of the bedsprings protesting and of Pavarotti's outraged wail as he clawed at the bedroom door. Then there was only heat, and a pooling of such urgency inside her that she sobbed, holding him with all her strength, totally dependent on him for the explosion that caught her at last and sent her whirling into a splintering release.

Clinging tight, they slowly spiraled down to the fractured notes of Pavarotti, in full, indignant voice.

"I swear to God, I'm gonna drown that cat in the lake. Right after I oil these bedsprings." Exasperation and wry amusement mingled in Cam's husky whisper, and Alex giggled and closed her eyes, snuggling close to him.

There was a blanket on the end of the bed, and he drew it up over them.

"We really ought to go upstairs, to our own bed," she murmured.

"In a minute. Just lie still for now and let me hold you. It's been too long since I held you like this."

He folded her close.

Safe, secure in the shelter of her husband's body, she let consciousness slip away.

ALEX AWOKE HOURS LATER, in the middle of the night. Loons were calling on the lake. Cameron slept beside her, one arm still holding her close.

She felt troubled, as if she'd had a bad dream she couldn't quite remember, and in that first instant of awakening, she realized it was because they'd never really talked out the issues that had been bothering her. They would, though. Things were better between them, and they'd talk....

She snuggled closer to him, closed her eyes and slept.

NANCY TOWNSEND PHONED Alex at eight the following morning. Cam had left for work an hour earlier, and Alex was having a cup of coffee on the porch outside the kitchen, feeling wonderfully lazy and contented as she watched Pavarotti stalk the small birds that flitted in and out of the water on the shoreline below. They were much too fast for the cat, but he went right on trying, crouching motionless and then springing at them an instant too late.

In a hesitant voice, Nancy asked if Alex was settled in, and she offered suggestions as to where the best bakery and meat market were located, and how to go about having fresh farmer's milk and eggs delivered to the door. There was a moment of awkward silence, and then in a tense voice she added, "I hate to be a nuisance, but I'd really be grateful if you'd have a look at Jason." Her concern was palpable. "He's throwing up more than ever.

I've been feeding him every hour all night, and to me it looks as if he throws it all up again and then some. I'll bring him over if you like, or—I don't suppose you were planning to come into town?''

"I was, as a matter of fact," Alex lied. "I'd be happy to come by. I haven't even showered yet, so it'll be a half hour or so." She craned her head to see the clock on the kitchen wall. "About nine-thirty, if that's convenient for you?"

"That's perfect. I can't thank you enough." It was obvious that Nancy was near tears. She added in a shaky voice, "I'm really worried, Alex."

It was only quarter past nine when Alex, medical bag in hand, tapped on Nancy's front door. She was shocked at the other woman's appearance. Nancy looked totally exhausted. There were dark circles under her eyes, and her bright smile was forced. "Come in. I feel so awful dragging you out on your first morning in your new house. I know how busy you must be." She sounded both apologetic and distracted. She led the way into the kitchen, where the baby was in the bassinet on his tummy, lying still and quiet.

"I'm not busy at all, honest. Cam's a neat freak, and he has everything in good shape. He's a lot better housekeeper than I am, I'm afraid. I was just sitting out on the deck being lazy when you called." Alex glanced around Nancy's spotless, gleaming kitchen, thinking of the dirty dishes she'd left in the sink, the unmade beds, the stack of laundry she'd forgotten to bring with her into town to wash.

Lucky she was good at medicine, she mused. When it came right down to it, she didn't really give a damn about a tidy house. People with medical problems were far more interesting—like tiny Jason.

She bent over the baby, turning him so she could see his face, and the moment she really looked at him, alarm bells went off in her head.

"Morning, sweetface. Let's just slip these clothes off so I can have a good look at you here," she crooned. She picked him up and smiled down at him, hiding her reaction to his pallor, the dark circles under his eyes, the fact that he didn't startle or open his eyes when she lifted him. She noticed that the fontanel on the top of his head was sunken.

Nancy had already put a folded blanket covered by a fresh sheet on the table, and Alex quickly laid the baby there and stripped off his clothing, further alarmed by the swollen and bloated belly and the sagging skin at his minute shoulder joints, all clear indicators that he was seriously dehydrated.

"He threw up all day yesterday, too, so I called Dr. King last night," Nancy said.

"And what'd King say?" Alex was palpating the baby's stomach.

Nancy suddenly burst into tears. "That—that I was a new mo-mother, imagining problems where there weren't any."

Jason's eyelids flickered and he, too, began crying—not the demanding cry of a healthy baby, but a weak, tired whimper.

"Is he wetting his diaper at all?" Dehydration in babies was a very serious matter.

Nancy shook her head. "Not since last night."

It wasn't a good sign. "When he vomits, Nancy, what's it like?" Alex probed the baby's abdomen once more, and again her fingers encountered the hard, telltale lump on the pyloric valve.

Nancy sniffed and blew her nose on a tissue. "It's r
ally forceful, almost like an explosion. It happens abo
ten or fifteen minutes after he's eaten, and it goes rig
across the room sometimes."

"Projectile vomiting."

Nancy's eyes were filled with dread. "He's really sic]
isn't he, Alex? I know it, inside of me, in a way I can
explain."

Alex looked over at the other woman, compassion ar
sympathy in her tone. "He *is* sick, Nance. I can't be su
without some tests, but I think he might have a conditio
called pyloric stenosis. That's when a valve between t
stomach and intestine swells and closes off the digesti
tract. I can feel a little lump right here—" She took Nar
cy's fingers and guided them to the spot. "There, in h
abdomen, and one of the primary symptoms is projecti
vomiting. If I'm right, he'll need an operation to corre
it."

"Oh, my God." Nancy's hand flew up to cover h
mouth, and there was outright panic in her eyes.

Alex reached out and gripped her shoulder. "It's
fairly minor operation, but it can't be done here. It need
to be performed by a trained pediatric surgeon. Babie
with this condition are always sent to Vancouver becaus
it's a specialized technique. The real danger is that Ja
son's quite dehydrated right now. There's not much tim
to lose." Alex refastened the tiny diaper, her mind rac
ing. She replaced the sleepers and booties and handed th
baby to Nancy.

Alex knew what she was about to do would likely mak
her future relationship with Dr. King less than amicable
but there was no choice. From what Nancy had said, Kin
had obviously and repeatedly overlooked a serious med
cal condition, and if Alex didn't take action, there was

good possibility that within twenty-four hours, Jason would die.

"I want you to go right now and pack a bag for yourself and for Jason. Take enough to last you both at least a week. I'm going next door to contact the BC Air Ambulance Service." With their help, Alex explained, she'd arrange for an ambulance to transport Jason to the airport in Cranbrook, an hour and a half's drive away, where a charter aircraft out of Vancouver would be waiting to transport the baby to Children's Hospital and the expert surgical care he required.

"Please, could you get hold of Greg for me?" Nancy was trembling.

"Absolutely. I'll get Lorna to radio him."

Nancy nodded, her chin wobbling. "Thanks. Thanks so much, Alex." Nancy's face was stark white, and the arms that cradled her baby shook, but her tears had stopped, and she seemed to have gained determination and strength as she hurried from the room.

Next door Alex quickly outlined the situation for Lorna, grateful that the other woman didn't ask any unnecessary questions. "How can I help?" was all she said.

At Alex's direction, she contacted Greg and Cameron. Alex was on the phone to BC Air Ambulance when Greg hurried into the office. Cameron was only a moment or two behind him.

The air ambulance service was fast and efficient. They assured Alex that an aircraft would be dispatched immediately and that the paramedics' van stationed in Korbin Lake would arrive in moments to pick up the baby, Alex, and Nancy and transport them to the airport. Alex made certain they'd have equipment for her to begin the intravenous drip that Jason required, and when she hung up the phone she quietly explained to Greg and Cameron what was going on.

The blood drained from Greg's florid countenance, and he made a choked, wordless sound before he managed to speak. "Are we going to lose him?" His voice quavered. "I don't think Nance could bear it if we lost this baby, too."

"That's not going to happen," Alex assured him with a note of confidence in her voice that she didn't actually feel. "We're going to get Jason to the best surgeon I know, and within a few weeks, he'll be completely well." She hesitated. She hated to frighten him more, but he had to be aware of the facts. "It's very important we get him there as soon as possible, though."

"You'll want to be with Nancy and the baby in Vancouver," Cameron said to Greg. "Go change and pack. Lorna will make arrangements for a seat on the next commercial flight out of Cranbrook, so you can be with your family in Vancouver by this evening at the latest. I'll put in for emergency leave for you and handle your shifts until you get back."

Greg was unable to respond for a moment. His throat worked, and then he managed to say, "Thanks, Cam. Both of you, thanks."

"Go get ready." Cam gave him a gentle punch on the shoulder, and the other man swallowed hard and hurried away.

Lorna was busy making calls, and for a moment Alex and Cameron were alone.

"Will the little guy make it?" Cameron's voice was pitched low, so that only Alex could hear.

"I think so, but another couple of hours could have been fatal." Her voice betrayed her feelings. "What I'd like to know is what the hell is wrong with King, missing something like this? It's not a difficult diagnosis."

"Good thing Nancy called you. If you're going with her in the ambulance, you'll need money in case you stop on the way back for a meal or something." He pulled out his wallet and extracted bills, handing them to her.

Alex shook her head. He knew her so well; she never thought of mundane matters like having cash in her purse.

Cam planted a quick, intense kiss on her lips, and another lighter one on her nose.

"Get Lorna to give me a call the minute you get back. And if anything comes up and you need me, call here. You've got the number with you?"

"I have it. Thanks, Cam." She was the one in charge, but it was enormously comforting to have his support.

There wasn't time for anything more. The ambulance arrived, and it took Alex only a few moments to ascertain that the two paramedics on board were highly competent.

Martha Davis was plump, probably in her late fifties, with a head of snow-white hair and an air of serene calm. Her partner, Daniel Brandt, was younger, forty perhaps, with craggy good looks, an athletic, well-muscled build, a head of thick, curling brown hair and a captivating grin.

The ambulance was equipped with an isolette, and with the paramedics' assistance, Alex inserted an IV drip of normal saline solution into the frontal vein on Jason's head. When the procedure was completed, Nancy climbed in, and within moments, they were speeding down the highway with Daniel at the wheel.

The trip was uneventful, the conversation limited to comments about Jason. The baby weathered the trip well, and it didn't seem long at all to Alex before the ambulance reached the Cranbrook airport.

The landing field had been cleared, and the small, sleek aircraft chartered by Air Ambulance was waiting. The highly trained members of the infant transport team hurried over with a transporter isolette the instant the ambulance stopped, and Alex gave them a concise summary of her diagnosis and Jason's condition, turning the responsibility for her tiny patient over to their expert care. "Hang in there, tiger," she whispered as she helped them transfer him from one isolette to the other.

In less than ten minutes, she and the two paramedics watched as the aircraft sped down the runway and lifted into the blue, sun-filled afternoon sky with Jason and Nancy on board.

Alex heaved a sigh of relief. Jason would be in the care of the senior pediatrician at Children's within a couple of hours. The adrenaline that had surged through her veins suddenly gave way to a feeling of weary satisfaction and a sudden realization that she hadn't had anything to eat yet today. Her stomach rumbled, and she turned to the paramedics.

"I have to make a couple of calls, and then do we have time for some food in the cafeteria before we head back? I'm starving."

Martha smiled and nodded. "You bet. I didn't have any lunch, either. How about you, Daniel?"

"Sounds good to me." He gave Alex his wide smile and a tiny salute. "We'll save you a seat in the cafeteria, Doctor Ross." There was respect and open admiration in his tone, and Alex couldn't help but smile at him in response.

"Call me Alex, please." She hurried over to the bank of phones adjacent to the small cafeteria. First, she called Children's Hospital and spoke to the pediatrician in Emergency, telling her all she knew about Jason. She realized that the ambulance service would have alerted Children's, but she wanted to make Jason's arrival personal. She wanted every detail taken care of.

She hung up and redialed a number she knew by heart, St. Joe's switchboard. Morgan Jacobsen was often over at Children's, checking on one of her babies, and perhaps she'd keep an eye on little Jason, as well.

When Morgan finally came on the line, Alex's eyes unexpectedly filled with tears. Lord, but she missed her old friend. Even though they hadn't seen each other that often, she'd always known that Morgan was just a few floors above her at St. Joe's. Now, there were untold miles between them, and the distance made Alex ache with homesickness.

She smiled and wiped her wet eyes when her friend's deep and distinctive voice caroled a greeting over the wire.

"Alex, sweetie, it's so good to hear your voice. So how's life in the boonies? Anybody pregnant there?"

They chatted for a moment, and then Alex told Morgan about Jason. "As a favor to me, I wondered if you'd sort of keep an eye on him? He's my first patient here in Korbin Lake."

"Consider him tucked safely under my wing," Morgan said instantly, and after another few moments, Alex hung up the phone.

Fishing a tissue from her purse, she blew her nose hard, trying to quell the awful loneliness the call had created inside of her. She closed her eyes for a long moment, willing the emotion away, aware that Martha and Daniel were sitting just a few feet away.

She was also aware that Daniel Brandt was watching her, his gaze sympathetic. As she blew her nose, Alex caught his eye and then avoided looking at him again, embarrassed by her tears. She made her way to the counter and placed her order, and by the time she sat down, she was in control.

Over soup and a thick lettuce-and-tomato sandwich, Alex got to know the other two a little. Martha had been a nurse's aide for years, and when her children were grown she'd taken training to become an emergency medical attendant. She and her carpenter husband had moved to Korbin Lake five years before, and she'd been on ambulance service for two years now.

"And what about you, Daniel?"

"I was a criminal defense lawyer in Vancouver, but I quit that two years ago and moved out here. I decided it made a lot more sense to drive ambulances than to chase them."

Alex laughed. "What made you choose Korbin Lake when you left the city?"

A shadow came and went on his face. "My grandfather lived here, and he was dying. He pretty much raised me, and I wanted to be with him for whatever time he had left. He died last spring, and I just stayed on."

"I see." She didn't, not really. There were gaps in his story that intrigued her. He was an interesting man, and she liked him.

"We already know all about you, of course." His voice and smile were openly teasing, and he ticked off items on his fingers as he listed them. "Married to our new Mountie, a highly skilled physician about to start work at the clinic, living in old Mrs. Rathbone's house down by the lake with a noisy cat named Pavarotti who'll only eat one specific kind of tinned cat food..."

Alex raised her eyebrows and had to laugh. "How on earth did you find all that out so fast?"

"From Evelyn—she works as a checkout clerk at the Overwaitea supermarket. She's an excellent source. People talk to her."

"I see. Well, I'm going to have to keep that in mind the next time I unburden myself at the cash register."

They all laughed, and then Martha said, "You'll be working with Dr. King at the clinic."

"Starting next Monday," Alex confirmed. "I haven't actually met Dr. King yet. I suppose both of you know him well?" She knew the ambulance crew in a small town sometimes had to call a doctor, depending on the severity of the emergency.

Martha and Daniel exchanged a telling look. "We know Dr. King, all right," Martha confirmed, her voice expressionless. "Other doctors come and go, but King's sort of a fixture in Korbin Lake."

"I'm looking forward to meeting him," Alex lied. Actually, the more she thought about it, the more she dreaded the encounter. "And I'd like to carry an ambulance pager if that's all right with you," Alex continued. "It would make it lots easier to reach me if you ever needed to."

Again, Martha and Daniel exchanged looks. "We'd be delighted to supply one," Daniel said. "We've had the odd problem with that in the past."

Alex knew he meant King, and a shiver of foreboding went skidding up and down her spine.

The more she learned about the man she'd be working with, the more apprehensive she became.

CHAPTER NINE

THE TRIP BACK TO Korbin Lake was relaxed and enjoyable.

Daniel told clever, outrageous stories about his days as a lawyer, and Martha added vignettes about her time as a nurse's aide. Alex found herself relating funny things that had happened in Emergency over the years and laughing more than she had for a long while.

Daniel dropped Alex at the detachment, and he and Martha drove off, waving and calling friendly goodbyes, with assurances they'd provide her with an ambulance beeper very soon.

Alex walked into the office feeling both optimistic and more relaxed than she'd been for weeks, and she gave Lorna Berringer a grateful smile. "Thanks for all your help this morning, Lorna. Everything went fine. I'm quite sure Jason's at Children's already, and I made arrangements for Nancy and Greg to stay at Parent's Shelter, which is only a block from the hospital."

Tears shimmered in Lorna's green eyes. "Is the baby gonna be okay, you figure?"

"Absolutely. Think positive here."

"Good thing Nancy called you instead of going back to the clinic again to see King," Lorna declared with vehemence. She shook her head. Her shiny hair, sprayed into place, didn't move an inch. "That old nincompoop of a doctor, he should have retired a long time ago. I wouldn't take my gerbil to him, and yet mostly everybody else in this town seems to figure the sun shines out of his... nose.''

Alex didn't respond. Lorna's outburst and the guarded reactions of the ambulance crew confirmed her own disturbing suspicions about the doctor she'd be working closely with. The now-familiar sense of foreboding returned.

King wouldn't be grateful for the actions she'd taken today. He was bound to resent her for making him look bad, even if she'd done the only thing possible.

''The sergeant just called. He's on his way in if you want to wait a minute.''

Cameron hurried in a few moments later, and she related the details of the trip to Cranbrook. Then he strolled out to Alex's car with her.

''You're something else, Doc, you know that?'' He tipped her chin up and kissed her lightly on the lips. ''This town's mighty lucky, getting someone of your caliber.''

She appreciated his approval, but more than anything right now, she wanted to talk to him about King. She needed to hear Cam's opinion of the whole situation, but the sidewalk in front of the police office wasn't exactly the place to have a confidential discussion.

Alex slid into the car, grimacing as her bare legs touched the hot upholstery. ''Oww! It's scalding in here. I'm going home to jump in the lake. Any chance you could join me for a quick dip, Copper? I'd sure like to talk to you.''

He sighed and shook his head. ''Sorry, love. Not a chance. With Greg gone, I'm the law in these parts. I may even have to bunk here at the office for a couple of days, depending on how busy we get.''

''Oh, Cameron, no,'' she groaned. ''And here I figured our frantic days were over.'' She'd told herself that the one really positive factor about this move to Korbin Lake was that she and Cam would have much more time to spend together, time to rebuild the emotional intimacy they seemed to have lost. Now, it seemed they'd have less time than ever, at least for a while.

Well, the circumstances certainly weren't Cam's fault. She hid her disappointment and said cheerfully, "I'm stopping at the deli to pick up dinner, so it'll be in the fridge if and when you get there."

"Good thinking. It's far too hot to cook."

She grinned up at him. "Potato salad from the deli's my idea of gourmet, remember?"

"You do have other talents, Doc." He winked and gave her a suggestive look, obviously remembering the passion they'd shared the night before.

The portable radio on his belt crackled, and when he spoke into it, Lorna's distorted voice relayed a message Alex's untrained ear couldn't begin to decipher.

Cam responded, and then said, "Gotta go, I'll call you later. Don't wait up for me." He loped toward the patrol car parked at the curb and drove off.

Feeling absurdly lonely and abandoned, Alex started her own car, wondering irritably when the time would ever be right for her and Cameron to have a discussion about something besides potato salad.

The house seemed lonely and deserted when she made her way down the long, twisting driveway. She gathered up the deli bags from the car and went inside. The answering machine indicated there were two messages.

She'd left the kitchen door open, and her cup sat where she'd left it on the porch, a gray skin on the top of the cold coffee. For a moment she stood and looked out at the lake, remembering the feeling of peace and tranquility she'd experienced for such a little while, sitting here this morning. Those idyllic few moments before Nancy's call seemed so long ago.

"Pavarotti, where are you? Come here, cat." The animal came strolling in from the deck and wound himself around Alex's ankles, bemoaning the lack of food in his dish at the top of his voice. "Spoiled thing," she chided, bending to stroke him. "Aren't you supposed to be able to catch rodents or something if you're hungry?" She opened a tin for him and scratched his ears before pressing the button on the machine to retrieve her messages.

The first terse message was from her mother.

"Alexandra, surely you've arrived by now. *Please* give your father and I a quick call and reassure us that you're safe. We've become pathetically paranoid about our children lately."

Alex cursed under her breath, and an all-too-familiar feeling of guilt overwhelmed her. She'd planned to call her parents last evening and, with Cameron's lovemaking, she'd forgotten. She'd thought of it again when she woke up this morning, figured it was too early to disturb them, and then Nancy's call had driven it out of her head.

The second message was from Cameron's brother, David.

"Hey, country people, how's life out there in the mountains? I might just drive down and visit you guys, see if there's any jobs out there. There's sure nothing here on the coast. Gotta square it with my parole officer and fix the carburetor on the Chevy before I take off, though, so I'm not too sure when I'll get there. Talk to ya when I see ya."

Alex scowled at the machine and her heart sank. She wasn't ready for houseguests, that was certain. She considered calling David and diplomatically telling him so, and then decided she'd better talk it over with Cam first.

She dialed the police office, but of course Cam wasn't there. Lorna promised to have him call.

Alex unloaded the deli bags and set the containers in the fridge. The chocolate ice cream she'd bought was melting, and she was about to put it in the freezer when the phone rang.

"What's up, Alex?"

"Cam, your brother called. It sounded as if he was planning on coming for a visit."

"Hey, that's great. Did he say when?"

Her hand tightened on the phone. "Within the next few days, I think. He's apparently driving through. Cam, I really don't feel up for company just yet."

"Dave's not company, sweetheart. He's family. It'll do him good to get out of the city for a while. The crowd he hangs with are a bad influence. I worry about him."

Alex sank down into a chair, twisting the phone cord around her fingers. "But he'd be staying right here with us."

"Yeah. Of course. At least for a while." Cameron sounded rushed. "That's all right with you, isn't it? I mean, there's plenty of room. He could have that downstairs bedroom—the shower's right there, so it wouldn't disturb us at all." He didn't even wait for an answer. "Look, honey, I've gotta run. Things are piling up on me."

Alex hung up the phone and slammed the freezer door closed as annoyance and frustration built inside of her. She should have known Cam would want David to come and stay. The house was huge, there were all those empty bedrooms and, as he said, David was family.

But damn it to hell, the last thing she wanted at this particular time was her brother-in-law living with her and her husband. She felt that she and Cam had difficult issues to work out between them, things that affected their marriage, things that needed privacy and time. She was trying to make the best of it, but she still deeply resented the way Cam had arbitrarily changed their lives.

But the negative feelings she had about David staying with them had nothing whatsoever to do with him, she reminded herself. She sincerely liked David—it was impossible not to. Her feelings had to do with Cam, with a growing awareness that the relaxed life-style, the intimacy, the opportunity for shared confidences that she'd dreamed of having with her husband here in Korbin Lake might just be a fantasy. And they sure as heck weren't going to materialize if a third party was around.

She could feel anxiety and anger pulsing in every cell in her body, and she needed to do something to release it. She ran up the stairs and stripped off her shorts and crumpled cotton shirt, pulling on her bikini.

She was hot and tired and out of sorts. Maybe a swim would cool her down so she wouldn't jump down Cameron's throat about this David thing the moment he walked in the door tonight. *If* he walked in the door tonight, she corrected herself, remembering what he'd said about sleeping at the office. All of a sudden she sat down hard on the bed and anger turned to weary frustration.

How could she even fight with her husband properly if he wasn't ever around?

CAMERON CAME HOME that night, but not until three in the morning. Alex half woke and gazed in a fuzzy stupor at the bedside clock when he collapsed into bed beside her.

"S'late," she croaked. "Where've you been?"

"Partying at the local juke joint," he said, amusement in his tone. "Go back to sleep. I'll tell you about it in the morning." He kissed her lips and gathered her tight against him.

It had taken her hours to get to sleep and she was far too groggy to do more than mumble and then slide back into oblivion, comforted by his warm body folded around her. They'd talk in the morning.

She came fully awake when the phone rang at seven. Cameron answered it, and she realized he was already up. His hair was still wet from the shower, and he was wearing an unbuttoned uniform shirt, snug black briefs and navy socks.

"Yeah, tell him I'll be there in fifteen minutes," she heard him say before he hung up the receiver.

Alex struggled to a sitting position, rubbed at her eyes and yawned. "Are you going out again? You only just got home."

"Morning to you, too, sleepyhead." He tousled her hair and tipped her chin up for a fast kiss, then stepped into his navy slacks and tucked in his shirt. "Somebody broke into the drugstore last night. The security alarm went off, but by the time I got there, whoever did it was long gone. I couldn't locate the owner. He wasn't at home, and his wife wasn't cooperative at all." He threaded a belt swiftly through the pant loops and fastened it. "He called the office just now. Seems he was over at his girlfriend's place." He sat down on the bed and put on his shoes, then stood up and strapped on his gun belt. "No wonder the wife wasn't cooperative, huh?"

"Will you be back for lunch?"

"I doubt it. Are you nervous out here by yourself, hon?"

"Of course not. I love it here. I'd just like us to have some time together, that's all."

"I know, but with Greg away, I'm on deck. Y'know, I'll feel a lot better about you being alone out here if David's around. Not that this is a major crime center or anything, but for the next while you're liable to be by yourself a lot. Things'll slow down some when Greg gets back, but until then, I'm going to be working long hours. And even with two of us, it's damned busy, much worse than I figured it would be. We could really use another man at this detachment. We're seriously understaffed."

"Can't you tell Headquarters that?" His words confirmed her worst fears—instead of more time off, it seemed he'd have even less.

"I intend to if I ever get time to draft a full report." He glanced at his watch and bent to press a quick kiss on her mouth. "Gotta run, baby. I'll call you later."

She heard him trotting down the stairs, and a moment later the front door closed. The engine on his Jeep roared to life, and the sound gradually faded as the vehicle climbed the driveway.

Alex plopped back on the pillows, disappointed and irritated in equal measure. Was she getting paranoid, or was Cameron deliberately avoiding any intimate discussions? Was her overwhelming feeling of frustration simply due to the fact that she hadn't started work yet herself and consequently had too much time on her hands while Cameron was apparently run off his feet?

Well, the obvious answer to that was to go back to work herself, which she'd do in just a few days. In the meantime, surely she could find plenty of things to keep her busy. She reached for the phone and the list of numbers she'd left beside it the night before.

The first call was to Children's Hospital, and she learned that Jason Townsend was rehydrating nicely and was scheduled for surgery at three that afternoon.

The second call was to St. Joe's, to Wade's doctor, Mike Parsons. Alex had called her mother the previous afternoon, and Eleanor had sounded frantic. Wade was still refusing to see his family, although Thea was ignoring his wishes and camping out in his room anyway, which incensed Eleanor; if she, Wade's own mother, respected his desire for privacy, then surely *that woman* ought to do the same. Physically, Wade was improving very gradually, but Eleanor reiterated her belief that he needed intensive counseling—her standard formula for any sort of emotional conflict with her children.

For once, though, Alex thought her mother might be right.

She waited impatiently while the switchboard operator paged Dr. Parsons. Alex was hoping to catch him before he began his morning rounds.

In a few moments, Mike's deep, hearty voice came on the line, and Alex asked about Wade. Her heart sank as Mike repeated pretty much what Eleanor had said.

"Physically, he's progressing as well as we'd hoped," Mike said. "The sensation in his legs is a very positive sign, and the swelling in his spinal cord seems to be decreasing. We'll be able to take the tongs off fairly soon." He recited details of Wade's medical treatment and then added, "Emotionally, he's not so good, though. As you know, depression's the norm in cases of spinal injury. He's still insisting that he doesn't want to see anybody, that he's best left totally to himself. Thea still goes and sits beside him, but he either refuses to talk to her or else he becomes verbally abusive. Harve Franklin keeps trying, but Wade won't say much, except to tell him to get the hell out of his room."

Harve Franklin was a staff psychiatrist at St. Joe's, a big, friendly bear of a man whom Alex liked and respected.

"Wade's not suicidal, is he, Mike?" It was a possibility that had haunted Alex half the night, and she shivered as she heard the slight hesitation in Mike's tone.

"I don't think so. We're all keeping a close eye on him."

Alex hung up feeling chilled and slightly sick, wondering whether or not she should return to Vancouver in an effort to help her brother. The problem was, she didn't know what she'd be able to do if she did go. And going back to Vancouver right now certainly wasn't the answer to the problems she and Cam were having, either. She blew out a pent-up breath and dialed the phone again.

This call was to Thea. Alex had tried to reach her the night before with no success. This morning the phone rang over and over, and at last Thea's husky voice responded, thick with sleep.

Alex apologized, and instead of making polite conversation, she went straight to her reason for calling. "Thea, I'm worried sick about Wade and I need to talk to you," she confessed, quickly relating what Mike had told her a few moments before.

"Is there anything, anything at all, that you think would help Wade? Do you think I could do any good if I came down and tried to talk to him?"

Thea was silent for so long Alex thought the connection had been broken. "Thea? Are you still there?"

A sniffle came over the line, and Alex realized with a pang of sympathy that Thea was weeping. "I don't think there's anything anyone can do," the other woman finally managed to sob. "Everybody's tried, but you know how—how damned *stubborn* he can be."

"Yeah, I do. He's a lot like Dad that way, although he'd never admit it."

"No, for sure he wouldn't." There was a pause, and Alex heard Thea blowing her nose. "If I knew what to do," she finally continued, "I'd do it, Alex. See, he's—he's trying to force me to leave him. He either treats me like a stranger or else—" Thea sobbed again and finally gained control, and now her voice was angry. "Or else he uses every dirty trick he can think of to hurt me. Yesterday he said he doesn't really love me, that what we had together was just physical, that I'm—I'm one hell of a lay but—la-lacking in the brain department." There was heartbreak as well as anger in her tone, and Alex felt sympathy well up inside her.

"When I left the hospital last night, I went and sat through three movies," Thea went on in a desolate tone, "and I don't remember the first thing about any of them. I feel as if he's making me crazy." The sobs began again, deep and agonizing.

Alex's heart went out to Thea. Tears filled her eyes, and she couldn't think of what to say for comfort. She waited, and after a moment Thea managed to add, "He—he thinks just because his spine is injured, I won't want to be with him anymore. He won't listen when the doctors say there's a good chance he'll walk again. He's locked himself away from me emotionally, and I don't know what to do to get him back. I don't know what the *hell* to do, Alex. All I know is, I love him."

The words seemed to echo in Alex's head. She did her best to reassure and comfort Thea, feeling uncomfortably like her mother when she suggested a therapist at St. Joe's, a practical woman Alex knew and trusted.

"And if you feel like talking to me, I'm here. If it would help for me to come down, I'll come. Just please keep me posted as to what's really going on, won't you, Thea?"

Thea promised, and Alex hung up the phone with a terrible sense of helplessness and the knowledge that she'd been no real help at all.

He's locked himself away emotionally, and I don't know what the hell to do about it.

The words seemed to lodge like cement in the pit of Alex's stomach, and she leaped out of bed, tossed her outsize cotton sleep shirt in the laundry basket and headed naked for the shower, frantically going over all the things she needed to do that day.

Go to the bank, transfer her accounts, send out address changes, find a decent hairdresser, buy tampons and moisturizer, get a couple of paperbacks to read, empty her suitcases into the closets, organize her clothes for work...

She lathered her hair with shampoo and then stood under the spray long after the soap was gone, her heart thudding with anxiety.

Was Cameron, too, locking himself away emotionally?

Was he using his job to keep from having to discuss any of the issues they'd left unresolved? Because if he was, Alex felt exactly the same way Thea did.

And she didn't know what in hell to do about it, either.

THAT DAY, and the days that followed, seemed to confirm her fears. She hardly saw Cameron. He called four or five times each day, hurried calls that always seemed to be interrupted by some emergency. "I've decided to sleep in the single officer's quarters at the detachment rather than have the night calls routed to the house," he told her at one point with perfect logic. "I'm just too far away at the lake. It takes too much time to get back to the detachment.''

Alex began to see distinct advantages to living next to the police office.

They ate dinner together three times, once at home and twice at Luigi's, a family-style restaurant in town. None of the three meals was leisurely or relaxed; at home, Cameron's radio interrupted their meal continually, and the calls left him distracted.

At the restaurant, Alex learned that eating out with a policeman in uniform was similar to being an exhibit in a zoo. Everyone stared, either openly or covertly, and many of the town's citizens felt free to wander over and discuss some injustice or other. Some introduced themselves and welcomed Alex and Cameron to Korbin Lake, which was nice but certainly didn't make for an intimate or relaxing meal. She was beginning to realize that in this town, Sergeant Cameron Ross was public property, and it irritated the hell out of her.

Oh, they talked, of course, in hurried, interrupted bursts that made her want to scream. She managed to tell Cam about Wade, and she relayed the happy news that Jason's surgery had been a resounding success; the baby was recovering at an amazing speed, and the Townsends would be back in a few days.

Their return couldn't come too soon for Alex. She'd made up her mind that the instant the pressure of work had lessened for Cameron, she was going to confront him and really work through all the issues he seemed to be avoiding so adroitly.

And added to everything else, the closer she came to starting work, the more Alex found herself dreading it. Dr. Hollister King was not going to thank her for taking

over the treatment of little Jason Townsend. She knew
that for damned sure.

The emergency room at St. Joe's was beginning to seem
a veritable rest home compared to the intricacies of life in
a small town.

CHAPTER TEN

MONDAY MORNING and her first day of work came all too soon for Alex.

Cameron had come home after all late Sunday night, but a call had come at three in the morning, a report of domestic violence, and he'd hurriedly dressed and gone out again. Nerves on edge at the thought of her new job, Alex didn't sleep much after that.

At five, she got up and showered and then dressed for work, knowing it was far too early but needing to get the day started. She was accustomed to being alone in the big house by now, but this morning she felt especially lonely and abandoned.

It was childish of her, she knew, but it would have been so nice to have Cameron there to reassure her, to tell her that the pretty blue patterned cotton skirt and matching vest, the white silk tee and pearl studs were the right choices for a day at the clinic. She dried her hair and fluffed out the curls, again needing Cameron's assurance that the shorter haircut she'd had on Saturday was a good one.

She wanted him to tell her that of course Dr. King was a reasonable man, that he and Alex would work easily and well together, that all her misgivings were unfounded.

Damn it all, Cam, why can't you be here for me when I need you? But he wasn't there, so instead, she chattered nonstop to Pavarotti as she made herself a cup of instant coffee.

She was too keyed up to eat the single slice of toast after it popped up in the toaster, and the cat got bored with her stream of nervous chatter and bolted out the back door.

"Traitor," Alex called after him. She glanced at the clock. It was still too early, but she had to get out, do something. She gathered up her medical bag and her purse and went out into the early-morning sunshine, locking the door behind her and wondering how she'd feel when she unlocked it again that night.

The medical facilities were on the outskirts of town, far enough from both houses and highway to seem almost pastoral. Korbin Lake Medical Clinic was housed in a small frame building just a hundred yards or so from the twenty-six bed hospital. Both structures were pleasantly situated on wide lawns interspersed with flower beds, set against a thick backdrop of emerald green pine trees.

At this early hour sprinklers sent water cascading over the grass and flowers, the spray catching rays of sunlight and making rainbows.

Alex compared the idyllic scene to the frantic early-morning traffic in front of St. Joe's and smiled wistfully as she pulled her car into the nearly deserted lot. Driving to work in the city had sent adrenaline pumping through her veins. This was a lot more like meditation.

Alex glanced at her watch. It was barely seven. She was slated to meet Dr. King at eight at the clinic, and then Harry Perkins, the hospital administrator, over at the hospital. Well, what the heck. Maybe being an hour early would give her a chance to familiarize herself with both hospital and clinic before the workday started.

She walked slowly across to the main entrance and into the hospital, heading straight over to the nursing station and smiling at the pretty nurse with the long strawberry blond hair who returned her smile with a gamine's wide grin and a cheerful greeting.

"Morning. What can I do for you?" She had a sprinkling of freckles on her nose and a dimple beside her mouth.

"I'm Doctor Ross. I—"

"*You're* our new doctor? Holy smokes." The young nurse's hazel eyes widened, and she held out her hand. "You're an early bird. Our director of nursing won't be here until around eight. How d'ya do? I'm Rebecca Jones. Everyone calls me Becky."

There was an engaging openness to her manner that put Alex immediately at ease. "Hi, Becky. I'm Alexandra, but everyone calls me Alex." They both smiled as Alex shook the other woman's hand. "I'd just like to look around if you don't mind."

The nurse's intelligent eyes were assessing Alex, from the tip of her curly head to the leather sandals on her bare toes, and there was approval and admiration in her expression and her tone. "Wanna poke around on your own or would you like the guided tour?" Again, her wide smile came and went. "No extra charge."

"Well, if it's free, of course I'll take the tour." Already, Alex liked this friendly woman, and a little of the tension inside her eased. If all the staff were like Rebecca Jones, it would be a pleasure to work here.

For the next fifteen minutes, Becky walked Alex through the hospital, introducing staff and patients alike. The rest of the staff consisted of a senior nurse who acted as evening supervisor, two RNs on duty at night, four more during the day, and one orderly.

Becky introduced the other nurse, Pam Walker, a quiet woman in her midforties, and the two aides collecting breakfast trays. Alex was delighted to find the small lab extremely well-equipped, the operating room state-of-the-art.

"Complex surgical cases are sent to either Vancouver or Calgary, we don't have a full-time anesthesiologist or enough trained staff to do more than the routine stuff here. Doc King does vasectomies, appendixes, circumcisions and hysterectomies," Becky explained. "But you already know all that. I guess you'll be doing anesthesia for him."

Alex did know, and she wasn't delighted about that aspect of her new job, although of course she didn't say so to Becky.

Although she'd sat in on a refresher course in basic anesthesia before she left Vancouver, she was well aware that it was a specialty for which she wasn't fully trained. She also knew, however, that applying for a position as a GP in a small community like Korbin Lake meant performing several other medical procedures for which she'd routinely call in specialists at St. Joe's.

And maybe that was the good news, she told herself firmly. She'd be getting back to the grass roots of medicine here, and although she was a bit nervous, it would be a great learning experience.

She tried to shove her uncertainty to the back of her mind and concentrate only on the patients Becky was introducing. There were a dozen or so of them, housed in small, sunny rooms, and Becky knew every one on a first-name basis. It was obvious from their responses that she was not only a caring and compassionate nurse, but a beloved one, as well.

She led Alex into one last room, where an elderly woman was sitting up in bed, sewing together the knitted portions of a child's indigo blue sweater. The woman's fingers were twisted from arthritis, she breathed with difficulty and there were nasal prongs in her nostrils, attached to an oxygen outlet.

"This is a very special lady, Alex. I've saved the best for last. This is my grandma, Winifred Lawrence. Gram, this is our new doctor, Alex Ross."

Hazel eyes, identical to Becky's own, shone intelligently from the wrinkled face. She laid down the knitting and held out a gnarled hand. "How d'ya do?"

Alex shook it gently, noting how blue the nails were. "I'm very pleased to meet you, Mrs. Lawrence."

"Call me Winifred, it's more neighborly. Mrs. Lawrence makes me feel like the parson's wife or something." A smile came and went, again a facsimile of Becky's.

"What are you knitting?" Alex fingered the soft wool.

"A sweater for my granddaughter. Becky's little girl, Emily. It's almost done."

"Emily's going to love it, Gram." Becky kissed the woman's wrinkled cheek and drew the covers up over her thin legs. She checked the oxygen mix and stroked the withered arm that protruded from the pink hospital gown. "Blue's always been Em's favorite color." Becky lowered her voice to a conspirational whisper. "I'll smuggle her in to see you this afternoon."

When they were again in the hallway, Alex asked quietly, "What's your grandmother in for?"

"Pneumonia, caused by her heart. Myocardial ischemea."

*Lack of oxygen supply to the heart with consequent al-
tered cardiac function.* The prognosis wasn't great for a
woman Winifred's age.

"She's improving, but it's slow this time. She's almost
seventy-seven." Becky's voice was determinedly cheerful, although Alex knew the nurse had to be aware that at
her grandmother's age, there was no question of bypass
surgery.

As if Becky had read her mind, she said softly, "It's
tough when you know exactly what the odds are, isn't it?"

Alex nodded. "It sure is. My brother had a motorcycle
accident just a short while ago, and I've realized it's much
more difficult to be a relative when you're in the medical
field."

"How's he making out?"

Alex briefly outlined Wade's condition. It was a relief
to be able to tell someone about her brother, particularly
someone as responsive and sympathetic as Becky.

"It must have been tough for you, leaving Vancouver
just after that happened," she said, and the compassion
and understanding in her voice was deeply comforting to
Alex.

At last Becky opened the door to a small staff lounge
and gestured at the coffeemaker. "This is the end of the
tour—you've seen the whole joint. Want a cup? It's fresh.
I just made it before you got here."

Alex checked her watch and then nodded. There were
still ten minutes or so before she was due to meet Dr. King
at the clinic.

Becky rinsed out two mugs and filled them. "The hospital grapevine says you're married to our new Mountie.
You have any kids, Alex?"

"Nope, not yet. Maybe in a few years. A baby needs
more time and attention than we'd be able to provide right

now. I have trouble taking good care of our cat, never mind a baby.''

And a baby needs parents with a secure marriage.

Becky nodded. "Kids are lots of work, all right. I'm lucky. Mom and Grandma have always lived with me. They care for Emily when I can't be around.'' She sipped her coffee and then added, "I'm a single parent.'' Her voice took on a bitter note. "Emily's genetic donor walked out just after she was born, never to be heard from again.''

Alex felt touched by the confidence. Before she could reply, however, the door of the coffee room opened and an older nurse walked in. She was tall and thin, ramrod straight, and every detail of her uniform was impeccable. She was even wearing a cap, the only one in the hospital to do so. From behind the tinted lenses of her designer glasses, her cool gray eyes flicked from Becky to Alex. Instantly, the atmosphere in the room changed.

Becky set her barely touched coffee on the scarred table and sat up a little straighter.

"Morning, Shirley. This is our new doctor, Alex Ross. Alex, Shirley Boyd, the director of nursing.''

Shirley didn't offer her hand. She gave Alex a cool glance and a nod. "I suppose you'd like a look at our facilities,'' she said in a grudging tone.

"No problem, Shirley,'' Becky said in a breezy voice. "I've already shown Alex around. I knew you'd be busy when you came on shift, and I had time.''

Shirley shot her a glacial look, and then pointedly glanced at the clock on the wall. "I believe rounds start at eight-thirty, and I imagine Dr. King will be waiting for those charts, Becky.''

Becky didn't spring to her feet, although it was plain Shirley thought it would be appropriate.

Alex, however, got the message loud and clear. "I really appreciate your help, Becky. I'm meeting Dr. King in a few moments myself, so I'd better be on my way. Nice to meet you, Shirley," she lied.

She hurried out, mentally putting Becky on one side of an imaginary ledger and Shirley on the other. One positive, one negative. And where would Hollister King fall?

She hurried along the sidewalk that bordered the clinic's parking lot.

"Doctor Ross?" The deep, officious male voice sounded from behind her, and Alex stopped and turned.

"Hollister King." He was exceptionally tall and very broad, with a full mane of white hair and a sizable paunch. Alex knew he was fifty-nine, and for his age King was still an impressive figure. She instantly felt both physically intimidated and improperly dressed—her colleague was wearing an impeccably tailored light brown summer suit with starched white shirt, conservative necktie and highly polished brown leather shoes. His snowy brows grew in bushy profusion above penetrating pale blue eyes, and he was scowling at her through horn-rimmed glasses.

Conscious of her bare, sandaled feet and casual clothing, Alex still managed to sound more confident than she felt. "How do you do, Dr. King? I've been looking forward to meeting you." She extended her hand and dredged up a smile.

To her horror, King ignored the polite gesture. He looked straight into Alex's eyes with cold animosity. "What's this nonsense I hear about you sending the Townsend baby off to Vancouver by Air Ambulance last week without so much as a by-your-leave from me? I was the physician on the case, madam. I *am* the Townsends' doctor. I *delivered* young Jason Townsend. You, on the other hand, could hardly have known him a day, and still you took it upon yourself to take over a patient of mine. Bloody cheek, I call it. Who do you think you are?"

Alex dropped her hand and stared straight back into King's eyes. She'd encountered enough doctors like him during her career to have perfected a way of dealing with them, but superficial bravery didn't do anything for the trembling deep in her insides.

"Jason was operated on at Children's three days ago for pyloric stenosis, Doctor King." She kept her voice even, her tone nonjudgmental. "When I saw him, he was already dangerously dehydrated. As you know, in a baby Jason's age, severe dehydration is often terminal. I took immediate action because I felt the situation warranted it."

"You should have contacted *me* before taking any such action," King roared, oblivious to three people who'd just pulled up in the parking lot a few yards away and were getting out of their car. All of them froze, staring curiously at the two doctors.

Alex shot a meaningful look at their audience and said in a steely tone, "Perhaps we should continue this conversation somewhere a little more private, Doctor?"

King's large, already florid countenance turned magenta, but he wheeled around and stalked through the front door of the clinic without another word, leaving Alex to trail behind, her anger and sense of outrage boiling up inside her like a volcano as she walked in behind him.

King didn't pause at the reception area, and the woman behind the desk stared openly at both of them as they passed.

Alex followed hard on King's heels, making it through the door of his office a bare instant before he slammed it.

The rude, insufferable old . . . walrus!

She was damned if she was going to let him get the better of her, especially when *he* had been the one to make the diagnostic mistake. The opinionated old stuffed shirt ought to be thanking her for saving his patient instead of acting this way, she fumed.

King ignored her presence, picking up a file folder from his desk and pretending to study it.

Alex stood and stared at him, letting the silence lengthen.

At last, he shot her a look. "You do have an office down the hall, young woman. I have rounds to make at the hospital and patients waiting to be seen. And as far as patients are concerned, you will be sent only the new ones. From now on, my patients are off-limits. Do I make myself clear?"

Alex could barely contain her temper. Her voice trembled, but she stared him straight in the eye, her chin held high. "I will see any patient who asks to consult me. I am a physician, and my responsibility is to the public, not to you, Doctor. We have to work closely together here, and it would be far more pleasant to be congenial, but if this is your attitude, then I shall have no choice except to be as rude to you as you have been to me."

She opened the door and stepped through it, closing it softly behind her. Her face and neck felt as though they were on fire, and her entire body was trembling. She took a moment to draw in several deep breaths before she walked over to the tiny, birdlike woman behind the reception desk.

"Morning." Lord, her voice had a quaver. She cleared her throat, pasted on a smile and held out her hand. "I'm Dr. Ross. How do you do?"

The woman smiled hesitantly and took Alex's hand, her small dark eyes wary. "I'm Ruthie Amorelli. Welcome to Korbin Lake Medical Clinic. I'll be handling your appointment book and doing your billing."

"I'd appreciate it if you could quickly show me the facilities and point out which office I'll be using, Ruthie," Alex said as pleasantly as she could, fully aware that the dividing walls were thin and the entire altercation with King had undoubtedly been overheard.

Well, now everyone in the clinic knew exactly what was going on, so there'd be no surprises. "I'll be seeing any new patients that arrive. Are there many new patients, Ruthie?"

"Well, there's always new families moving into the area," Ruthie said uncertainly. "But right at the moment, I don't think there are any coming in that I know about. Not this morning, for sure." She flashed a false, bright smile. "You'll have plenty of time to get settled in, anyway, Doctor." She led the way down the hall, scurrying past the closed door of King's office.

"There are two examining rooms down here, and we use the lab over at the hospital, of course. This is your office." She opened the door to a small, bare but pleasant room with a wide window looking out onto a wooded area. The room contained only a stained beige carpet, a scarred desk, a telephone and two chairs.

"That connecting door is to one of the examining rooms, and the bathroom's over here. There's a little lunchroom at the back, and I guess that's about it."

Alex thanked Ruthie, went into her office and closed the door, slumping against it with her fists clenched, staring out at the peaceful green pine trees and seeing instead the morning bustle at St. Joe's ER.

Monday mornings could be quiet. The staff would be having coffee, chatting about the weather, laughing at one another's jokes, trading friendly insults and gossiping about some weird incident or other that had occurred over the weekend.

Bella would be taking up a collection for somebody's wedding shower, and Helen would be showing off pictures of her latest grandchild. They were an insular family in the E.R., Alex thought with a wistful smile, bonded by the intimacy of combating illness and death.

They were *her* family, beloved, familiar, caring. They were her friends. They respected and acknowledged her ability as a physician, they liked her as a person. She missed them so much at this moment that her chest ached.

What in heaven's name was she doing in this alien place, in this barren room, subject to the rude tirades of a man who thought his name represented his station? She didn't have a patient to her name, and from the sound of things, no real prospects of getting many. Her fists curled and she fought the rush of self-pitying tears that burned at the back of her eyeballs.

Damn you, Cameron Ross. What have you done to my career?

THE MEETING WITH Harry Perkins was pleasant and unremarkable. Short, fat and well over sixty, the administrator puffed on a cigar the entire time Alex was with him, making her wonder if anyone had ever talked to him about the connection between smoking, arteriosclerosis and obesity.

She also wondered if the smell of cigar smoke would linger in her hair and clothing for the rest of the day, and decided it would.

He asked about her father and made flattering comments about Bruce's ability as a surgeon—Bruce had apparently successfully operated on Harry's brother at some point. He didn't indicate what for, and Alex didn't ask, desperate to get out and breathe some pure air as soon as she decently could.

"We won't need to have you apply for admitting privileges," he said in his gravely smoker's voice. "We're all very glad to have you here."

With one obvious exception, Alex thought. Surely Perkins had to know how Hollister King felt, but if he did, he didn't mention it. Instead he went on to say that he hoped Alex would enjoy a long and pleasant career in Korbin Lake and then invited her down to the hospital cafeteria for coffee and doughnuts, which she declined. He was available at any time, he emphasized, if she should need anything. His door was always open.

And that was that.

She made her way back over to the clinic at half past ten, and from then until four in the afternoon she treated two patients, one a senile old man with a bladder infection who for some reason refused to be treated by King. The old man was probably smarter than the rest of the waiting room full of people, Alex thought cynically.

Her second patient was a tourist who'd stopped in Korbin Lake for lunch at a diner and stepped the wrong way off the curb, ending up with a severely sprained ankle. He arrived at Emergency, and Dr. King declared himself too busy to see him, actually referring the man to Alex.

Alms for the poor, Alex decided ungraciously.

The hours dragged endlessly. She read outdated magazines from the waiting room and listed supplies she needed to make her barren office personal and inviting. When the loneliness grew intolerable, she placed a call to the nursing desk on Wade's floor at St. Joe's and asked if she could speak to him. A long time passed, and then the nurse came on the line.

"I'm so sorry, Dr. Ross, but he refuses to talk to anyone."

Alex hung up. She dialed Thea and got her machine, called her mother and father and got theirs, tried Verna with no success, then tried to reach Morgan, only to learn that her friend was in the delivery room.

Alex shook her head and had to smile. Where else would Morgan be? The delivery room was her all-time favorite location.

Desperate now, Alex called the RCMP office and asked Lorna if Cam was available.

"Gosh, I'm sorry, Alex. He's up at the mine. I can reach him if it's urgent."

She was on a roll, and it wasn't a good one. "No, not at all. I just wondered if he was free for a late lunch. Just tell him I called."

She hung the phone up and considered an overdose of something lethal. It seemed everyone in the world was busy except her.

At four-fifteen, she was getting ready to go home at last when the telephone rang.

"Is this Doctor Ross, the ravishing new GP? Do you make house calls, Doctor? Because I seem to have this swelling—'

"Cameron?" Just hearing his voice brought tears of self-pity to her eyes.

"Hi, sweetheart. How's your first day going?"

She swallowed back the urge to tell him exactly how it was going. "Slow," she managed to reply instead, trying to sound unconcerned. Ruthie could come in any moment, and she didn't want to be overheard when she told Cam exactly what she felt about Doctor King.

"Very slow. In fact, I'm going to head home in a few minutes." *Please, Cam, come home with me, just for a little while.* "How about joining me?" She waited, praying that he'd say he could break off early.

If ever she needed to talk to him, it was now.

"I wish I could," Cam said, and a feeling of intense loneliness swept over Alex.

"Things are nuts around here. I was away all day, and now there's a stack of complaint sheets to sort out, and I still have to drive out to some ranch and check on a complaint that they're mistreating their horses. Thank heaven Greg's coming back tonight. Listen, honey, could you do me a big favor and stop on your way home for a case of beer? If I ever get free here, I'm gonna sit on our deck and sip a cold one, and the way my day's going, I'll miss the store. Don't worry about supper. I'll bring home Chinese about six." A radio squawked in the background. "Gotta go, love. Talk to you later."

And that was that. Alex hung up slowly. At least the frustration that came from trying to have any sort of meaningful conversation with Cam was becoming familiar.

CHAPTER ELEVEN

STEERING CAREFULLY down her twisting driveway, Alex saw a battered old red Chevy she recognized parked in front of the house, and her heart sank.

David had obviously arrived. She'd hardly had time to unpack, and now she had a houseguest. She tried to plaster a welcoming smile on her face, a smile that felt as strained as an overstretched rubber band.

Her brother-in-law didn't seem to notice. He came loping up from the lakeshore, a wide grin on his handsome, tanned face. His hair was tousled, his T-shirt bragged Packing The Goods, and his rugby shorts bared long, heavily muscled legs. Like his older brother, he was drop-dead handsome, and he was going to cause quite a stir among Korbin Lake's female population, Alex surmised as he wrapped his arms around her, lifted her off her feet and planted a kiss on her cheek.

"Hey, Alex, hope you don't mind me dropping in like this. I got things in order in Vancouver and just decided to take off. How's it goin' with you? You're as gorgeous as ever, sister-in-law. You cut your hair shorter—it looks great. God, it's good to see ya. Mom sends her regards, and she sent a box of baking along, as well."

He wrapped his arms around her in another exuberant hug and lifted her again, swinging her around.

She squealed and laughed in spite of herself at his ebullient good nature. No one could stay down for long around David—he had a little-boy innocence and charm that was captivating, as about half the women in Vancouver could attest to. Some of the tension inside her eased, and her smile suddenly felt more natural.

"So where's The Man? Off chasing bad guys?" He pretended to draw firearms from an invisible holster.

"Horses, the last I heard. He'll be here at supper time. Come and help me carry the beer in. It should still be cold."

"Wow, you shop right, sis. I've been fantasizing about cold beer the last two hundred miles. Let's grab a couple and go for a swim. Hey, I just can't believe this place—it's next thing to paradise. Is the water warm?"

"Not bad. Refreshing, I'd say."

"Liquid ice, huh?"

"Two degrees off."

They laughed together, and she showed David the downstairs bedroom and located bedding for him. While he brought his things in, she left a message at the office for Cam, telling him David had arrived, and then she changed into her bikini.

For the next hour, they swam and chatted and relaxed in the sunshine, and although they discussed Wade and the problems he was having, gossiped about mutual acquaintances in Vancouver and laughed at Pavarotti's futile efforts to catch birds on the shoreline, there was still a hurting part of Alex that felt as though it were on hold, waiting, always waiting, for Cameron. The devastating quarrel with King, the empty, endless frustrating day she'd just spent was still there just under the surface, and she needed Cam to help her exorcise it.

He arrived at last, laden with paper bags filled with cardboard containers of food and an immense bucket of rice. Alex watched as the brothers embraced, pounding each other on the shoulder and exchanging friendly insults.

Again she thought of Wade, and a lump rose in her throat, remembering the way he used to hug her so hard her ribs ached. Now he wouldn't even speak to her on the telephone.

"You going for a swim before we eat, Cameron?"

At her question, he turned to her, taking her into his arms and planting a quick, sexy kiss on her mouth, and she snaked her arms around his lean middle, taking comfort at least in his physical presence.

But he shook his head at swimming. "I have to eat and go back to the office. Gotta catch up on my paperwork so Greg knows what's going on when he comes on shift tomorrow morning."

"But you'll be back later, won't you? Not too late?" She tried to keep the plaintive entreaty out of her voice and didn't entirely succeed, but Cameron didn't seem to even notice. When had he stopped picking up the small signals they'd always used to communicate things they couldn't say?

"I could be quite a while. Don't wait up for me, honey."

Don't wait up for me? How many times had he said that this past week? She felt her temper rising. "I had a few problems at work I wanted to talk over with you, Cam."

"You been butting heads with old Doc King right off the bat?" He shook his head and grinned as if the idea were amusing. "I've met him. He's a pompous old guy, isn't he? Is he upset with you over Jason?"

"Something like that." With David right there, she couldn't bring herself to relate the humiliating details of her scene with King the way she needed to do.

"Well, just be patient. He's been the head honcho here since you and I were in diapers. It'll probably take time for him to accept you, honey."

Be patient? She glanced at David and swallowed the furious retort that sprang to her lips. *Wrong, Cameron. You're dead wrong. He'll never accept me—and you don't even have time to hear about it.*

They trooped up to the house and ate, and still Alex waited for an opportunity to have a private word with Cameron. It didn't come. As soon as the meal was over, David said, "Hey, Cam, c'mon out and have a look at the relic. There's a knock in the engine I can't seem to locate."

"Sure thing, and then I'll have to be getting back to the office. Bye, Alex."

He reached for her, but she avoided his embrace.

On Tuesday and Wednesday, Alex awoke with a feeling of absolute dread in the pit of her stomach. She'd always bounded out of bed, filled with enthusiasm for her job. Now, she had to force herself to get up and go to work. She dreaded the encounters with King that were inevitable in an area as small as the clinic, but hardest of all to bear were the empty hours spent in her office, dutifully reading medical journals she'd never had time to do more than glance at before, waiting for patients who didn't materialize.

Each morning, she walked into the clinic to find people sitting on the chairs, already waiting for King. She came to hate the sympathetic expression on Ruthie's face and the slight shake of her head, indicating there was no one for Alex to see.

Thursday morning, however, Ruthie's smile was wide. "Mrs. Townsend and the baby are waiting in your office,

Doctor," she chirped. "And you have an eleven and a one o'clock appointment, and another at three."

"Heavens!" Alex clasped her hands together in mock horror. "How will I ever find time for lunch?"

Ruthie laughed, and Alex hurried eagerly down the hall to her office.

Nancy, holding a peacefully sleeping Jason, beamed at Alex when she came through the door.

"Nancy, it's great to see you. And how's our big boy doing?" Alex took the baby, loving the warm, fragrant feel of him in her arms. He looked a little pale and drawn, but relaxed and complacent, and the mark on his head where she'd inserted the IV was already covered with a healthy-looking scab.

"Oh, Alex, he's a different baby. He's so contented, he just eats and eats and then sleeps. I actually wake him up sometimes just to make sure he's okay. And he smiled at me for the first time this morning when I was changing him." She looked from her baby over at Alex, and there were tears in her eyes. "We can't ever thank you enough for what you did for us. I'm convinced Jason would have died if it hadn't been for you. I've told everybody I know what a great doctor you are. I feel like taking out an ad in the paper."

"Better not. I'd probably face bribery charges." Alex was embarrassed, but the praise was sweet balm for her battered ego right now. "Let's just take this handsome fellow into the examining room and see how his incision's doing."

Jason startled and woke as Alex undressed him. He pouted a little, but he didn't cry when she unfastened his clothing and removed the small dressing covering the surgical site.

"This looks just fine, Nancy. Keep it clean and dry, and by the look of it, he'll be totally healed in another week." She changed the dressing and replaced the tiny clothes, then cradled the little boy against her for a long, satisfying moment before she reluctantly handed him back to his mother.

"He's pretty special, this fellow," she said with a grin. "He's my very first patient here in Korbin Lake."

Nancy nodded. "Greg and I talked it over, and we'd like you to be our family doctor from now on, Alex. I'd never go back to Doctor King after what happened." She shook her head and shuddered. "You know, I saw him on the street yesterday, and he barely even said hello, much less asked me how Jason's doing."

King wasn't saying so much as hello to Alex, but she didn't mention it. It would be unprofessional for her to talk about King to Nancy, but fortunately it didn't work the other way.

"I wrote Doc King a letter the minute I got home, you know, telling him we were going to be your patients from now on and why, as if he couldn't guess. If that's all right with you, of course?"

King probably hyperventilated, Alex thought with grim satisfaction. "I'm absolutely delighted to have the Townsend family as my patients," she said with a wide smile.

"Good. Because I need some advice right away about dieting." Nancy grimaced and indicated her stomach and hips. "What do you suggest I do about this weight, Alex? I gained ten pounds each time I lost a baby, and then with Jason, I really went over the top. I'm ashamed to admit it, but I'm about fifty pounds over what I was when Greg and I got married. I'd sure like to lose it, but each time I manage to go down even five pounds, I gain it right back again."

"First we'll make sure there's no medical problem causing it." For the next half hour, Alex did a thorough physical, taking blood and urine samples to rule out any medical reason for the weight gain. Then she counseled Nancy about a low-fat, high-fiber diet, suggesting she eat seven small meals each day instead of three large ones and set aside time every day for a long walk with Jason. "A combination of exercise and frequent low-fat meals will do it, you watch and see," she reassured the other woman.

Nancy's gratitude was heartwarming. When she left, there was plenty of time before her next patient, so Alex strolled next door to the hospital lab with the specimens she wanted tests run on.

"Hey, Alex, how's it going?" Becky Jones was just coming out of a patient's room, and she flashed her wide, friendly smile.

They were alone in the hallway, and for some reason, Alex chose not to make the customary automatic response—that everything was just great.

"To tell you the truth, this is the first day this week I haven't seriously considered drowning myself in the lake," she said impulsively. "I've actually got three appointments today. That's about the same number I've had all week long."

"So business has already increased a hundred percent. You're on a roll," Becky teased, but there was understanding in her eyes. "Thing'll get better, you wait and see. Look, we're having a little party over here later today for Gram. It's her seventy-seventh birthday. You wanna pop over later for some cake and coffee?"

"I'd love to. How's she doing? Did she get the sweater finished?"

"Yeah." A shadow passed over Becky's delicate features. "She's finished the sweater, but she's not doing too well. We'd hoped she was going to get home for her birthday, but it wasn't possible. Anyhow, come to her room at about four-thirty.''

"Sounds good. I'll be there.''

"Great. You can meet Emily. She's going to model the sweater.''

"I'll look forward to it.'' A buzzer rang insistently and Becky waved and hurried off. Alex walked outside and made her way along the sidewalk that led to the clinic, feeling more optimistic than she'd felt in days.

As the afternoon progressed, her spirits rose even more. Her day turned out to be almost busy; besides the three booked appointments and Nancy's visit, she saw four other patients: three newcomers to the community and one middle-aged woman. Etta Krantz, a longtime patient of King's, wanted a second opinion on estrogen-replacement therapy for menopause.

King had apparently told Etta he didn't recommend it—there was a history of breast cancer in her family. Feeling enormously relieved that she wouldn't have to disagree once again with King's diagnosis, Alex spent an hour explaining why. She sent Etta home with a list of reading material on menopause and several suggestions about alternate, more natural ways of controlling her annoying symptoms, including vitamin supplements and some herbal remedies Alex was familiar with.

Etta thanked her and left, and Alex went down the hall to get a coffee, taking it back to her desk. She was trying to decide what color to paint her office, and she had a selection of color chips from the hardware store spread out in front of her. She slipped off her shoes and propped her bare feet up beside the telephone, sipping her coffee and studying the samples.

There was a tap on the door, and thinking it was Ruthie, she called out, "Come on in."

"Hello there." Daniel Brandt stepped through the door.

Alex swung her feet off the desk like a child who'd been caught at mischief, and managed to upset her coffee in the process.

"Damn." She grabbed at a roll of paper towels to mop up the mess, and he knelt down beside her, dabbing away at coffee stains.

She looked at him and found that he was laughing, and she had to laugh, too. "Protestant work ethic," she said ruefully. "Makes for a guilty conscience over the darnedest things."

"Yeah. When I first got here, I used to have a panic attack if someone I knew saw me strolling down the street at ten in the morning. I expected them to shake their finger under my nose and say, 'Why aren't you gainfully employed, young man?'"

He got to his feet and she did, too. "Sit down, Daniel. I don't suppose you want a coffee of your own to spill?"

"Thanks, I'll pass on the coffee." He sat, relaxed and easy, one long denim-clad leg propped on the other knee. He looked around the office. "Nice place you got here. Minimalist decorating. I like that." His gray eyes sparkled with humor.

Alex laughed. "Actually, I was just trying to decide what color to paint it. What d'ya think?" She held out the color chips.

He considered them. "Not beige. Or mushroom. Everybody seems to be doing walls mushroom these days." He went through the chips and chose a bright, cheery red. "How about this? You'd never have to worry about bloodstains that way."

"You're no help at all, and you're also a trifle ghoulish."

"Why is it no one appreciates my practical nature? And speaking of practical—" he dug into the pocket of his shirt and put a beeper on her desk "—this was my excuse for coming by."

"Thanks. I appreciate it."

"Not half as much as we do. We'll try not to call on you unless it's something we absolutely can't handle."

"Hey, call me. I don't mind. At the moment, I'm not exactly overworked anyway."

"You're going to be. It just takes time in a small town for people to change their ideas. Hell, there's still the odd dinosaur to contend with here in Korbin Lake." He winked.

It dawned on Alex that Daniel was probably well aware of the situation here at the clinic with King. Working on the ambulance service, he'd know King well and also hear all the gossip that was a part of being around any hospital.

She remembered that he'd been a lawyer. "Do you ever miss the courtroom, the excitement of criminal law, Daniel?" *The way I miss the ER at St. Joe's?*

"I did for the first few months, yeah. I was hooked on the adrenaline rush you get in a courtroom, I guess. It takes a while to get over." He looked at her for a long moment. "You miss the city, huh?"

She nodded. He was easy to talk to. "It's a big adjustment, coming here. I'm sure I'll get used to it, but—"

To her absolute horror, she felt her eyes fill with tears. She ducked her head to hide them.

"You've got a tricky situation here, Alex." His voice was warm and intimate and filled with sympathy. "People get set in their ways when they get older. They're not open to new ideas or to the fact that maybe it's past time to step down." He didn't mention King's name, but they both knew what he meant. "If I can ever be of any help, even just to listen, call me." He reached for her prescription pad and scribbled down his home number and then got to his feet. "Gotta go." He tapped the beeper he'd set on her desk. "We sure appreciate you offering to carry this."

"Thanks, Daniel." She had the feeling she was thanking him for more than the beeper.

He paused with his hand on the doorknob. "About those color chips, Alex. Maybe get a second opinion. Unfortunately, I'm color-blind."

He left, and she laughed outright. Daniel Brandt was funny and kind, and both those traits were what she needed just now. Trouble was, she needed them from Cameron instead of Daniel Brandt.

But she was still smiling a short while later when she hurried into the hospital and down the corridor to Winifred Lawrence's room. She'd driven to the small nearby shopping mall a few minutes before and pondered over what she could bring the old woman, deciding finally on a pretty porcelain container of hand-and-body lotion. She'd had the clerk tie a huge red ribbon on the bottle, and she'd chosen a funny birthday card, as well.

She paused in the doorway, suddenly shy. The room was filled with a mixture of hospital personnel and visitors. A huge homemade chocolate cake sat on Winifred's bedside table along with a stack of cards. Her bed was littered with small and large packages in pretty satchels or wrapped in bright paper. The tiny old woman was obviously weaker and even more frail-looking than when Alex had first met her. Each breath was an effort, in spite of the oxygen she was receiving, but her wrinkled face was wreathed in smiles and her bright eyes shone with happiness and excitement.

A tiny girl in a white ruffled dress and the blue sweater Winifred had made was sitting on the end of the bed, her back to Alex.

"Hey, come on in. Glad you could make it." Becky quickly introduced some of the hospital staff whom Alex didn't know.

Still feeling a little awkward, she moved to the bedside to place her gift with the others. She touched the old woman's hand and smiled down at her. "Happy birthday, Winifred. You probably don't remember me. I'm—"

"Doctor Alex," Winifred wheezed, smiling and nodding up at Alex. "'Course I remember. Couldn't forget such a pretty face. I was just sewing up Emily's sweater when Becky introduced us the other day. Emily, honey, say hi to the new doctor."

Alex turned to the child with a wide smile, and shock rippled through every nerve ending. Emily had the distinctive slanted eyes, rounded face and protruding tongue of a child with Down's syndrome.

"This is my daughter, Emily," Becky said, and Alex reached out and gently took the tiny girl's hand in her own, crouching down so that she would be at the child's eye level.

"Hiya, Emily. Hey, don't you look pretty in your new sweater. Did Great-Grandma make you that?"

The little girl stared up at Alex for a long moment. Then a wide, happy grin lit up her features and she stretched her arms up in a plea to be held.

"C'mon, then." Alex scooped her up, and Emily's arms snaked around her neck, her head flopping on

Alex's shoulder, her mouth pressed into Alex's neck, breath wet and warm and fragrant.

"Well," Becky said with a note of surprise in her voice. "Seems you've made a conquest, Alex. She's not always that responsive to strangers."

"We're soul mates," Alex said lightly, cuddling the child against her. "Besides, she likes my perfume."

Everyone laughed and then called greetings to two new arrivals who'd just appeared in the doorway. One carried a cardboard box filled with sandwiches and the other a flat tray of fancy baking.

"Alex, this is my mother, Sadie Jones, and my aunt, Lily Keeling. They're the caterers for this gala event."

Sadie might well have been Becky's older sister. She was shorter than Becky but still slender, and she had the same startling red-gold hair and sparkling hazel eyes as her daughter. One had to look closely to see the fine lines around her mouth, the slight softening of the dramatic jawline that indicated she was, indeed, Becky's mother.

Lily was quite different, tall and heavy and wrinkled, with silver hair and glasses, but with the same ready smile. They greeted Alex warmly, and Lily remarked, "Looks like our wee Emily's adopted you, Doctor Alex." She planted a kiss on Emily's cheek. The child smiled at her but didn't loosen her hold on Alex's neck.

The women handed around sandwiches and sweets, and someone poured glasses of apple juice.

"Well, Winifred, if Doc King ever shows up, we can cut this cake and get you to open those presents," someone said, and Alex felt an alarm bell go off in her head. She should have guessed that King would be invited. She knew for a fact he wouldn't be pleased to see her here.

She had to get out. Being insulted by King would ruin what had turned into a pleasant day, and she'd feel humiliated in front of these kind people. Gently, she tried to untangle Emily's arms and set her back on the bed, but the little girl was having none of it. She shook her head no and tightened her clasp on Alex's neck. Alex tried to catch Becky's eye, but the nurse was talking to Lily, and both Lily and Sadie were busy handing around the food they'd brought.

"Well, well, Winifred, this is quite a party you're throwing." King's bluff, hearty voice had every head in the room turning toward the doorway, and Alex felt her heart begin to pound.

CHAPTER TWELVE

ALEX TURNED SLOWLY and faced Dr. King. He was holding a huge bouquet of long-stemmed roses, beautifully arranged in a cut-glass vase, and he looked past Alex and made his way to Winifred's bedside, setting the flowers down beside the chocolate cake.

"Olinda sends her regards. I can't take credit for the flowers—she arranged them," he said with great good humor.

Alex could see the pride and affection on Winifred's face when King bent and pressed a noisy kiss on her cheek.

"Happy birthday, my dear. And many, many more," he added gallantly. There were tears in many eyes at his words, because everyone was aware that Winifred had perhaps reached her final birthday.

"I made them all wait so you wouldn't miss out on the cake," Winifred said with difficulty. "We all know how you like chocolate cake, Doctor. Would you cut it for me?"

"I'd be honored, Winifred." With a wide smile, King wielded the knife and sliced the cake into neat, even portions, joking about his surgical skills as he slid each slice onto a small paper plate and personally handed them around.

Alex, her stomach in an anxious knot, stood as far away from him as she could get, murmuring quietly to Emily, waiting for an opportunity to hand the little girl to one of her relatives and escape.

But to her amazement, King cut an extra large piece of cake and brought it straight over to her. "I see you've made a friend, Dr. Ross," he remarked in an neutral tone. "I happen to know this young lady's as fond of cake as I am myself. I thought the two of you might like to share."

"Why...thank you, Doctor." Alex was so surprised she fumbled and nearly dropped the plate he handed her.

"Hollister. The name is Hollister. No need to stand on ceremony, Alexandra, isn't that so?" His gaze wasn't as friendly as his tone indicated, but at least he was offering an olive branch of sorts, and Alex accepted gladly.

"Of course, ummm, Hollister."

"If you're going to eat cake with Emily, you need a chair and a very large bib," Becky announced, guiding Alex to a seat next to Winifred's bed and spreading a towel across Alex's lap. "You'll probably need a shower, too, by the time you're done."

She removed the little blue sweater. "Don't want to get this all chocolatey, honey." She gave Alex an uncertain look. "You sure you don't want me to take over for this performance, Alex?"

"Not at all. We'll make out just fine."

Everyone seemed to be watching now, and affectionate laughter erupted when Emily crowed with delight. She squirmed around on Alex's lap so she could reach the plate and, with Alex holding on tightly to both cake and child, Emily happily began shoving pieces of it into her mouth. She scattered crumbs everywhere, smearing Alex and every exposed inch of her own white dress with liberal amounts of chocolate icing, all the while making sounds that indicated how very pleased she was with this windfall.

"Don't say I didn't warn you." Becky rolled her eyes and went for a washcloth and a basin, and King led the group in a rendition of "Happy Birthday." With his help, Winifred opened her gifts.

Smeared with cake, and aware that Emily had wet her diapers through, Alex watched the elderly doctor charm the entire roomful of women. For the first time, she began to understand something of the nature of the relationship that Korbin Lake shared with Hollister King. He was one of their own, Alex mused. He might make mistakes, serious ones, but the community indulged him because of his roots here and the kind of good fellowship he was displaying right now. When his eyes met Alex's, there was both triumph and challenge in his hard blue gaze.

I can afford to be magnanimous to you if I choose, his look said. *Because just like all the others who've been here before you, you'll lose. You'll leave, and I'll still be here.*

"Give her to me, Alex, now that she's totally wrecked you." Becky crouched and gently scrubbed Emily's face and hands and legs with a soapy cloth. "Gosh, I'm sorry about your blouse and slacks. Send me the dry-cleaning bill."

"Nonsense. They're cotton, and they wash like a dream."

Becky finished sponging Emily down and lifted her up into her arms. "Miss Muffet here needs to go home and have a bath and a nap." Becky's eyes were filled with gratitude and affection. "Thanks for being so patient with her."

"My pleasure." Alex's arms felt empty without the warm weight of the little girl. The other guests were all leaving now as well, and Winifred had fallen asleep, her head on one side, her breathing stertorous.

King chatted quietly for a moment with one of the nurses and then, with a curt nod to Alex and a gentle chuck under Emily's chin, he, too, left.

Sadie and Lily gathered up the remnants of the party, and Alex walked out to the parking lot with the family, helping to carry the food containers. She waited beside their battered old station wagon as Becky strapped Emily into an infant seat.

Alex bent and pressed a kiss into one of Emily's palms and folded the flaccid little fingers around it, smiling at the sleepy girl. "Bye, sweets. Thanks for befriending me."

"You must come over soon and have a cup of tea with us," Sadie insisted. "Emily's going to want to see you again real soon and she pretty much rules the household."

"I'm off on Saturday, if that's good for you, Alex," Becky added immediately. "Come about three. Emily'll be up from her nap by then. And maybe wear a scrub suit in case she decides to share food with you again."

They all laughed. "Here's our phone number. Call just before you leave and I'll give you directions." Becky scribbled on the back of an old grocery list. "Not that anybody could stay lost long in Korbin Lake."

"Don't bet on it. I'm not used to these small towns," Alex joked. They all laughed again and waved as Alex made her way to her own car.

She drove home feeling happier and more relaxed than she'd felt since her arrival in Korbin Lake, and it wasn't until she turned down her own driveway that she began to wonder if Becky Jones had deliberately orchestrated the meeting with King in Winifred's room.

Alex knew there were very few secrets among hospital staff, and of course Becky would know every detail of the feud between Alex and King. Perhaps she'd counted on the intimacy of the party to ease the situation. If so, Alex was indebted to the nurse. King would never be a bosom buddy, but at least now they were speaking, and it eased the tension for everyone.

Cameron's Jeep was in the yard, so he was home from work. Her heart soared, and she leaped out of the car and hurried into the house, eager to tell him all about her new patients, the party, Emily, and especially the fact that she and Hollister King were now on a first-name basis.

"Cam? Cam, where are you? You'll never guess what happened." Her voice echoed through the house, and Pavarotti came and wound around her ankles.

There was no answer, and Alex made her way into the kitchen.

There was a note taped to the fridge.

"Gone fishing with Dave. Packed a lunch, so don't wait supper. Love ya, Cam."

The cat meowed, and across the lake the inland gulls shrieked and dipped over the sun-speckled water. The empty house suddenly seemed too large and far too lonely. On impulse, she went to the telephone and dialed Thea's number, needing to talk to someone. To her surprise, Thea answered instantly.

"Alex, hi. How's it going up there? How's it feel, being a country doctor?"

"I'd starve if I had to depend on what I'm earning," Alex said with rueful honesty. "But I've met some nice people." She told Thea about Becky and her family, and the other woman asked questions and seemed interested.

Alex, feeling guilty at talking only about herself, said, "How's it going with you?"

"Busy. Nutty. We're doing a catalogue right now for next spring, heavy sweaters and leggings. We'll be shooting swimsuits in December, just as usual, and then I'll freeze my butt off.''

Alex laughed. ''How is it with Wade? I tried to phone him and he refused to speak to me, so I guess he's still pretty difficult.''

''He sure is, and I'm getting sick and tired of it.'' Thea sighed, and Alex could sense her exasperation. ''He's getting the tongs off tomorrow. He's regained a lot of sensation in his legs, and his other injuries are healing fast. Things are going so well, and yet he's still being such a bonehead, picking fights with me over nothing, doing everything he can to drive me away.'' Thea's voice revealed how upset she was.

''Honestly, Alex, I don't know how much more of this I can take. I talked to that therapist you suggested, and she says it's a deep fear of being abandoned that makes Wade act this way. He figures I'll leave him anyhow now that he's injured, so he's doing everything he can to make it happen.'' Thea's voice changed, and now she sounded really angry. ''Talk about not trusting me, the jerk. I still love him, but I sure don't like him very much right now. If he wasn't flat on his back, so help me, I'd give him a fat piece of my mind.''

''Why don't you do exactly that?'' The words were out before she had a chance to think about them, and Alex hoped to God she was giving Thea the right advice. ''Stop letting him get away with it, and tell him how you feel for a change.'' She thought of Cameron, and her own festering anger, and it dawned on her that maybe she ought to take her own advice.

''You think I should?'' Thea sounded uncertain. ''Your mother keeps on and on at me about not upsetting him, how we have to understand how he must be feeling.''

Alex snorted. "My mother's never had the slightest idea how Wade was feeling, or anyone else for that matter. Don't let her bully you." Again, her own words surprised her. She'd never really realized until this moment that her mother was a bully.

"I try not to, but it's hard. She's pretty overwhelming. But it's not her I want to live with, it's Wade. So you really figure I should level with him, huh?'

"I do." As she thought it over, Alex was sure it was the right thing. "It's time he started appreciating you a little more. If I were there, I'd tell him so."

"Thanks, Alex." Thea's voice was suddenly thick with emotion. "Y'know, I used to feel so inadequate around you—me a model with a measly grade-twelve education and you a doctor."

Alex protested, knowing all the while that she had harbored some of the wrong ideas about Thea, too.

"I want you to know I don't feel that way anymore," Thea went on. "I'm really glad we got to know each other, even though it took Wade's accident to do it."

Alex was deeply touched. She felt the same way, and when she hung up a few minutes later, it was with a sense of warm affection for Thea. She prayed she'd been right in suggesting a confrontation with Wade.

Again, she thought of Cameron and the problems the two of them were having. She hated confrontation, but it was cowardly of her to recommend it to Thea and avoid it herself.

"HEY ALEX, WE'RE HOME."

Cameron dumped three lake trout in the kitchen sink and rinsed his hands under the tap. He could hear the television in the small sitting room, and he went along the hallway and into the room where Alex was curled on the sofa watching an awards show, the cat asleep on her knees.

"Sorry we're late. We met a guy who took us out in his boat, and then we had a beer with him when we got back. He's a supervisor up at the mine, and he says there's a job opening that Dave should apply for."

Alex gave him a vague smile. "Where is David?"

"Gone to have a shower. He's going into town."

"You going with him?"

The tone of her voice set off a warning bell. "Of course not. He's probably going to check out the action at the local pub." He frowned at her. "What's the matter, honey? You mad at me because I went fishing? Tonight's practically the first free time I've had all week."

She shook her head. "It's not the fishing." There was a silence and then she said, "It does seem as if you're gone all the time, though. I thought when Greg got back we'd have some time to spend together, but it hasn't worked out that way, has it? Greg's been back all week, and still I've barely seen you."

He knew she was right, and guilt made him defensive. "That's ridiculous. I've been home every evening."

She nodded. "Yeah, you have. You're here, but we don't really communicate much anymore. You and David are either playing chess or fishing or watching football. I wait for you to come to bed, but I'm usually asleep before you get there."

For some reason Cam didn't care to explore, her accusation made him angry. "I didn't invite Dave out here, Alex, but you know as well as I do that he needed to get out of the city. And I can't just ignore him now that he's here, can I? I figure maybe he'll have a chance to straighten out his life, being with you and me. Obviously you don't see it that way."

She clicked off the television, moved the cat and wrapped her arms protectively around her drawn-up knees. "I admit I'm not overjoyed about David staying here right now." She drew a breath and let it out again with a whoosh. "But it's you I have a real problem with, Cam. You've been using David as a reason to distance yourself from me, and it hurts." Her voice trembled. "Do you realize that we've never once sat down and really discussed this move and the effect it's had on our lives? You talked a little about the reasons you felt it was necessary, but you seem blind to the fact that having to come here has affected my life, my work, just as much as it has yours."

Her voice wobbled, and he realized she was on the verge of tears. "Because of you, I left a job I loved to come to a place where my skills are being wasted. I sit around waiting for patients, grateful if I get two or three a day. Damn it, Cameron, I used to see fifty cases a day, maybe more, at busy times at St. Joe's. It's your choice we're here. The very least you owe me is sympathy and an opportunity to complain about what's bothering me without having to make an appointment with you to do it."

Your choice. Your fault. Cam could feel cold sweat trickling down his back, soaking his armpits. Again, guilt made him defensive, and he knew he sounded harsh, but he couldn't control it. "I've told you I'm sorry I screwed up our lives, what more can I say? You're not the only one having problems at work. I'm having a hell of a time learning everything I need to know to run this detachment. And I'm not working long hours to avoid you, Alex. I'm just trying to do my job as well as I know how."

"At the expense of our marriage, Cameron? You know, I still can't really understand why you made the decision to move here without so much as consulting me. We've never had a chance to talk it out between us."

"I've talked about it all I ever intend to, Alex. The move was a value decision on my part, and I made it. If that's not good enough for you, well, I'm sorry." He knew he was being hard and unfeeling, but at the moment he didn't care. His own emotions were threatening to overwhelm him. "I know you and your family feel the need to discuss everything to death, but believe it or not, there are people around who handle their problems differently."

"You call this handling a problem?" She was visibly trembling now, and part of him was ashamed, mortally ashamed for upsetting her this way.

"This is avoidance, Cameron. This is sticking your head in the sand and pretending that everything's fine. And in case you hadn't noticed, it's not fine at all. Whether you want to admit it or not, this move is affecting our relationship in a terrible way. And on top of that, you've closed yourself off from me, and no matter how hard I try, I can't communicate with you anymore."

"Communicate." He spat out the word. "You're beginning to sound exactly like your mother, Alex. That's her catchword for everything, *communicate*." He knew all too well that the last thing she ever wanted was to be compared to Eleanor. Again, a tiny part of him was horrified by his own cruelty, but he couldn't seem to stop. He snarled, "Just don't try to psychoanalyze me, okay, *Doctor Ross?*"

Shock and pain tracked parallel paths across her mobile features, and her full lips trembled. He watched her throat contract as she swallowed hard.

With visible effort she got to her feet and moved past him, careful not to touch him in any way. He heard her footsteps going up the stairs, and he heard their bedroom door close softly. He knew he should race up those stairs after her, drag her into his arms and apologize his fool head off. He should somehow make it right between them, this instant, he knew he should.

But it was like a treadmill. The moment he apologized, she'd want to talk, she'd ask again for an explanation of the whole mess, and he just didn't have one to offer. A sense of humiliation made him cringe whenever he realized how he'd messed up their lives, yet his pride wouldn't let him discuss it. He needed to forget about it all. Why didn't she understand that?

He cursed in a steady stream, located the keys to the Jeep in his pants pocket and headed for the front door. Being a policeman meant there were always stacks of reports to write, forms to fill out, requisitions to sign.

For the first time in his career, Cam thought of the endless paperwork on his desk as an advantage.

IT WAS THE WORST FIGHT they'd ever had, because it didn't get resolved.

Alex lay awake hour after hour that night, waiting for Cameron to come home, planning what to say. She heard David arrive just after midnight, and she lay, tense and expectant, thinking Cam would be right behind him. But when 2:00 a.m. came, and then 3:00, and still her husband hadn't returned, hurt turned to icy anger and rebellion.

She wouldn't allow him to control her like this. She wouldn't lie awake waiting for him to choose to come to her. With her pillow under her arm and an extra comforter from the closet, she moved into one of the spare bedrooms for the remainder of the night, finally slipping into exhausted slumber just at dawn.

She woke with a pounding headache to a silent house and the certain knowledge that she'd overslept—she hadn't brought the alarm clock in with her when she changed bedrooms. A quick survey indicated that although Cam hadn't slept in their bed, either, he must have returned at some point to shower and put on his uniform—his gun was gone from the dresser, and the towels in the bathroom were wet. He must have been especially quiet so as not to awaken her, and her spirits sank even further.

His actions confirmed what she already knew, what she'd accused him of doing—he was isolating himself from her.

As she quickly showered and dressed, her stomach in knots and her fingers clumsy, she recalled other quarrels they'd had. Always, within a few hours or a day at most, they'd been resolved, the wounds they'd both created with harsh words soothed and healed with lovemaking. Inevitably, at some point during the night, they'd ended up in each other's arms, which in turn made it possible to discuss whatever was wrong.

Maybe having extra bedrooms were more of a curse than a blessing, she thought miserably. She hurried down to the kitchen just in time to surprise Pavarotti up on the counter, happily finishing off three fresh fish Cam must have left in the sink.

She scolded him, cleaned up the mess, then put out fresh water and an open tin of cat food to try to keep him honest, reminding herself that she and Cam *had* made love since she'd come to Korbin Lake and it hadn't helped one bit.

Just as she was getting into the car to drive to work, her ambulance beeper went off, and she used her portable phone to make the call as she steered out onto the main road.

There'd been a car accident at a level crossing on the highway five miles east of town, and Alex hurried to the site.

There were already a half-dozen cars lined up, and she pulled onto the verge and got out, taking her medical bag and running along the row of cars to the scene of the accident.

A woman was screaming. Broken glass littered the pavement. A blue pickup truck lay wheels up in the ditch, and an older-model black car with its passenger side smashed in sat at an angle in the middle of the highway, blocking two lanes of traffic.

The ambulance crew was already there, as well as the police cruiser. Greg Townsend was directing traffic around the scene, and Cameron was crouched on his haunches beside three teenagers, two boys and one girl. It was the girl who was screaming and sobbing hysterically. The teens were sitting in the grass on the edge of the highway. One of the boys sat hunched over, his head resting on his knees. Martha was kneeling beside him, examining his shoulder.

Cameron looked up and saw Alex, and their eyes met. For just an instant she saw a mirror image of the desolation that she was feeling. In that same instant, though, it was gone, and there was no chance to say anything except a quick, cool hello.

Martha got to her feet as Alex hurried over and said, "Looks like just some scrapes here. I think the older man over there needs your attention the most."

Alex, panting a little, hurried over to where Daniel knelt beside an elderly man sprawled like a rag doll on the pavement. Blood oozed through a dressing on his forehead, and one ankle lay twisted at a crazy angle. His head was rolling from side to side, and his eyes were wide open but dazed with pain. He was making a steady moaning noise and clutching at Daniel's arm.

"What've we got?" Alex lifted the dressing and looked at the gash as Daniel recited the story.

"Pickup truck broadsided this man's car. He was wearing a shoulder belt, but his head hit the steering wheel. He was unconscious when we got here but he's coming around now. Airways clear, BP's 210 over 140, pulse 45. He's not coherent yet."

A nasty head wound, but hopefully not life threatening. Alex ran her hands down his body, knowing the ambulance crew would have checked but needing to make her own examination. She searched for traces of broken ribs, tenderness, indications that there might be internal bleeding, and she was relieved when she found none.

Alex checked the pupils of the man's eyes. They looked normal. "I'm Dr. Ross. Can you tell me your name, sir? What's your name?"

"Where am I?" The voice was feeble. "Who are you?"

"I'm Doctor Ross. Can you tell me your name, sir?"

"Henry Poulin. Please, my leg hurts. Oh, my leg—"

"We're going to get you to the hospital right away, Henry, and we'll fix your leg." Together, Alex and Daniel stabilized the broken ankle with a pillow splint.

Martha came hurrying over just as they loaded Mr. Poulin on a stretcher and slid it into the ambulance.

Alex turned to the paramedic. "Anybody else need looking at here?"

Martha motioned toward the teens. "The three kids over there were banged up pretty severely. They have cuts and bruises, but no signs of concussion. The girl's hysterical. Sergeant Ross is taking them to the hospital in the police car. He says to tell you he's got a spare set of keys for your car and Constable Townsend'll bring it over for you."

"Thanks." Alex climbed in beside her patient. Siren blaring, the ambulance drove off.

At the hospital the nurses were waiting, and Alex was impressed with the way they functioned under minor emergency conditions. As she'd realized the first day, the small hospital was exceptionally well equipped, and the tests she ordered on Poulin were performed quickly and efficiently. The only staff member Alex had any problems with was Shirley Boyd, the nursing director. Shirley made it very obvious that she disapproved of Alex and considered her an interloper.

"I've called Dr. King. He's just over at the clinic, and he'll be here in a few moments to take over," she announced in an imperious voice.

Alex stifled an angry retort. "Good," she said as evenly as she could. "As soon as he arrives, we can take Mr. Poulin into the OR, but right now I'd like those X rays as soon as possible, Shirley."

Just as she'd thought at the scene of the accident, Henry Poulin had no internal bleeding, no life-threatening injuries. Within fifteen minutes, King came bustling in, and because the fracture needed pinning, Alex administered the general and King set the broken ankle.

The older doctor was both confident and quick, doing a good job on the compound fracture. He whistled tunelessly and pointed out obvious techniques throughout the operation, and Alex felt he was putting on a bit of a show for her sake. She was glad, however, that her first experience at administering anesthesia was for such a minor procedure. She'd feel much more confident after this initial surgery.

Poulin was soon resting comfortably in the small intensive-care unit. The nurses had called his daughter, and she rushed in, very upset, so Alex spent time reassuring her that her father would be just fine.

By the time Alex was free, Cameron had left. He'd turned the teens over to Doctor King, and Alex sought the doctor out when she was done with Poulin's daughter. She wanted to know how the three youngsters were, and she felt grateful that at least she and the older physician were on speaking terms today.

King said, "Boys are fine. I sent them home, but I admitted the young lady. Didn't you realize she was pregnant?"

CHAPTER THIRTEEN

IT WAS OBVIOUS King was enjoying himself.

"I understand you were right at the scene with the ambulance crew, Doctor. Didn't you question her? It was the first thing *I* asked her. Or is she telling me the truth when she says you didn't even bother to talk to her before she came in?"

Alex opened her mouth to explain the circumstances, but he didn't give her a chance.

"I've always maintained that we doctors aren't infallible. Any one of us can make mistakes, wouldn't you agree, Alexandra?" His deliberate use of her first name was meant to demoralize, to put her in what he considered her place.

She wanted to slap him. She wanted to wipe the condescension, the smarmy superiority, from his face. Yet, at the same time, she knew that what he said was absolutely correct. Neither she, nor any other doctor alive, was infallible. Anyone, at any time, could make mistakes.

And she knew, as any conscientious doctor did, that those mistakes could mean the loss of a life.

She struggled to portray a composure she was far from feeling. "I didn't examine the girl at the accident scene," she admitted, uncomfortably aware that she'd taken the paramedics' word that there were no serious injuries without checking for herself. "She only appeared to be suffering from scrapes and bruises. Mr. Poulin was in far more distress." She stopped, mentally berating herself for her oversight.

King allowed the charged silence to stretch for an interminable time, and Alex knew he was relishing her agitation. A small, malicious smile came and went on his face before he finally added, "Actually, Doctor, it seems she's miscarrying. Twenty-six-week fetus, or so she tells me. Mind you, it's the best thing that could happen, her losing the baby. She's the daughter of one of our local pastors—hellfire and brimstone and all that. She's scared to death of him." He snorted and added in a malicious tone, "Maybe she should have paid more attention to his sermons."

"Was the miscarriage a direct result of the accident or had it already begun beforehand?"

"Doesn't really make much difference, does it?"

"I suppose not." Rage at King for baiting her mingled with compassion for the unfortunate teen. "Poor little kid," Alex said. "No wonder she was crying so hard at the accident scene. She must have already been in labor. What about the baby's father?"

King harrumphed. "Young punk. He's the one that was driving. Wanted to stay in here with her, but I sent him on his way. Wild young ne'er-do-well, not a penny to his name. I know his father, too. I've heard him complain that the boy spends everything he has on that idiotic truck of his."

There wasn't a trace of understanding in his voice. Alex thought of her brother with his motorcycle, of David with his beloved car. Didn't most young men spend their money on some vehicle or other? Wasn't King ever young himself?

"Do you have any kids, Hollister?" The question was out before she could stop it.

"Kids? What kind of question is that?" He frowned at her.

"I just wondered."

"Well, the answer is no, as a matter of fact. Olinda couldn't have children."

Alex nodded. It explained a great deal about his attitude.

"I'm sorry."

He snorted. "Sorry? Nothing to be sorry for. I never wanted kids. Far as I can see, they're just a pack of trouble. No respect, no ambition." He glanced at his watch. "Enough chitchat, Alexandra. You may have plenty of time, but I'm afraid I don't. My waiting room was already full when I was called over here."

She didn't point out that they shared a waiting room. His arrogance might have been funny if it wasn't so aggravating.

Alex followed him the short distance to the building that housed the clinic, expecting another quiet afternoon, but to her surprise, eight of the patients waiting there were booked to see her that afternoon.

In spite of Hollister King, business was indeed picking up.

Or could it be because of him?

CAMERON AND DAVID had dinner waiting when she got home that night. They'd packaged potatoes and carrots in foil and baked them, and they'd lit the barbecue to grill the fish before they realized that Pavarotti had eaten them. They'd cooked hot dogs instead, but Pavarotti was in disgrace.

"We considered grilling the damned cat, but we figured you might object," David said with a wink and a grin when Alex came in the back door. He had a tea towel over his shoulder and a frilly apron he'd unearthed from God only knew where tied around his waist over his cutoffs.

"I applied for that job today, Alex, and I've got a real good feeling about it. I should hear early next week."

"That's great news, David."

Cameron was washing a pot in the sink. He looked at her over his shoulder, and she could see the muscles in his jaw tense, but all he said was "Hello, Alex."

She gave him a long, level look. All the pain of their quarrel was there between them, but after the long, tense day, and with David right there, she didn't feel like bringing it up now. Obviously, Cameron felt the same.

When she stepped out on the porch, however, Cam came out and put his hands on her shoulders, turning her toward him and leaning down to kiss her.

Unable to stop herself, Alex quickly turned her head so his lips grazed her cheek instead of meeting her mouth, and her anger at him surfaced all over again. How could he even begin to pretend that everything was all right between them?

He pulled back and dropped his hands. He studied her face for a long moment, his gaze impassive. Then he stepped away from her without a word and went to tend the hot dogs.

DAVID WATCHED and listened as his brother and sister-in-law talked to each other as if they were strangers forced to make conversation in a difficult social situation. They were scrupulously polite to each other during dinner, and the strain was thick enough to cut with a knife.

What the hell was going on? It had gradually dawned on him during the time he'd been there that something wasn't quite right with Cameron, but David was damned if he could figure out what was wrong, and Cam certainly wasn't about to unburden himself. David was the first to admit that Cam wasn't easy to talk to.

Cameron was the original strong and silent type, the best brother a guy could have, but not into sharing any of his feelings. All week, Cam had been unusually eager to do things that David knew from experience weren't particularly popular with women—fishing, watching sports on television, tinkering with the engines of various vehicles. Between that and working ungodly hours, it was pretty obvious Cam wasn't spending much quality time with his wife, and now there was this general freeze-up.

It worried him. David had always viewed Cameron and Alex as the ideal married couple, and seeing them this way made him sad and scared as well as uncomfortable. Maybe he ought to get out and let them work it through. In his not-so-limited experience, the best way to solve a quarrel was in bed, but with him around, there probably wasn't much chance of that.

"Think I'll drive into town and check out what's playing at the movies," he said when the meal was finally over.

"I thought we were gonna watch the baseball game," Cameron said. "Anyhow, the theater in town only has one show a night, and you've missed it."

David frowned at his brother. Cameron was either getting to be damned slow on the uptake or else he really didn't want to be alone with Alex. As far as David knew, there was nothing wrong with Cam's brain, so the second possibility seemed the only rational one.

David glanced over at Alex, trying to gauge what was best for him to do. She met his eyes and gave him a phony smile that didn't fool him for a minute. She was miserable, all right.

"You two go ahead and watch the game," she said in a cheerful voice that wouldn't have fooled a two-year-old.

"I'll clean up. After that, I'm heading for a long soak in the tub and an early night."

"We'll clean up. You go ahead and have your bath." Cameron got up and began to scrape plates with a lot more energy than David figured the job required.

Alex watched her husband for a moment, her expression unreadable. "Well, thanks for dinner, you two," she finally said. "I'll see you in the morning, David. Night, Cameron. I'll probably be asleep before you come up to bed."

David got that message loud and clear. He waited to hear how his brother would handle it.

"Night, Alex. Oh, by the way, I have to go in to the office in the morning. There's a stack of files and the computer was down all afternoon."

She gave him another long look and nodded. "Fine. I'll be out myself for part of the day."

The two men finished the dishes in silence and made their way into the TV room. Cameron clicked on the game, and settled on the couch.

David flopped down beside him.

"So you figure you might enjoy working up at the mine?" Cam was obviously making conversation.

"Yeah, I think I would. There's the best benefit package I've ever heard of, and the pay's good."

"Great." Cam's tone was preoccupied, and David didn't think his brother had heard a word he'd said. He decided to pry.

"So what's going on with you and Alex? You guys have a fight or something?"

"Yeah, we did." Cameron's curt tone made it plain the conversation wasn't to his liking. He turned up the volume on the television.

David raised his voice. "Well, don't you think you oughta go talk to her?"

"Talking doesn't help." Cameron's jaw set in a way that brooked no more discussion. David could think of things besides talking that might do the trick, but who was he to give Cam advice? It had always been the other way around. David was always the one in a jam, with Cameron riding to the rescue.

So he must know what he was doing with his own wife, right?

Wrong. Even David could see that Cameron was making some pretty serious mistakes here, and Alex was hurting because of it. Maybe Cameron wasn't as infallible as he'd always seemed. The idea was shocking, but the evidence was right there. Unless Cam smartened up fast, his marriage could get real shaky, in David's opinion.

He tried to figure out what to do to help, but he came up blank. The very idea of him trying to give Cameron advice would be laughable if it wasn't so pathetic. His brother was the one who gave the lectures and figured out the solutions, David reminded himself.

He tried to concentrate on the game, but somehow it had lost its appeal.

ALEX SLEPT LATE the next morning, and when she awoke the bed beside her was empty. She was pretty certain Cameron didn't have to work Saturdays—filing wasn't exactly life or death, in her experience. He was doing so by choice, and it hurt her.

She lay there for a few minutes, her heart aching as she remembered rare but memorable Saturday mornings in Vancouver when she and Cam had the day off together.

She'd awaken in his arms, the sound of traffic loud outside their window, and they'd make slow, languorous love. He'd phone and order pizza for breakfast and they'd eat it in bed, getting cheese and bits of topping all over the sheets. They'd shower together and drive to Chinatown, joining the noisy crowds of shoppers on the narrow downtown streets, laughing together, talking nonstop, teasing, arguing, kissing.

Connecting. They didn't connect that way anymore.

She lay, terribly alone, in the beautiful sun-filled bedroom, with the peaceful sound of birds calling as they swooped over the lake, and tears burned at the back of her eyeballs.

When had she lost him, and why?

AT THREE THAT AFTERNOON, Alex parked in front of the address Becky had given her a short while before on the phone. It was a modest frame house with green-and-white trim, and it was set on a street of other houses identical in design. Sweet peas spilled over the picket fence, and majestic coral gladiolas bloomed along the narrow cobbled walkway.

Alex breathed in the perfume-laden air as she climbed the steps and knocked on the screen door.

"Alex, hi." Becky, barefoot, lavish hair loose around her shoulders and looking about twelve years old in blue jeans and a cropped T-shirt, opened the door and beckoned her in. "As usual, we're in the kitchen. Why is it women spend all their spare time in the kitchen? We could saw off the rest of this house and not really miss it much." She drew Alex past a tidy living room, along a narrow hallway and into a spacious, homey room where Sadie was busy stirring something in a pot on the stove.

Sadie greeted her with a smile, and Alex knelt to say hello to Emily, sitting on the worn but highly polished lino flooring with a circle of toys surrounding her. She dug in her shoulder bag for the sturdy little music box she'd found in a toy shop in the mall that morning and presented it to Emily, demonstrating how it worked several times before she placed it in the small, chubby hands.

With dark chocolate eyes, the little girl stared at the toy in wonder and then turned her attention to Alex's face. For several long moments she looked deep into Alex's eyes, and then her square face split in a wide, delighted grin. She dropped the new toy and reached out for a hug, instead.

Alex obliged, holding the warm, fragrant little body close against her.

"Come on over and sit down. Tea's ready," Sadie said with an indulgent shake of her head. "She's really got your number, that girl."

"It's mutual. She's a charmer, aren't you, Miss Emily?" Alex set the child gently back on the floor on her padded bottom, but Emily shoved herself to a standing position and grasped Alex's finger, toddling alongside her as she moved to the table.

"What a clever girl. I didn't even realize you could walk." Alex lifted Emily into her highchair. "When did she learn?"

Alex knew that each Down's syndrome child developed differently, although all were retarded on a scale from mild to profound. She guessed that Emily, like the majority of Down's kids, fell somewhere in the moderate range.

"She started six months ago, at two and a half, surprised us all. You're doin' real good, aren't you, munchkin?" Becky tied a bib around her daughter and put a slice of buttered bread in front of her. "Bread, Emily. You want some bread, sweetie?"

"We talk to her all the time, naming everything so that she'll match up sounds and objects," Sadie explained, passing Alex a plate of homemade bread and another of thinly sliced tomatoes. "She's not talking much yet, but she's trying hard."

"I'm so lucky with her," Becky said with patent pride. "She doesn't have a heart defect, which so many Down's kids have, and she's been fairly healthy ever since she was born, apart from some nasty respiratory infections. At first, feeding her was a problem, but she's gotten much better—except that she much prefers chocolate cake to broccoli. All in all, she's learning at a pretty fair pace."

As tea was poured and the delicious array of food devoured, they spoke sadly of Winifred, still in the hospital and showing little improvement. But Becky and her mother also related affectionate, humorous anecdotes about Emily, and Alex reflected on how lucky this small girl was, being raised in the midst of such unconditional love. With a pang, she wondered what would have happened to such a child in her parents' home, where love seemed to be meted out only in return for accomplishments.

Becky and Sadie asked questions about where Alex had worked before she came to Korbin Lake, and she explained about St. Joe's, adding that her father was a surgeon before his retirement. Both Sadie and Becky were wonderful listeners, and somehow, Alex found herself talking about Wade again, about his injury and the emotional effect it was having on him and on the rest of the family.

Becky said, "Mom, remember the story Gram always tells about your uncle Tom?"

"Heavens, yes." Sadie related it while Becky poured more tea. "Years ago, when Becky was just a baby, my uncle Tom, my father's brother, was hurt in the mine. He had to have both of his legs amputated, one below the knee, one above.''

Sadie shuddered at the memory. ''Doc King hadn't been here long at the time. He did the operation. Tom was married, with two little girls. The youngest, Carrie, was just the age you were at the time, Becky, not even six months old.''

Sadie shook her head as she reminisced. ''At first Tom was glad to be alive, but then apparently he got it in his head he wasn't good for anything, kept on about how he should have died, felt real sorry for himself and developed a terrible temper. He wouldn't get out of bed or even try to use his wheelchair, didn't want to see anybody.''

''Just like Wade,'' Alex said.

Sadie nodded and blew out a breath. ''He nearly drove my poor aunt crazy, he was so miserable after that accident. She's a nice woman, Aunt Isabelle, and she tried everything. She tried being patient, she tried to reason with him, she tried to ignore him, but one day she just couldn't take it anymore, and she walked out and left him high and dry.''

''The best part is, she left him with the kids,'' Becky added.

''She did at that,'' Sadie confirmed with a mischievous grin. ''She left him on his own with those two little babies. She knew they were their daddy's darlings, and if anything was going to snap him out of it, it would be his babies. She went to Vancouver and stayed with her sister. When Tom realized she'd really left him, he sent a neighbor to get my mother and I to come and take over.''

Becky laughed. ''But Gram was too smart to go. She says she knew what had gone on, how miserable Tom had been, so she said no, and she and Mom warned all the neighbor women to leave him on his own, let him find out he could manage if he tried. Right, Mom?''

Sadie nodded. ''It was tough to do, but we figured it was the only way, sort of throw him on his own resources. Mind you, we kept a close eye out to make sure the kids didn't come to any harm.'' She chuckled. ''He had a terrible time for a week or so, I guess. Mom and I worried sick about those babies, but next thing I knew, I saw him in the grocery store in his wheelchair. He had Carrie tied across his chest in a sling, and he'd rigged up a thing at the back of the chair for Roberta to stand in, and he was doing just fine. The girls were dressed quite peculiar—Tom was always color-blind—but apart from that, they seemed well fed and happy. He was so put out with Mother and I, he wouldn't speak to us for the longest time, but he was up and around, and that's all that mattered.''

Alex was fascinated by the story. ''Did his wife ever come back?''

''Yes, after a time,'' Sadie confirmed. ''They're still together. They moved to Edmonton a few years ago to be near Roberta and her husband. Mind you, Isabelle let him stew for a good long time before she gave in. It was at least six weeks before she came back. By the time she came home, he'd learned to cook and do laundry and care for those girls as good as Isabelle could herself, so she marched up to the mine office and got herself a job as a clerk and left him to it.''

Becky shook her head and giggled. ''I never would have guessed Aunt Isabelle had it in her. She's so unassuming.''

Sadie nodded. ''At first glance, she seems the quiet type, real shy, but she taught me a few things, I'll tell you. Whenever we had a real bad fight, I used to threaten your daddy that I was gonna ask Aunt Isabelle for her advice." They all laughed. "Scared him so bad he'd usually say he was sorry, even when it was my fault." Her face softened, and her eyes looked past them, and it was obvious she was peering into another time and place.

Becky was the one who answered Alex's unspoken question. "My dad was killed in an explosion in the mine when I was nine. Grandpa died in the same accident. He only had another six days to work before he was going to retire."

Becky's tone was matter-of-fact, but Alex was shocked at the thought of such tragedy being heaped upon one family. How had these women borne it all? Becky, Sadie, Winifred—all of them had been touched by tragedy, not once, but many times. All of them had struggled with heartbreak in one form or another.

For the first time in weeks, the ever-present worry in Alex's heart about herself and Cameron eased slightly, and even her concerns about Wade lightened. The story about Uncle Tom had helped in a way that nothing else could have done. She was going to tell Thea the story, too, Alex decided.

"Lots of men died in that accident, twenty-six in all," Sadie added. "We sure weren't the only ones to lose our men that day. Back then, we used to call the mine the widow maker."

The casual way deaths and accidents at the mine were discussed among these women gave Alex a startling glimpse into what it really meant to be a coal miner's family.

"My brother-in-law just applied for a job at the mine," she said. She'd never even stopped to consider that if he was hired, David's job might be dangerous. "He'd be operating heavy equipment."

"Well, don't let all this talk about accidents scare you, Alex. The mines are a lot safer now than they were years ago," Becky reassured her.

"And the compensation settlements are better now, too," Sadie said, adding without a trace of malice, "Back then, the mine owned most of the housing. A week after my husband was killed, I was given three months to move. They wanted the house for another miner and his family. Widows with kids didn't qualify for company housing in those days."

"That's how we all ended up living here with Gram," Becky told Alex. "Grandpa had bought this house years before, and Mom and I moved in and just never left. Oh, I was gone while I did my training and for the first year after I got married, but when Emily was born and Ryan walked out on us, we came back here, too." She laughed. "We joke about it being Gram's haven for homeless women."

Alex had wondered about the all-female household and how it came to be. She was touched by the women's blatant honesty, their willingness to share intimate details of their lives with her.

Sadie got to her feet. "This poor wee girl's falling asleep sitting up. I'll go put her down for a nap. C'mon, princess." She lifted Emily, whose head was nodding, and kissed her. "Why don't you girls go on out in the backyard and sit where it's cooler? I'll clean up here and join you when I'm done."

Becky caught Alex's eye and rolled her eyes and grinned.

"C'mon, *girl*, " she teased. "Seems we're getting out of dishes. Let's disappear before Mom changes her mind." She led the way out the kitchen door and along a wooden walkway to where several lawn chairs sat in the shade of a huge weeping willow.

"To your mother, you're a girl no matter how old you get," she commented. "I never understood that until I had Emily."

It had been years since Alex thought of herself as a girl, and under different circumstances, she might even have taken offense at the moniker. But here, in this modest house, with these incredibly strong and loving generations of women, the label touched and deeply comforted her, as though she'd been initiated into a small, exclusive fraternity of females, accepted as one of them, supported by them, even loved just because she was a woman, with a woman's special problems.

And at this particular time in her life, she'd never needed anything so much.

"When I was a little girl," Becky was saying, "I used to pretend this tree was my castle and I was the queen." She flopped into one of the chairs as Alex sank into the other. The trailing willow branches reached almost to the lawn, forming a sort of green cave that at least gave the illusion of coolness.

"I'd play dress up and have tea parties under here. Gram and Mom would play right along and call me Your Majesty and let me wear their good shoes. They spoiled me something awful, the same way they spoil Emily."

Becky shook her head and laughed, but her hazel eyes were sad, her voice filled with fathomless pain. "I wonder sometimes if Emily'll ever be able to even pretend. As you know, there's absolutely no way of even guessing how profound her retardation will be until she's older." She turned to Alex, and tears shimmered in her hazel eyes. "It's not the big things that bother me. I don't give a hoot that she'll never be a rocket scientist. What hurts so much are the little things, the stupid remarks people make, the things that Emily will never be able to do, like have a baby herself." A wistful smile flickered across her face and disappeared. "When I found out I was pregnant, I wanted a little girl so much, Alex. I never thought for a moment I'd have a boy, and before she was born, I used to dream we were having long conversations, you know, talking about clothes and hairdos, silly things, and also the intimate stuff you don't talk about with anybody but your mother."

Alex shrugged and shook her head. "I guess I don't really know what mothers and daughters talk about, Becky. I envy you the relationship you have with Sadie and Winifred. I've never had anything like that with my mother." She explained about Eleanor, about the intellectual analysis that always took the place of intimacy and warmth. "The only person I've ever really been able to talk with is Cam."

But not anymore. Even that's gone now—

"He's gorgeous, your husband. I can tell you, he caused quite a stir when he first came to town," Becky remarked. "There were lots of broken hearts when he told everyone he was married to a beautiful woman."

"He *said* that?" It was gratifying to hear.

"Absolutely." Becky giggled. "You probably haven't noticed, but we've got a couple of bimbos on staff at the hospital, and they came on pretty strong to him the first time he turned up there with an accident victim. He let them know that his wife was arriving from Vancouver, that she was not only beautiful but a hot shot big-time doctor, as well, and he did it so tactfully they didn't even realize for a while that they'd been put down."

Alex smiled. This was a side of Cam she'd never heard about before, and today it comforted the sore place in her heart.

"Mind you, hearing that the sergeant's beautiful wife was the new doctor in town didn't exactly make Doc King jump for joy." Becky shook her head. "He's such an old chauvinist."

"I've noticed." Alex kept her tone carefully neutral.

Becky was silent for a moment, her forehead creased in a frown. She seemed to be pondering something. Her voice was sober when she said, "You've probably heard that we've had a lot of doctors come and go here over the past five years, Alex."

Alex nodded. "I asked Ruthie how many, and she said four, which seems a pretty high turnover."

"Doc King drives them away," Becky said flatly. "I know it's not news to you that he isn't the easiest guy to get along with. You're the first woman doctor we've had, and very selfishly, I'd like to see you stay here." She looked straight at Alex. "I hate to sound like a gossip, but I'm going to anyway. I think there's some stuff you ought to know if you're going to survive around here."

CHAPTER FOURTEEN

BECKY PAUSED for a moment, obviously pondering where to begin. "You understand what a hospital's like. Everybody knows everything, Alex. Or they think they do. Anyway, the word is King's giving you an exceptionally bad time."

Pride made Alex want to deny it, but there wasn't much point—just as Becky said, there were few secrets around a hospital. "This week's been pretty rough, all right," she conceded. "I'd really appreciate anything you could tell me that might help."

Becky nodded and heaved a sigh. "Well, it's all pretty tacky, but here goes. Shirley Boyd, our illustrious director of nursing, has been involved with King for years and years."

"Sexually involved?" The concept of straitlaced Shirley in any sort of passionate scene was difficult for Alex to imagine.

"At first it was definitely a sexual affair. Apparently they were spotted more than once coming out of a motel in Cranbrook. It might not be hot and heavy anymore, but there's still a strong bond between them. It started a long time ago, and they now wield a lot of power, not just at the hospital, but in the politics of the town generally. You see, King is on the town council, and she's on the school board. They both chair various committees. Anyhow, she has a nephew, Rodney Boyd, who just recently finished an internship in Toronto. It was no secret that she and King both wanted him to take over here when Dr. Lee left so suddenly."

"I see." Suddenly, the open animosity Alex had endured from both King and Boyd made sense.

"All of us nurses figured it was a done deal," Becky went on. "We were absolutely stunned when we found out you got the job instead of Rodney."

Alex's mind was working furiously. She was thinking about how and why she *had* gotten the position at Korbin Lake. With a sick feeling in her stomach, she remembered the connection between her father and Harry Perkins. Could Bruce have pulled strings, drawn in some old debt Perkins felt he owed, to make sure Alex got the job instead of Shirley Boyd's nephew? It was all too possible, considering her father's ambitions for her.

She suddenly felt nauseous at the idea that it hadn't been her qualifications at all that got her hired on at the clinic. Chances were good that she was on staff solely because of her father's influence. If King knew that—and he undoubtedly did—no damned wonder he had no respect for her.

"You look upset." Becky's forehead puckered in a frown. "I'm sorry. I'm probably way out of line, telling you all this stuff. I shouldn't have said anything."

Alex mustered a reassuring smile and shook her head. "It's not what you said, it's—it's something else, something that just occurred to me. Believe me, Becky, I very much appreciate knowing where I stand and what's going on under the surface."

Becky gave her a troubled look. "It's just that Doc King's going to do everything he can to get you to leave, and I'd hate to see that happen. And I'm afraid I have no loyalty at all to Shirley. She's a proper witch to work with."

Alex thought over the situation. "King's married. What does his wife think about this thing with Shirley Boyd?"

Becky grinned. "The hospital grapevine's speculated about that often enough. You haven't met Olinda?"

Alex shook her head.

"Well, she's petite, still very pretty, vivacious, and unfortunately not very bright. The consensus is that she was put on this earth to shop and party, and as long as Hollister keeps bringing in the bucks, she couldn't care less what he does. He's made a lot of money over the years. They have a condo in Hawaii and another in Mexico, and Olinda spends about half the year in one or the other. Even when she's here, she flies to Vancouver or Edmonton most weekends to shop."

"What about Shirley? Doesn't she want King to marry her eventually?"

Becky shrugged. "Who knows about Shirley? She doesn't confide in anyone. My guess is she likes things just the way they are. She's got lots of clout around town and a good job, and her independence, as well." She shot a worried glance at Alex. "Damn, I was afraid of this. I sound like the worst kind of gossipmonger."

Alex shook her head and gripped Becky's hand for a moment in reassurance. "I'm grateful for what you've told me. It makes everything a lot clearer." She managed a crooked smile. "See, I sort of thought Hollister and Shirley disliked me because of the way I dressed or something. At least now I know it's not only my jeans they take offense to."

Their laughter was interrupted by Sadie. "You two want some lemonade?" She came across the lawn bearing a tray with three icy glasses, and the conversation became general. The women chatted until at last Alex reluctantly got to her feet.

"I hate to go—this has been such fun—but I have to go grocery shopping. Cam's working today and there's not a thing in the house for dinner." She *did* hate to go. The afternoon had been an oasis in an otherwise barren day, and she suddenly wanted to see Becky and Sadie again soon.

"Listen, why don't you both come out to the lake tomorrow afternoon? We'll go for a swim and have a barbecue. Emily'll love the water—it's really gotten warm this past week."

Sadie shook her head uncertainly. "We have to go visit Mom in the hospital, and besides, what would your husband say, all of us females descending on him that way?"

"Cam will love it." Alex was sure he would—he loved informal get-togethers. Besides, he'd made it plain enough that he didn't particularly want to be alone with her, she thought dismally. "My brother-in-law, David's, staying with us, so Cam's got all the male support he needs, and I'd enjoy not being outnumbered by men for a few hours."

"We could go see Gram early, and Aunt Lily will gladly stay with her the rest of the afternoon, Mom," Becky said.

They looked at one another, and then Becky grinned at Alex. "We're acting like this because we don't get invited out much. We're real hicks when it comes to socializing. I haven't even been on a date since I divorced, and Mom's not much better. We've stuck pretty close to home ever since Emily was born. And she hasn't been around men much at all."

"She needs to practice her flirting, then," Alex declared. "Come about four. The guys will adore her."

Sadie said hesitantly, "Thanks. We'd love to come. But you must let us bring the potato salad."

"No argument there," Alex said instantly. "I should warn you, I'm not much of a cook, but Cam and David make up for it. Their mother, Verna's, a wonderful cook, and fortunately she taught them."

"We'll be looking forward to it."

JUST AS SHE'D EXPECTED Cameron was pleased Alex had invited people over, and he suggested they also include the Townsends. Greg was officially on duty, but Cam said he could monitor his calls from a portable.

David and Cameron got up early Sunday morning, sweeping the porch and cleaning the barbecue, marinating the steaks and chicken Alex had bought.

"What're we serving for dessert?" Cameron was putting beer cans in the fridge while Alex mixed up a huge green salad.

"Strawberries and cream," she said absently. She was still mulling over the things Becky had confided the day before. David was outside putting up extra chairs Cameron had unearthed from the basement, and she and Cam were alone for a few moments at least.

"Cam, I knew my father used his influence when I applied for this job in Korbin Lake," Alex blurted out. "What I didn't know was that Hollister King had someone else in mind for it. Dad must have really turned the screws, and that's how I got the position. It's also why King's so resentful of me."

Cameron finished shoving one last can into a corner of the bottom shelf. He got to his feet and closed the fridge. "Is King giving you lots of flak?"

Alex shrugged. "He's made it plain he doesn't want me interfering with his patients. He's not what I'd call friendly, but at least he speaks to me now." She chopped fresh tomato and dumped it into the bowl. "It's not King I'm upset about right now. It's my father." She slammed the knife down. "Damn it all, Cam, I'm furious with him. I had no idea there was another candidate. I knew Dad put in a good word for me, but I also believed I'd gotten this job because of my qualifications. Now I feel terrible because Dad really pulled rank, and there was this other doctor who wanted the job just as much as I did, and for all I know, was just as well qualified. I feel like some spoiled, greenhorn kid who can't land a job on her own."

Cam folded his arms across his chest and leaned back on the cupboard. "I'm sure you'd never have been hired if there was any question at all about your ability. They'd never even have considered you if you weren't qualified for the job, regardless of your dad."

Why didn't he see that the issue was really her independence? "But I wanted to do it on my own, Cam. I *needed* to do it on my own." She punctuated the words by banging her fist on the counter.

He leaned against the cupboard and picked up a piece of celery and munched on it. "If Bruce tipped the scales so that you got this job, then I'm grateful to him. We could have ended up with you working in Vancouver and me here, with our off time eaten up commuting from one place to the other, never seeing each other."

Outraged that he didn't understand her feelings at all, she started to tell him that their marriage wasn't working even with them both in the same place, but suddenly the front doorbell rang and David came bounding up the back stairs.

"Company's here," he announced, his eyes wide with excitement. "Man, that redhead's somethin' else, Alex. Why didn't you warn me?"

"She's my good friend, David. She's off-limits, so no moves, okay?" Alex swallowed her anger and tried for a smile as she and Cam and David went to the door to greet their guests.

DAVID TOOK THE SLENDER, chapped hand that Becky offered, and afterward he wondered what he might have said when Alex introduced them, because he didn't remember a word of it.

The only thing he knew with absolute certainty was that this was the woman he'd waited his entire life to meet.

He'd asked Cam once how he'd known Alex was the right woman for him. Cam had thought it over and then said, "It's a different feeling from any you've ever had before. It's not something you can make a mistake about. You just look at her and you know."

Looking at Becky, David knew.

She was small, with pixie features and thick, red-gold hair tied up in a knot at the back of her head. Her hair shone like polished copper in the sun. She had big, sad hazel eyes that didn't reflect the wide smile on her lovely mouth, and her white shorts and pale blue blouse revealed a lushly rounded shape and curvaceous legs.

Her voice was husky and a trifle shy, and he recognized instantly her defensiveness when Alex said, "And this little angel is Emily."

David had listened with casual sympathy and scant attention when Alex described this baby and the problems she was born with. It was too bad, he'd thought, but it really wasn't anything to do with him.

Now, all of a sudden, it got up close and personal.

Now, this tiny, fragile girl with her flattened little face and dark, innocent eyes had suddenly become part of a future David never in his wildest fantasy envisioned for himself.

The one thing he'd never knowingly done was date a woman with kids. His mother had been single, and he knew all too well the awful mixture of hope and dread and fear a little kid felt when his mother went out with a man. A child had no choice in the matter. A child had to go along with whatever his mother decided to do, and David didn't want any kid ever feeling the way he had when he was a little boy.

And still he hadn't said more than a few words to Becky. He hadn't kissed her or held her in his arms or made exquisite love to her the way he planned on doing. He knew she'd never allow him any closer than arm's length unless he found a straight path to the heart of this baby.

It scared the living hell out of him, and Becky hadn't the slightest idea of the depth of commitment he was making when he reached out to the little girl and said with his best grin and his most charming tone, "Wanna come and talk to Uncle Dave, princess?"

And with an entirely feminine dip of her head and a sidelong glance of pure flirtatiousness that astonished her mother and grandmother, Emily held out her arms to him.

ALL THAT HOT AFTERNOON, Alex felt as if there were two of her. One talked and laughed and played hostess and even felt smugly pleased at how well everything was going at this, her first party in Korbin Lake. The other part watched Cameron as if he were a stranger, marveling at his easy charm, impartially admiring his male beauty, and wondering if she'd ever really known him or if she'd only imagined the kind of husband she'd thought she had.

He was a wonderful host, quietly finding time to talk with each of their guests and making them feel welcome. He paid particular attention to Sadie, who might otherwise have felt a little out of place with all the young people. He and Dave and Greg took over the cooking of the chicken and steaks, and Alex was free to sit with the women on the porch in the late-afternoon sun and talk of babies and books and clothes and dreams.

"Your husband is a very fine gentleman," Sadie declared when they were leaving.

"Thank you." Alex knew it was so. She hated herself for feeling jealous, for resenting the fact that Cameron had paid far more attention to their guests that day than he'd paid to his wife in the past week.

Later that night, alone in their bedroom, Cam shucked off his sleeveless gray T-shirt and stretched.

Alex watched him with the same detached feeling she'd had all day, wondering if she'd ever had the slightest inkling what really went on his head. She used to think she did.

She questioned so many things these days, herself most of all, now that she'd learned how she'd gotten her job.

"That was a good party, honey." Cam sounded more relaxed than he had for days, and he seemed unaware of her tension. "Everybody seemed to have a great time."

"I hope they did." She sat down on the edge of the bed and kicked her sandals off, then lay back on the spread and closed her eyes. She felt infinitely weary, and at the same time, edgy. She couldn't seem to relax.

"This house is ideal for entertaining." She tried to sound normal. She absolutely didn't want to fight with Cam again tonight. "Everybody got along really well."

Cameron's voice seemed to come from a long way off. "It's hard to believe Sadie's old enough to be Rebecca's mom. Apparently she's been a widow for years, I wonder why she never remarried?"

Alex shook her head, eyes still closed. "Becky says her mother's had friends over the years, but Sadie just never wanted to get married again." A disturbing thought made her open her eyes and sit up. "Speaking of Becky, did I overhear David asking her out to dinner?"

Cam shrugged his bare shoulders and undid the snap on his shorts. "You got me. He didn't mention it. But it was obvious he couldn't take his eyes off her, so asking her out would be the logical next step."

Alex nodded, and her voice was harsher than she intended when she said, "Becky has enough problems in her life without getting mixed up with David. I particularly asked him not to mess around with her."

Cameron stepped out of his shorts and stood in his blue briefs, looking at her. There was a defensive note in his voice. "Why's that? Dave's not exactly an ax murderer."

"He's the original love-'em-and-leave-'em type, that's why, and I don't want Becky to get her heart broken. She hasn't had a single date since Emily was born. She's just not in David's league."

"She's an adult, Alex. But I'll speak to him if you like."

"Would you please? For Becky's sake, and also for Emily's."

"I've never been around a kid with Down's syndrome before. What's her future going to be?"

Alex explained that each child was different, and there was no way of telling. "Early training's important. Those women are doing a great job with Emily."

"Sure seems that way. And little Jason's looking good, too. Greg was changing him and he showed me his scar. It's almost fully healed."

Alex's mind wasn't really on the conversation they were having. Instead, she was wondering bitterly why Cam could talk so freely about everyone and everything except the specific issues that affected the two of them.

He came over and knelt on the rug beside the bed, his hands resting gently on her shoulders, his head on a level with hers. "You need any help getting out of these clothes, pretty lady?"

His voice was a husky, suggestive whisper, and his hands slid down to cup her breasts before finding the button on her shorts and beginning to undo it. His lips wandered from her temple to her throat, nibbling along her jawline, leisurely capturing her lips. His hands moved to cup her bottom, drawing her nearer to the edge of the bed.

Desire flared within her, and for a brief, automatic moment she responded to his kiss the way she always had done. This, at least, was still good between them. This was familiar, intoxicating. This was her husband, loving her the way she needed loving.... "My beautiful woman." He slipped her brief top up and over her head, deftly unfastening the bra beneath, weighing her breasts in his palms, caressing the already hardening nipples, making her breath catch in her throat.

And then, like an icy tide, all the things unsaid and unresolved between them rose up and overwhelmed her. She tried to shove them away, to stay rooted in the here and now, lost in the red haze of passion that was beginning to envelop her, but her body was suddenly cold and empty, swamped by a wash of negative emotion. The anger she'd been suppressing returned, and for the first time ever her body was deadened to the sensual invitation Cam was extending.

She stiffened in his embrace, scrabbling back across the bed, grabbing a nightshirt from under her pillow and tugging it over her head.

"I can't, Cam." The words burst out of her. "I just can't make love with you as if nothing's wrong between us. There's too much unfinished business, and it's bothering me. It won't go away until we talk about it."

For a long moment, terrible desire and an awful yearning burned in his dark eyes and sharpened the carved lines of his face. Then, with a visible effort, he gained control. He got to his feet and turned away, snatching up his shorts and pulling them on, his movements abrupt and stiff.

He was angry. She waited with both dread and eagerness for the inevitable confrontation. Now, at last, they'd have it out.

"This is still about the other night," he growled.

She nodded, her throat dry and tight. "Yes, it is. That, and—"

He cut her off. "I'm sorry, I probably said some things I shouldn't have." His voice was flat, and she couldn't read his expression.

"It's not what we said, Cam." She drew her legs up under the long cotton shirt and hugged them tight. "It's what we didn't say that's bothering me. Oh, Cam, couldn't we just talk, the way we used to?" Her voice trembled a little, and she waited for his answer, her heart pounding.

He was silent for what seemed a long time, and then he sighed and ran his fingers through his hair. "Look, Alex, I know you're stressed out with moving, changing jobs and worrying about Wade. I'm sorry you're having a rough time. You made it plain the other day that you blame me for screwing up your life, and you're right. Apart from Wade, I know I'm to blame. I take full responsibility for all of it." His dark eyes burned, not with passion now, but anger. "But damn it all, I can't wave some magic wand and make it right for you, and no matter how much you want me to, I refuse to spend every free moment wading through my subconscious and wallowing in guilt and despair. It's just not my style."

Her voice on the edge of breaking, Alex whispered, "You honestly don't see what's happening to us, do you, Cameron? You don't want to see."

His face was closed, hard and tight and cold. "Nothing's happening except what you imagine, Alex. Get a grip on yourself. You're creating problems where there aren't any."

His words seemed to bruise a tender place in her chest. If he'd struck her a hard, physical blow, it might not have hurt as much as his indifference.

"I think I'll go down and watch TV for a while." His voice was almost normal, and in disbelief she watched him grab up a shirt, thrust his arms through the sleeves and leave the bedroom, closing the door gently behind him.

Alex sat frozen for a long time. She was married to a stranger!

CHAPTER FIFTEEN

CAMERON STOOD ON the other side of the closed door, his palms sweating, a deep, roiling sickness in his gut that threatened to expel whatever was left of his dinner.

He hated himself for hurting Alex.

He resented her for forcing him into it.

Why couldn't she see that all that emotional crap was better left alone? He swallowed hard and wiped his palms on the seat of his shorts, slowly making his way down the rest of the stairs, telling himself he had every right to be furious with her.

He wanted her, he needed the comfort of her body, the reassurance of her love, the oblivion of sexual release, and she'd turned away from him. For the first time ever in their marriage, Alex had refused him, and it was devastating to his ego. His body ached, and there was a peculiar emptiness in his chest. He didn't want to remember the look on her face when he'd left the bedroom, or the hopeless tone of her voice.

The door to the study was closed, and from behind it he could hear the muted sound of the television. Relief swept over him. David was still up. The last thing Cam wanted right now was to be alone.

His brother was sprawled on the couch, a pillow wedged behind his head, a beer can near at hand. The television was tuned to a rugby game. He looked up surprised to see

Cameron. "Hey, bro, thought you'd packed it in for the night."

"Couldn't sleep." Cameron lowered himself into an armchair and squinted at the screen. "Who's playing?"

"Scotland and Australia. Two tries for the Scots, zip for Australia. There's only a few minutes left to play. Looks like the Aussies are outta luck."

They watched in silence as the game ended, and slowly, Cameron began to feel a little more relaxed.

Dave flipped the mute as the inevitable postgame interviews began. "Watching rugby makes ya think of Wade, huh?"

Cameron nodded. It was gut wrenching, watching the game his brother-in-law had loved and excelled at.

"I went to see him a coupla times at the hospital," Dave said. "It's tough to know what to talk about. Think he'll ever walk again?"

"Hard to say. The odds are pretty good. He's getting sensation back in his legs, but it'll take lots of effort, according to Alex."

"God. And he was a world-class athlete." Dave shuddered. "Makes you realize just how fast your life can change."

Cam was all too aware of how fast life could change, and he didn't want to think about it. They sat in silence for a moment, and then he deliberately changed the subject. "So, think you can stick it out here in the boonies if that job comes through?"

"Yeah, sure. It was kinda weird being here at first. Small towns are way different than the city, but I'm getting to like it now, better every day." His voice took on a note of pride. "If I get hired on, I'll do a good job, too. I'm damned good at operating heavy machines. That's one thing I really know how to do."

Cam bit back the urge to say that if David had stayed in school the way he'd wanted him to, there'd be a lot more things his brother knew how to do. It was a contentious subject between them, better left alone.

There was a lengthy silence before Cameron spoke again, feeling uncomfortable but also wanting to honor the promise he'd made to Alex. God knew he wasn't doing much else for her these days.

"Alex figures you're putting the moves on her friend, Becky."

"Oh, yeah?" Dave took a long swallow of beer, and there was a defensive note in his voice when he spoke. "I asked the lady out, figured we'd have some dinner, take in a movie." He flashed his cocky grin at Cam, but there was an open warning in his green eyes. "No big deal. I didn't exactly propose, y'know."

"Yeah." Cameron knew he was on delicate territory, but he felt compelled to say something more. "Well, just be up front with her, okay? She's got a lot on her plate with that kid, and she doesn't need her heart broken into the bargain."

Dave slammed his beer down. "Jeez, Cam, I'm a big boy now. I don't need a lecture on my love life from you of all people. Lay off."

Cameron was all too familiar with David's hair-trigger temper. "I happen to know your track record in that department. Remember Kim?" Several years before, Kim had been one of the numerous women Dave was involved with briefly and disastrously. Kim had become obsessive when Dave tried to break off with her, following him, calling, writing notes doused with her perfume, threatening suicide and finally actually slashing her wrists before she agreed to psychiatric help.

Cameron didn't blame Dave entirely—the woman was unbalanced to begin with—but there was no doubt Dave seemed to have a devastating effect on women.

"I don't want to see a nice lady wrecked because you get bored with the situation, that's all."

Dave got to his feet, his face livid. "For your information, I don't intend to do anything, *ever,* that will hurt Becky. And I don't figure you're in any position to lecture me, big brother. Looks to me as if you could use some counseling yourself. You're not exactly Mr. Congeniality with Alex these days, are you? Maybe you oughta take a look at your own marriage before you start giving me advice." He stalked out of the room, slamming the door behind him.

Furious, Cam leaped to his feet to go after him and then slumped back on the sofa, his head in his hands. Damn it all, he didn't want to fight with David. He didn't want to fight with *anyone.*

He wanted peace and quiet, without soul-searching or angry confrontations. He'd had enough of that to last him a lifetime back on the drug squad.

Why couldn't his wife and his brother get the hell off his case?

He reached for the remote and turned up the sound, willing the noise and the action on the screen to dull the emotions that tore at his guts, but the attempt was futile. Much as he hated to admit it, Dave's accusation was right on the money.

He was being unfair to Alex; he knew that. He'd make more of an effort, he promised himself.

Starting tomorrow.

THE FOLLOWING DAY, Cameron spent almost the entire morning out at the mine. There'd been a staggering number of thefts lately—electrical equipment, small motors and tools—and the mine officials had a good idea which employees were responsible. This morning Cam had set up a scheme to catch the perpetrators in the act, with search warrants prepared for their homes, as well, and he was feeling good about the operation.

He drove down the winding road that led back to town, going over his careful preparations and trying to second-guess the way the scene would play. His fingers were tight on the steering wheel, and when he glanced in the rear-view mirror, he caught a glimpse of his own expression, intense and concentrated. Excited.

All of a sudden he realized how ridiculous it was, getting himself all hyped up over a matter of some petty thievery. He was making a mountain out of a molehill, his mother would say.

It's not a major drug bust, Ross, he reminded himself bitterly, and the feeling of excitement slowly disappeared. He had to get used to the idea that from here on in, the odd high-speed chase would be as exciting as it was liable to get.

His work so far in Korbin Lake had consisted mostly of traffic enforcement, petty thievery, minor assault, some shoplifting and a few complaints about cruelty to animals on outlying farms. He figured his job was about as different from the drug squad as night from day, and it was still too soon to say whether or not he'd want to stay at it for an extended period.

For now, he did his best to convince himself that it was fine. It might even give him a chance to drive out whatever perverse demons were haunting him.

He thought again about the things his brother had accused him of the night before, of screwing up his marriage and being unfair to his wife. Part of him knew all too well that he was being a proper jerk, but he couldn't seem to stop.

Just thinking of Alex brought a surge of heat to his groin. No matter how bad things were between them, he still couldn't think of her without wanting her. It hurt that she'd turned away from him last night. How long had it been since they'd made love? He wasn't sure of the exact number of days, but for sure it was longer than it had ever been.

He was on the edge of town when he suddenly decided to drop in on her, take her out to lunch, try his best to smooth the atmosphere between them. He wheeled the car around and picked up the radio.

"Korbin Lake, 851, I'll be 10-7 at the Med Center for lunch."

Suddenly he couldn't wait to see his wife.

FOR ALEX, the morning had seemed endless, even though she'd had four patients. Two were new mothers, friends of Nancy Townsend. Their visits were routine checkups for themselves and their babies, and both related Nancy's glowing recommendations of Alex as a family doctor.

She maintained a professional cheerfulness for her patients, but inside, Alex was miserable. Cameron's actions and words the previous night had hurt her deeply, and in what seemed to be a pattern here in Korbin Lake, he'd left for work by the time she awoke that morning.

Shortly before noon, the intercom buzzed.

"Mr. Brandt is on line three, Doctor Ross."

"Thanks, Ruthie." Alex made the connection, and the warm male voice that responded to her greeting made her smile.

"So, what color did you decide on for the office?"

"I think eggshell, with accents in primary colors," she said, looking around at the dismal surroundings and imagining it colorful and cheery. "I'm buying an unfinished bookshelf and lacquering it bright red," she decided on the spur of the moment. "And I'll put toys on the lower shelves for the kids."

Becky had brought over several trailing plants that morning, gifts from Sadie to say thank-you for the Sunday party, and Alex had set them in front of the window. "I'm going to spray-paint some hanging baskets yellow and blue and green and hang plants all across the window, and I'll bet even a color-blind person is going to like it here when I'm done," she teased with a grin.

"That's a low blow. I'm deeply hurt. But you could apologize by joining me for lunch. I'm over in the hospital cafeteria."

She hesitated, all too aware of hospital gossip. But eating lunch with an ambulance attendant in a crowded cafeteria surely couldn't be misconstrued, could it? She had no more appointments until two, and talking to Daniel might take her mind off her problems. "I'll see you over there in five minutes."

She quickly ran a brush through her hair, applied lip gloss, and made her way across the lawn to the hospital.

Daniel was already seated by the window, and she waved at him and joined the lineup at the food counter, choosing a chicken salad sandwich and a coffee. A few moments later, she slid into a chair across from him. He greeted her cheerfully, and they ate and chatted easily about the weather, the ambulance service and the hospital food. Alex was almost finished her sandwich when Cameron suddenly appeared at her elbow, seemingly out of nowhere.

"Cameron?" Alex stared up at him, amazed to see him. In the time she'd been at the clinic, Cam had never once come to have lunch with her. She felt flustered, thrown off balance, by having him appear this way with no warning.

"Hi, Alex." He shifted his gaze from her to Daniel and nodded. "Brandt," he said. The look he gave Daniel was hard and somehow frightening.

"Hello, Sergeant Ross." Daniel's greeting was accompanied by a friendly smile, but Cam didn't respond, and his grimness irritated Alex all of a sudden.

"Sit down, Cam." She was aware that her voice was sharper than normal. "Have you eaten? Do you want to get a tray and join us for lunch?"

He looked positively formidable in his uniform, and the level look he gave her added to the effect. "I'm not really hungry, thanks." He dragged a chair out, however, and lowered himself into it.

Sudden alarm gripped Alex. "Nothing's wrong, is it, Cam? It's not Wade or—" Her thoughts went to David, her family, Cam's mother....

He gave her an apologetic smile and shook his head in reassurance. "No, no, of course nothing's wrong. I was just in the area and I thought I'd drop by for a few minutes, that's all."

She slumped with relief. "Oh, thank God. You scared me there for a minute."

"It's a hell of a note when the sight of your own husband scares you." His tone was dry, and his attempt at humor fell flat.

Daniel, obviously aware of the tension between them, cleared his throat and said, "I think I'll get a refill on this coffee. Can I bring you some, Sergeant? Alex?"

Cameron shook his head and Alex nodded and handed Daniel her paper cup. "Please."

"One cream, no sugar, right?"

"Right." She smiled at him, although her mouth felt stiff and dry. "You've got a good memory."

There was a charged silence as Alex watched Daniel maneuver his way through the lunchtime crowd to the counter.

Cameron, too, watched him go and then slowly turned his attention to Alex. "Sorry I interrupted your lunch. I guess I should have phoned first. I wanted to see you, to tell you I'm sorry about last night."

She waited, but he didn't elaborate, and her heart sank. "I'm sorry, too, Cam, but I don't think just saying we're sorry is enough. There's still so much we haven't discussed—"

"Damn it!" He shook his head and slumped back in his chair. "I don't know what you want from me anymore, Alex. I say I'm sorry and you say it's not enough." His tone was angry, and the accusatory look he directed at her stunned her for a moment and then made her furious.

"I keep telling you what I want, but you don't listen, Cam. I'm not spelling it out for you again." She was so angry her voice was trembling.

His eyes seemed to burn a hole in her skin, and after an endless, silent moment, he got slowly to his feet. In a deceptively soft tone, he said, "I'll see you at home."

Shaken, she watched him go. She regained a semblance of control and forced a smile to her lips when Daniel came back. He set her brimming coffee container in front of her and gave her a quick, assessing look.

"He had to leave so soon?"

She nodded and swallowed hard, not daring to trust herself to speak. Tears were dangerously close.

"I was married for four years once," he said abruptly. "It's one hell of a hard thing to do, marriage."

"I'll say it is," she managed to say. She cleared her throat. "What—what happened to yours?" She realized instantly that the question was much too personal.

"I'm sorry. I shouldn't have asked that—"

"I'd like to tell you." His gentle gray eyes met hers, and the pain in them made her shiver. "I was a workaholic lawyer, typical Type A personality, never a moment to waste. She tried hard with me, but eventually she found somebody else, a laid-back musician with more sense than I had at the time. The marriage breakup was my fault. It nearly killed me when I lost her, but I still didn't smarten up. I took on even more files and gave up sleeping for cigarettes and alcohol, and then I had a heart attack." He laughed mirthlessly, "A minor one, fortunately, but it scared the hell out of me. I was only thirty-seven. The day I got out of the hospital, my grandfather called—first time I'd spoken to him in months." He shook his head and said with grim sarcasm, "I was a real busy guy in those days, no time to make idle phone calls. Anyhow, he'd heard I was sick, and he was worried. Ironic as hell because it turned out he was the one dying with cancer. I got in my car that afternoon and drove up here, and I've been here ever since. Sold my share in the law firm and never looked back." His smile didn't quite make it to his eyes. "I guess you could say I ran away from my problems, and for the most part, running away worked for me."

Is that what Cameron was trying to do, too, run away from his problems on Drug Squad? Alex wondered. If so, it didn't seem to be working at all, for him—or for her.

"And you've never tried marriage again?"

He shook his head. "Nope. Like I said, it's a hard thing to do, and I've gotten lazy in my old age. I like the easy life."

He grinned at her, and she managed to smile back, but she felt that for all his joking manner, Daniel was telling her something important. Marriages fell apart when two people stopped communicating.

"I'd better get back to the office." She got to her feet and so did he. "It's been good talking with you, Daniel."

"Seems I did most of the talking. Anytime you want to turn that around, I promise I'll shut up and listen. That's what friends are for."

"It's a deal." But she didn't want to confide in Daniel Brandt. It was her husband she wanted to talk to. Cameron was still her best friend, wasn't he?

For the first time since they'd met, she wasn't absolutely sure of that, and it terrified her.

CHAPTER SIXTEEN

FOR ONCE, Cameron's Jeep was in the driveway and David's car was gone when she got home that evening.

The brothers had bought a wreck of an old car from a farmer the week before and had begun spending all their spare time out in the garage repairing it, but tonight the garage, too, was dark and deserted.

Alex thought of the appalling scene with Cameron at lunchtime, and her stomach tensed as she walked into the house. She bent down to stroke Pavarotti, delaying the moment when she'd have to face her husband and bear the brunt of his anger.

"Cameron? Cam, where are you?"

"I'm in the kitchen."

She squared her shoulders and walked in, chin high, feeling like a boxer entering the ring.

He was chopping onions at the counter, and to her amazement he looked up and smiled.

The sight of that familiar, crooked half smile made her heart ache with nostalgia.

"Rough day at the office, Doc?"

She listened closely for undercurrents of sarcasm but there didn't appear to be any. She blew out the breath she'd been holding. "Yeah. Sort of." She longed to blurt out all of her concerns about King. A few short months ago, she'd have had no reservations about doing so, knowing he'd offer her the best of advice. But things were different now. He no longer confided in her, and she found it impossible to share her own worries with him.

"How about you, Copper?" She forced a lightness into her tone that she was far from feeling, wondering when he was going to bring up the subject of their disastrous lunch. "Any shootouts on Main Street this afternoon?"

He shook his head and grinned, and the hard angles and deep shadows of his face softened for an instant. His thick black hair had grown out a little, and it hung down over his forehead. Alex impulsively reached out and brushed it back, tears burning behind her eyes. He was such a complicated, beautiful man, this husband of hers.

Touching him, a rush of physical longing suddenly overwhelmed her. More than anything in the world just now, she wanted the blind comfort of his arms, the reassurance of his loving, but she didn't know how to break through the barriers they'd somehow erected between themselves.

Cameron looked up and their eyes locked. Alex's breath caught, because instead of the anger she'd braced herself to expect, she could see the same desire that burned in her begin to kindle in the depths of his brown gaze, and relief spilled through her. The powerful physical attraction that had drawn them to each other the very first time they met was still there between them. Maybe it could heal.

Slowly, he laid down his paring knife and reached for her, his strong hands drawing her gently into his embrace.

"C'mere, beautiful stranger," he whispered, and with a half sob she raised her arms and slipped them around his neck. It felt wonderful, being held by the man she loved, familiar and safe and exciting all at the same time.

"Alex, I was way out of line today. The plain truth is I was black bloody jealous. I came hoping to have lunch with you and found Brandt there. It dawned on me that he's a good-looking guy, and you're so beautiful..."

The forthright explanation was all she needed to forgive him. She buried her nose in his neck, smelling the beer he'd been sipping, his shaving lotion, the musky, familiar personal scent of his body, and her heart missed a beat and then hammered against her cotton shirt in a crazy, erratic rhythm.

This was her husband. She wanted him, needed him. Maybe the intimacy of lovemaking would reopen the pathways to the closeness she longed to recapture. She forced the hurt of the past weeks out of her mind, concentrating instead on the purely physical reactions he aroused in her.

He kissed her, his tongue plunging deep and urgent, and she responded, pressing her breasts and thighs against him.

"I need you, Alex. I need you," he growled and cupped her bottom, pulling her into intimate alignment with his pelvis, rocking against her in a way that left no doubt about the intensity of his desire.

"It's been so long." His lips found her ear, her neck, the tender spot under her chin. Feverish, impatient heat pooled in her abdomen, and she refused to allow herself any second thoughts.

"Our bedroom?" Cameron's voice was thick.

She shook her head, and gasped, "Here. Now." It was too dangerous, that interval between kitchen and bedroom. It would leave time to think, time for all the old baggage to once again throw icy caution on what was happening inside her body.

He stripped off her slacks and her underpants in one efficient motion, undoing the snap and zipper on his shorts, shoving them down and kicking them off. She locked her arms tighter around his neck as he lifted her, resting her bottom on the edge of the table, cupping her buttocks and supporting her with his hands, both of them trembling and wild with need.

Then, simultaneously, the telephone on the kitchen counter rang and they heard the unmistakable sound of David's car pulling into the driveway at the front of the house, followed in quick succession by the slam of the car door, his cheerful whistle, and the sound of his size-thirteen boots taking the outside stairs two at a time.

Alex snatched up her clothing and dashed for the stairs. Behind her she could hear Cameron swearing in a steady, vicious stream. The telephone was still ringing when she slammed the bedroom door and leaned against it, panting and trembling, her heartbeat thundering in her ears. Pavarotti was curled snugly in the middle of the bed, and he raised his head and gave her an affronted look.

From below she heard David's voice and the muted rumble of Cameron's as he picked up the phone.

She was tying her housecoat when Cameron came into the bedroom. His shorts were on, but his chest was still bare, and she could tell the intimacy they'd shared was over. He was distracted now, his mind elsewhere.

"Gotta go up to the mine," he stated tersely. "We've nabbed some guys who've been stealing." He took off the shorts and pulled on a pair of jeans and a sweatshirt. He buckled his gun on, and almost as an afterthought came over to her, drawing her into his arms for a quick kiss.

"David's going out again. He got the job at the mine, and he's going to celebrate. I probably won't make it home until late. We've got warrants in place to search these guys' houses for the rest of the stolen goods, and we have to do it tonight, before anybody gets a chance to move anything."

She wondered if he felt as frustrated and let down as she did.

"I'm sorry, sweetheart" was all he said. He kissed her again lightly. "Be sure to lock the doors before you head for bed," he warned, and hurried down the stairs.

With Pavarotti complaining at her heels, Alex made her way down to the kitchen. David was at the counter, building himself a massive sandwich, and the look he shot her was rueful. "Sorry I barged in on you guys," he said without any pretense. He was slathering mustard and mayonnaise on top of tomatoes and cheese. "You oughta put a candle in the window or something to warn me off." He lifted the concoction to his mouth and took an immense bite, chewing and swallowing before he spoke again. When he did, his voice was thoughtful. "Alex, what're the odds for having more than one kid with Down's syndrome?"

She plugged in the kettle to make some instant coffee, giving herself time to absorb the implications of his unexpected question. "Down's kids are born with an extra chromosome in their cells," she explained, spooning granules into a cup. "They have three number 21 chromosomes, rather than two. Older mothers are more likely to have Down's children, but there aren't any hard and fast rules. And as far as predicting whether a mother will have more than one, I believe there's a slightly higher risk factor, but we can do amniocentesis and determine whether or not the fetus has Down's. Then the parents have the choice of aborting." She poured boiling water into the cup and took a sip too soon, burning her lip.

"Ow. Damn." She sat down at the table and looked at David. "We're talking about Becky and Emily, right?"

He nodded. "Yeah. I want to know everything there is to know about Down's. Can you get me some reading material on it?"

"I can, yes." She studied him for a moment. "Aren't you getting ahead of yourself just a little? You've only met Becky once."

"I know. I just want to be prepared when the subject of Down's comes up between us."

"Look, David—"

He held up a warning hand. "If this is lecture number seventy-seven, don't bother. I'm not gonna do anything to hurt Becky—you can take that to the bank. She deserves to be happy, and I intend to do whatever I can to see she gets a shot at it." He looked straight into Alex's eyes. "I know it sounds crazy, but I fell for her the minute I laid eyes on her." He shook his head. "Cam always said that's how it was for you and him, so I guess that's how it works for us Ross men." He swallowed the last of his sandwich. "Gotta go shower. I'm gonna drop over at her house and tell her I got the job." He started out of the room and stopped at the doorway. "Look, I really do feel bad about barging in just when you and Cam were getting it on, Alex. I'm gonna look for an apartment now I've got some income. You two need privacy."

Her face flamed, and she shook her head dejectedly. "I'm not sure what we need, David. Cam's different these days. I just can't seem to reach him." The all-too-familiar tears threatened, and she struggled to hold them back, lifting the cup to her lips and forcing herself to sip at the coffee she no longer wanted.

David came back to the table and sat down. "Hey, he loves you, Alex. Don't ever doubt that." He frowned, groping for words. "I never realized it till lately, but Cam had it rough when we were kids. Mom— Well, she's great, but she wasn't like other kids' moms who had a husband to help them. Cam and me, we had no father to pick up the pieces when things went wrong. So Cam took over that role in the family. He took care of Mom and me both, and it's only now that I see how tough it must have been for him. I mean, it was a huge responsibility, and he was only a little kid, right? Kids shouldn't have to take that much on their shoulders. And he takes things seriously, way more than I ever have. Right now, something's got him tied in knots—I don't have a clue what. But cut him some slack if you can, and I know he'll work it through.''

''I'm trying to do exactly that, but he doesn't make it easy.'' Alex was surprised at the depth of bitterness in her tone.

David nodded. ''He's not an easy guy. And he's acting like a bozo. I told him so, for all the good it did.'' He got up and awkwardly patted her shoulder. ''I gotta go. If there's anything I can do to help, say the word.'' He grinned. ''Just as long as it's not knocking some sense into Cam. I figure he could still take me if it came to a fist-fight.''

''Never that.'' Alex tried for a smile and almost managed it. ''Thanks, David. And—and best of luck with Becky.''

''Thanks.'' His smile flashed. He hurried up the stairs, and Alex heard the shower start.

She sat, hands cupping her now cold coffee, thinking over what David had said. Cameron never spoke much of his childhood, and her heart softened toward him, thinking of the small boy he'd been and the weight of the responsibility he must have borne. In many ways, he'd always taken care of her, too, she realized.

Except now he wasn't taking care of her in the ways she needed. She'd been pushing him hard, trying to get him

to listen to her. Maybe things would be better if she
backed off, let him come to her in his own time, on his
terms. The problem was, waiting was lonely, and there
were no guarantees he would confide in her anytime soon.
Her patience was already worn thin. Nevertheless, she'd
give it a try.

And please, Cam, you try too....

TWO WEEKS PASSED and she did her best, but nothing
changed. Cameron seemed to spend even more time at
work, and although they made love, the camaraderie
they'd once shared was ended.

Summer was ending as well. Outside Alex's office window this late afternoon, the leaves on the poplars were
already turning from green to bright orange-gold.

She forced her attention to the anxious-looking little
woman with the square face and weary blue eyes sitting
across from her. Alex glanced down at the chart on the
desk, checking for a name, and smiled reassuringly.

"What can I do for you today, Mrs. Mattera?"

She had to concentrate, Alex told herself. She couldn't
allow her personal problems to interfere with her job, but
it was becoming harder and harder to separate them as the
distance between her and Cam seemed to increase instead
of diminish.

Alex tried to maintain a smiling countenance for the
world, but inside, her heart ached. She had to force herself to pay attention to what Mrs. Mattera was saying.

"I bin havin' these spells," the woman began in a hesitant voice. "I get real dizzy and fall down. Burned myself quite bad on the oven door yesterday." She pulled up
her sleeve and revealed a sizable bandage on her right
arm.

"Do you lose consciousness when you have these attacks, Mrs. Mattera?"

"Sometimes. Wesley, that's my husband, he said I had to come see you, even though Doc King's been my doctor for years and years."

Slowly but surely now, Alex was building a patient roster. Some, thanks to Nancy Townsend's word-of-mouth advertising, were young pregnant women who wanted her to deliver their babies and become their family's general practitioner. Others, like Mrs. Mattera, appeared in her office like fugitives, choosing a time to consult her when Dr. King wasn't in.

"Wes ain't happy about the way Doc King gives out pills," Mrs. Mattera was saying. "Calls him a pill doctor. Wes don't believe in pills, but that's just Wes." She snorted. "Easy fer him. He ain't been sick a day in his life. Me, now, I need my pills just to keep goin'." She tugged her polyester skirt down over her plump legs and frowned. "Don't wanna hurt Doc King's feelin's, though. Ruthie said he ain't in this mornin', so no need fer him ta know I came ta you, right?"

"If you want the visit to be confidential, I'll certainly respect your wishes. Now, what medicines are you taking?"

"I brung 'em all with me so's you could see." She opened her handbag and pulled out a plastic bag stuffed with vials. "I bin feelin' poorly fer a long time. This here's fer my heart, and this is fer water—I get bad bloat—and this's fer my chest, to keep from getting pleurisy, and this's my little nerve pills because I don't sleep good without 'em—can't do without those. This one's fer my kidneys, this one's to help my arthritics, and this's fer my digestion, and this is fer my blood pressure."

Appalled at the array, Alex lifted each vial and studied the label. It was the second time this week she'd encountered this same situation. It seemed Hollister King wrote prescriptions with mad abandon and total disregard for the side effects each potent drug could produce. He didn't seem to be concerned about the cumulative effect of the drugs, nor did he seem to keep track of what other medications his patients were taking each time he dispensed a new drug.

"Wesley says all these different pills could be makin' me dizzy. You think that's right, Doctor?"

In Alex's opinion, this combination of pharmaceuticals was potent enough to knock an elephant to its knees, but of course she couldn't say so. "We're going to start with a thorough physical, Mrs. Mattera, and then we can make some decisions about medication."

Forty minutes later, it was clear to Alex that at least some of the symptoms that had led King to prescribe still another medication for Mrs. Mattera were in fact only side effects from a previous drug. She ordered an array of tests to confirm her suspicions, and when she sat down at her desk again and saw the plastic bag full of pills, she felt like scooping the entire mess into the garbage.

She knew it would take great diplomacy to convince Mrs. Mattera she had to stop taking the majority of the pills she'd come to rely on. And it was difficult for Alex to recommend stopping the pills without implying blame at Dr. King for prescribing them in the first place.

The medication that concerned her the most was the powerful tranquilizer Mrs. Mattera called her "little nerve pills." They were highly addictive, and Alex began by suggesting as strongly as she could that Mrs. Mattera gradually decrease the number she was taking, doing her best to explain in simple terms how dangerous and addictive the pills could be.

"But Doc King wouldn't've told me to take 'em if I didn't need 'em, now, would he?'' the woman objected, carefully tucking her plastic bag back into her purse.

When Mrs. Mattera left the office, Alex sank down into her chair and shook her head in frustration. How could King have prescribed such a drug in the first place, when Alex's careful questioning revealed that Mrs. Mattera had never even suffered a serious nervous disorder? Even more disturbing was the fact that King had then complacently renewed the prescription over a period of years simply at Mrs. Mattera's request.

Alex pondered the difficult situation she was in. More and more often, she was seeing disturbing evidence that King made serious errors in judgment. It wasn't just his misuse of drugs that bothered her, either. She'd witnessed a far more serious incident three days before, when she'd administered anesthetic while he did an emergency cesarean section on a young mother. It had happened late in the afternoon, and although King's hands were less than steady and he appeared distracted and tired, he seemed determined to work at top speed.

"Two minutes, Alexandra," he stated in a condescending tone. "A good surgeon can always get a baby out in two minutes. But of course, you know that. Didn't I hear that your father was a fine surgeon? Retired now, but still carries a lot of influence, I understand. Can't be that old, your father, but I guess the tempo in those city hospitals wears a man out."

Alex ignored King's barbs, concentrating on her patient's vital signs, but her stomach tightened as Shirley Boyd slapped a scalpel into his trembling hand and he made the first bold incision from the symphysis, the bone at the bottom of the pelvis, almost up to the navel. To Alex, he didn't seem to have the control that was necessary as he sliced through the abdominal layers to the uterus, and she began to perspire as she watched him come within a hairbreadth of nicking the bladder.

Becky was present as well as Shirley, and in Becky's hazel eyes above her mask, Alex caught a reflection of her own concern.

Alex realized she was holding her breath as King cut across the front of the uterus and shoved the bladder out of the way. Shirley was handing him instruments, and at one horrifying point Alex realized that King had become aphasic—he couldn't find the correct words for the instruments he needed. Instead of a Balfour retractor, he kept asking for a Kelly clamp. Shirley covered for him, handing him the proper instrument in spite of what he asked for, but Alex was utterly appalled. There was something very wrong with King.

By some miracle, the baby girl was delivered safely, the mother's abdomen cleaned and repaired adequately. By the end of the procedure, King was visibly trembling, and Alex's own hands shook for hours afterward. She devoutly prayed that she wouldn't have to spend much time with King in the operating room. And she wouldn't allow his scalpel within a mile of one of her patients, she vowed, even if it meant sending each and every one to Cranbrook or even Vancouver.

The Hippocratic oath each doctor took upon graduation stated that a doctor's colleagues should be treated as brothers. So what did one do when a brother was no longer capable of performing the tasks his job required? When, as was the case with Mrs. Mattera, his carelessness caused illness instead of alleviating it?

It was too bad, because Alex was beginning to enjoy her work in Korbin Lake. She was finding she took great pleasure in meeting and treating patients she'd likely see again; in the ER, the work was more hectic, with less chance for prolonged personal contact. This suited her.

If things were right with Cameron, and if she didn't have to deal with Dr. King, she could be very happy here, she reflected with a wry half smile, picking up the first of the charts she needed to update before she could go home.

Cam's mother had a saying that was appropriate here: If wishes were horses beggars would ride.

IT WAS PAST SIX by the time Alex was finally done, and she slumped in her chair and propped her legs up on the desk, realizing that she was dreading going home. She leaned her head back and closed her eyes.

Physician, heal thyself. Easier said than done.

Suddenly there was a peremptory knock on her door, and before she could say a word, or even swing her legs down, the door burst open and Hollister King stood there, larger than life, dressed as formally as usual in an impeccably tailored navy blue suit and light blue dress shirt and silk tie.

He took in Alex's casual blue cotton pants and matching shirt, her bare feet propped on the desk. He looked around at the homey atmosphere she'd created, and he frowned.

"Well, Alexandra, it's nice that at least one of us has time to relax."

"Evening, Hollister." She refused to move—it was her office, damn it! "Come on in, why don't you?"

"Can't." Her sarcasm was entirely lost on him.

"I'm on my way to a meeting. Just wanted you to know I'm operating first thing tomorrow morning. I'll expect you in at seven to assist me with the anesthetic." He turned on his heel, ready to close the door again.

Alex's heart sank, and she swung her legs to the floor.

"Hollister, wait a minute. What sort of operation?"

"Gall bladder. I'll fill you in on the details in the morning." Oozing impatience, he threw the answer over his shoulder and slammed the door.

Alex stared at the closed door, unable to shake the sick foreboding inside of her. The very last thing she wanted to do was be a part of King's surgical team again, but there was absolutely nothing she could do to avoid it.

CHAPTER SEVENTEEN

ALEX AT LAST got to her feet, wearily locked her office door and drove slowly home. Cameron was working afternoon shift, and David seemed to be spending every moment he wasn't working at Becky's, so the house was empty except for Pavarotti.

The telephone rang just as she came through the door, and she hurried into the kitchen to pick it up.

"Alexandra?"

Just by the way her mother said her name, Alex knew that Eleanor was angry, and her heart sank. That was all she needed tonight, another problem.

"I don't suppose you've heard the news?"

Alex muffled a sigh. It couldn't be good, judging by her mother's tone of voice.

"What news is that, Mother?"

"That woman—" the words held a wealth of scorn and impotent rage "—that woman has somehow *bullied* your poor brother into marriage. Some—some ridiculous ceremony was held at the hospital this afternoon. Your father and I weren't even invited! Can you imagine such a thing? It surely can't be legal, considering Wade's condition."

Alex clutched the receiver, feeling a slow, incredulous grin spread across her face. "Thea and Wade got *married?*"

"Apparently. As I just said, your father and I weren't even informed until afterward. In my opinion, your brother isn't well enough to make any such decision. I find it utterly appalling."

"Well, I don't." Alex was too elated to play the usual game of placating Eleanor. "I think it's wonderful. It means that Wade has decided to take control of his life again."

"Rubbish." Eleanor was too angry even to analyze the issue. "She's simply taken unfair advantage of him when he's vulnerable, that's all. And she was insufferably rude to me, Alex, when I expressed my very valid objections to this—this *travesty*. Would you believe she actually said that *I* needed counseling?"

"I've thought so myself at times." The words were out before Alex could stop them, and she heard her mother gasp. Before Eleanor could say another word, Alex added in a firm tone, "I'm absolutely delighted for both of them."

And then she did something she'd never dreamed of doing before. "I'm going to hang up now, Mother, so I can call the hospital and give them my love and best wishes."

Her mother's outraged voice was still audible even as Alex depressed the Disconnect button.

An instant later, she dialed St. Joe's, and the sound of Wade's excited voice made her happier than she'd been in weeks.

"Alex? Hey, sis, we were just about to call you. Thea and I got married an hour ago." He sounded strong, and, oh, he sounded glad. There were voices in the background, and laughter, and the clink of glasses. "Half the hospital's in here right now, helping us celebrate. Mike brought champagne."

Alex's eyes filled with tears.

"Wade, that's wonderful, I can't tell you how pleased I am."

"And, sis?" There was naked elation in his tone. "I stood up for the ceremony. I had to have support, but these old pins are gonna work fine again, I just know it now."

"Oh, Wade." Tears of joy were coursing down her face, and Alex could barely speak. "I'm—I'm so very happy for you, for both of you. And tell Thea I'm delighted to finally have a sister."

"Tell her yourself."

There was a moment's pause, and then Thea came on the line, euphoria palpable in her voice. "We're both sorry you can't be here to celebrate with us, Alex." Her voice grew soft against the background noise. "Thanks, from the bottom of my heart. I took your advice, and you were absolutely bang on the money."

"You told him off?" Alex was incredulous.

"I did. And when he got over being furious, he asked me to marry him. So I took him up on it right away, before he had a chance to change his mind."

Both women giggled.

"I love you, Thea. Welcome to the family."

Alex hung up. She reached down and lifted Pavarotti into her lap, terribly aware that even in this moment of absolute joy, she was alone.

Once again, Cameron wasn't there when she needed him.

HE FINALLY CAME HOME at 3:30 a.m., totally exhausted. There'd been a brawl at a bar, and of course by then her news about Wade and Thea had lost its first bright glitter. He dozed off while Alex was still talking, and she couldn't get back to sleep again. At daybreak she got up, all too aware that with morning came her duties as anesthetist to Hollister King.

She drove to work with a lump of apprehension in her stomach.

During her internship, Alex had always been aware of the peculiar intimacy of an operating room with its gowned figures hovering over the supine body of an unconscious patient like a gathering of priests in some ancient temple. She'd been aware as well of the sense of absolute unity between the medical team, a single-minded determination to do the very best possible for the patient.

This morning, that sense of unity was noticeable only by its absence. To Alex, it seemed that she and Becky were on one side of an invisible glass wall, with Shirley and Hollister on the other. Apart from the friendly remarks between herself and Becky, there was no chitchat before the operation began, and no tangible sense of teamwork as Alex meticulously gauged the amounts of chemicals needed to render the figure on the table unconscious.

"Do you think we could proceed anytime in the next decade, Dr. Ross?" King's voice dripped with sarcasm.

Alex did her best to ignore him. She checked and rechecked her calculations before she finally administered the proper dosage through the infusion tubing.

The patient was a stout young man in his midthirties named Johnnie Williams. Alex had talked with him a half hour before. Even feeling extremely ill, Johnnie seemed a gentle and likable person, although not terribly bright. He told Alex about his recent marriage, adding proudly that Laura, his new wife, insisted on being in the waiting room all during the operation, even though Doc King had laughed at the idea of her being worried.

"He said fixing this gall bladder would be easier on me than getting a root canal." Johnnie smiled. "So I asked him why not fix my teeth while he was at it?"

Alex laughed with him to put him at ease, but her own sense of foreboding refused to go away. She carefully studied Johnnie's chart and questioned him, confirming to her own satisfaction King's diagnosis of acute infection of the gall bladder.

Johnnie had come to the clinic late the previous afternoon with severe right-sided abdominal pain and extreme nausea. His white blood count was elevated and he was running a low-grade fever. King had admitted him, and the abdominal X rays he'd ordered had confirmed that the gall bladder was enlarged and inflamed.

Johnnie was now unconscious, covered with a sterile green sheet through which a window had been cut to expose the surgical site. Alex checked his eyes, then ran a finger along his eyelashes. There was no response. "He's under," she announced.

She felt her own heartbeat accelerate as Shirley slapped a scalpel into King's waiting palm. The elderly doctor looked puffy and flushed this morning, although his hands seemed steadier than they'd been during the cesarean section the week before. Maybe he was better early in the morning. Alex fervently hoped so.

With a flourish, King made the incision in Johnnie's abdomen, extending it from the sternal notch along the rib cage to a lateral point. Just as before, the doctor seemed to feel the need to hurry; within seconds, and with less caution than Alex felt advisable, he'd isolated the gall bladder, and Shirley slapped another scalpel into his palm so he could cut it free.

So far so good. Alex glanced down at Johnnie's face and checked his vital signs, which were fine. At a muffled gasp from Becky, however, her head jerked up again just in time to see that somehow King had dropped the scalpel into the opening in the abdomen.

He cursed and reached for it, and simultaneously rich, red blood welled from the incision and spilled in rivulets across the green sheet covering the patient's stomach and legs.

It was obvious that the scalpel had somehow sliced the liver and that King needed to locate the cut and repair it with due haste, but as Alex and the two nurses watched in horror, King began to fumble, muttering under his breath, demanding clamps and then throwing them to the floor.

"Blood pressure's dropping, 90 over 60. Heart rate 120." Alex flew into action, starting a large bore intravenous to elevate the blood pressure with intravenous solution.

The patient was bleeding out. "80 over 50, heart rate 140. Get him cross matched, and I want four units of O negative, stat." She quickly grabbed Ringer's Lactate to hang on the initial IV line.

If only one of the pharmacological agents would work—but she knew all too well that no drugs helped hypovolemia, diminished blood volume.

King's head wobbled and his hands trembled, and precious minutes passed while he groped around ineffectually, trying to find the site of the bleeding.

"Blood pressure's dropping, 60, palpable," Alex warned again, and almost before the last word was out of her mouth, the heart monitor warned that Johnnie's heartbeat was irregular.

"He's going to arrest, Hollister." Alex's voice was loud, even though her throat felt constricted. Her entire body was icy cold. "The patient is in hypovolemic shock."

Events seemed to slow, until to Alex everything was happening in the terrible slow motion of a nightmare.

"Do something, Hollister, for God's sake," she pleaded. "He's in r-fib. He's bleeding out—"

"Stop hollering at me and help me here, Doctor Ross." King's voice was panicked. There was blood everywhere. "Get those paddles ready, Becky," he bellowed.

Becky snatched the defibrillator paddles and shoved them into King's hands, even though the bleeding was continuing unabated and they all knew the paddles were useless if the patient bled to death.

Alex plunged her gloved hand into the incision, desperately trying to find the exact source of the bleeding. She groped and groped again, but there was no way of telling where it originated.

The beeping of the heart monitor changed abruptly, giving the flat, uninterrupted wail that signaled cardiac arrest, and in a loud, agitated voice, King began giving orders to use the defibrillator paddles, but of course it was no use.

Blood still seeped from the abdominal incision but it was evident to everyone except perhaps Hollister King that Johnnie Williams was dead.

SLOWLY, BECKY UNHOOKED the monitors, and for a moment they simply stood around the table and stared down at the body. Alex felt stunned, as if she'd been struck on the head by a heavy object.

She'd seen patients die before, far too many of them over the years, but never had she been involved in such a clumsy and utterly appalling foul-up as this. She looked over at Becky, and then at Shirley, and in their eyes she saw a reflection of her own horror.

To her amazement, King was the first to recover.

"That was most unfortunate, but these things happen. No point standing around. Let's get this incision closed."

Shirley handed him the materials and he went to work, seemingly quite calm now, his hands steady.

Alex gaped at him, astounded at his callousness, his refusal to take responsibility for what had just happened. She knew if she didn't get out of the room, she'd say exactly what she thought—that Hollister King was guilty of criminal negligence, that he ought never to operate on anyone again.

She burst through the doors of the operating theater and stood with her back against the wall, breathing in deep, ragged gulps, trying to regain some semblance of control. She thought of Johnnie Williams's new wife, waiting nervously somewhere nearby. What in God's name would Hollister King tell that poor woman?

She stood up straight and looked through the double windows into the operating room.

King was talking earnestly to the nurses, and Shirley was nodding in agreement. Alex stumbled over to the sinks and stripped off her bloody gloves, tossing them into the trash. She turned on the water and scrubbed her arms, but the blood seemed to cling, refusing to be washed away.

Behind her, the hinged doors from the operating room burst open, and King came out. Alex flinched at the sight of him. Blood was spattered on the lenses of his glasses and all over his face. His gown was drenched with it. He looked as if he'd participated in a slaughter.

But he did, her mind screamed. *We all did.*

He was solemn-faced, composed. "As soon as I wash up, I have to speak to next of kin, so I won't be through here for a while, Alexandra. Would you tell Ruthie to apologize to the patients who are waiting over at the clinic and ask my afternoon appointments to reschedule?"

All in a day's work. Alex was certain she was going to vomit. She swallowed hard against the bile in her throat. "I'd like a word with you, Hollister."

"No time at the moment," he snapped.

"Then I'll come to your office at the end of the day, about six." Her voice was tight and thin, and she didn't wait for a response. She turned her back on him and headed off to have a shower.

ALEX TAPPED ON Hollister King's office door at 6:00 p.m.

"Come in, come in. Well, Alexandra, it's been a long, hard day, and I still have house calls. What is this about? Can we make it brief?"

He was sitting behind his desk smoking a cigar. As always, he was impeccably tailored, his white-on-white striped shirt bandbox fresh, his glasses sparkling in the gleam of the overhead light.

Not a trace of blood anywhere, Alex thought wearily. He'd washed it all away, and from the looks of him, he'd also put it out of his mind.

"I'd like to talk to you about what happened this morning in the operating room." She didn't wait for an invitation to sit—she still felt ill, and she slid into one of the large oak armchairs. Every muscle in her body ached, and her head was pounding. Getting through the day had taken a major effort.

He puffed, and a cloud of smoke wafted toward her. She nearly gagged.

"Regrettable," he said with a shake of his head and a somber look. "A most regrettable accident. I feel terrible about it. But as I explained to Mrs. Williams, we doctors aren't God. There wasn't the slightest hint of any cardiac dysfunction. I did an EKG and it was normal. There was no way to guess that his heart would give out during the operation."

Alex was flabbergasted. She looked him straight in the eye. "You know as well as I do that Mr. Williams's heart wouldn't have failed if he hadn't been hemorrhaging. You dropped a scalpel, Hollister. You nicked the liver. The patient bled out—he didn't die from a heart attack. The autopsy will confirm it."

"We all make mistakes, Alexandra. You of all people should know that." He glared at her, his bushy eyebrows drawn into a single severe line across his forehead. The light caught the lenses of his glasses so that she couldn't see his eyes. "Before you point the finger of blame at me, you should remember that you're no more exempt than I am from errors in judgment. I distinctly remember a situation recently in which a young woman was miscarrying and you didn't even bother to examine her. She, too, could easily have died."

Alex was speechless for a moment. "You can't think of comparing that situation to this, Hollister. That was an accident scene. The girl was brought into hospital immediately and treated."

"*I* treated her. It was only because of me there were no serious repercussions from your carelessness."

Alex stared at him, and her outrage and anger overcame her. The man's ego was monstrous. She'd hoped to be as diplomatic as possible, but now she didn't give a damn about diplomacy. Her voice was firm, her words harsh and honest. "In my opinion, Hollister, you shouldn't be operating on anyone any longer. I've watched you twice now in surgery, and it's clear to me you're no longer capable."

"No longer capable? Is that so?" King's face grew purple. "Well, as far as I'm concerned, madam, your opinion is less than worthless around here." With short, vicious movements he stubbed out his cigar in an ornate silver ashtray. "I've been operating since you were in diapers, and I'll continue to do so long after you get tired of playing country doctor and run back to the city where you belong. You're only here because your father used his influence to get you the job. I told the board at the time you were hired that you wouldn't last."

Alex's voice rose. "I hate to disappoint you, but I'm staying, Hollister. I'll be around a long while, and from here on, I will no longer administer anesthetic for any surgical procedure you decide to perform. I intend to notify the administrator of that decision immediately."

King's voice, too, was out of control. He lumbered to his feet, leaning his palms on the desk and looming over her, his voice and his expression menacing. "We'll just see about that, madam. Being able to administer anesthesia was one of the requirements of your employment here. If you refuse to fulfill the terms of your employment, we'll simply have to get ourselves another doctor, won't we?"

He was utterly furious, and Alex herself was angrier than she could ever remember being. She gave him back glare for glare, but inside her, a tiny voice reminded her that this dreadful fighting wasn't accomplishing anything.

With an immense effort, Alex lowered her voice and tried for a reasonable approach. "Look, Hollister, I feel rotten having to say these things to you. I know this is hard for you, but for the sake of your patients, you have to face facts. During that cesarean the other day you became aphasic. You couldn't remember the names of the instruments, and you endangered a mother and child. And this—this disaster this morning—Hollister, you dropped a scalpel, and then you became confused. When the bleeding began, you wasted precious seconds, time that young man didn't have to waste. I can't sit back and pretend this was an unavoidable accident. I believe you were negligent in your duties as a physician, and I'd be just as negligent if I didn't draw it to your attention now."

She drew in a deep breath and said quietly, "Unless you voluntarily stop performing surgery, I feel I have no choice but to write a letter to the College of Physicians and Surgeons, telling them exactly what happened this morning. I will also speak to Harry Perkins, of course."

He let out a derisive snort. "Go right ahead. It's your word against mine. Harry Perkins and I go back a long way. As far as the college goes, I'll simply tell them the truth, that from the moment you arrived here you've done your best to undermine me to the community at large."

Alex gasped, and he blustered on. "You're an ambitious woman, and you'd rather I wasn't standing in your way. There's a great deal of money to be made in a community like this, and policemen don't get rich, isn't that a fact?"

Furious and disgusted, Alex still refused to let him bully her into another outburst. Instead, she quietly listed the sequence of events that would follow, praying that he'd back down. "You know there'll be an investigation as soon as I lodge a complaint, Hollister. Becky and Shirley will both have to give statements. There'll be an independent autopsy."

"My nurses will fully support me." There was complete confidence in his tone. "They'll swear I did everything in my power to save that young man's life, because, of course, I did. The autopsy will undoubtedly indicate that there was a heart defect that didn't manifest on the tests, and you show me a doctor who hasn't dropped an instrument at one time or another. I warn you, you'll come out of this looking both vindictive and dangerously ambitious, *Doctor* Ross. This will not benefit your career, believe me.''

Alex got to her feet. Her knees felt shaky, and the nausea was rising again in her throat. ''You leave me no choice in this matter, Hollister.'' She walked to the door. ''I'm taking action to see that nothing of this sort has a chance to happen again.''

CHAPTER EIGHTEEN

"ALEX OPENED THE DOOR and walked out, King's raised voice following her into the hallway. "You're going to be sorry you ever started this, madam. Remember, you're the newcomer in this town, not me. The people here are all my friends. You'll find that out the hard way, Alexandra."

She shut the door softly, cutting off his voice. She was trembling violently. She wondered if she could make it down the hall to her own office without having her knees give away. She knew she was doing the right thing, but it felt awful.

And the trouble was, much of what King said was absolutely true; she knew the college would be very careful about taking disciplinary action.

He was dead wrong about one thing, however, and it was like a lifeline to Alex in the midst of all the ugliness. Shirley would lie to save King's neck, but Alex was positive Becky would tell the truth. Becky would back her up as to what had really happened in that operating room this morning. Becky would probably be home by now. Her shift had ended hours ago.

Alex reached for the phone, then laid it back in its cradle. She wouldn't phone. She'd drive over instead and talk to Becky in person. She felt better already.

"I CAN'T DO IT, ALEX. I'm sorry." There was anguish in Becky's voice, but her refusal was adamant. She stared down at her hands, clasped tightly in her lap, and wouldn't meet Alex's disbelieving gaze.

"I guess if it came down to a court case, I'd have to say what happened. But writing it down and sending it to the College of Physicians and Surgeons voluntarily? Lodging a complaint against King?" She shook her head, and her bright hair gleamed in the fading light from the window.

"There's too much at stake for me, don't you see that, Alex? Apart from small pensions, the only household income is mine. And I've seen what happens to nurses when they cross King. More than one has lodged complaints during the four years I've worked at the hospital. He and Shirley made their lives so miserable they had no choice except to get out of here."

Alex felt stunned. She couldn't believe Becky's reaction. She struggled to find the words that would convince the other woman. "But—but there are other places, Becky, other hospitals. You could get a job anywhere, you—you're a wonderful nurse."

Becky shook her head again, more vehemently this time, and now there was anger in her tone. "Maybe so, but for me—for us—that's just not possible, Alex. Apart from the fact that all our friends and relatives are here in Korbin Lake, there's the matter of housing. We couldn't afford to buy a house somewhere else with the little that we'd get for this. And sure, Mom could probably get a job of some sort—God knows she waitressed and cleaned houses when I was a kid—but there's Emily. Em needs all the time and attention Mom and I can give her, you know that. And Gram... She hasn't much time left. How could we drag her out of the hospital, move her somewhere else, at the—the end of her life?"

Becky looked at Alex at last, and her eyes were filled with both resentment and abject misery. "I'm sick over what happened, don't think I'm not. I knew Johnnie. He was two grades behind me at school. He was nice." Tears welled up and spilled over. "Dr. King made it clear this morning after you left the operating room that he expects Shirley and I to support his claim that what happened was an accident and that everyone did everything possible to save Johnnie's life."

Alex nodded. She'd suspected as much. She'd just never dreamed that Becky would go along with him. There was nothing to do now except leave the other woman as much dignity as possible. "I'm sorry I put you in this position, Becky. I—I guess I didn't think the whole thing through enough."

"What—are you going to do?" Becky wiped her wet cheeks.

Alex thought it over for a moment, trying to formulate a plan now that she was alone in this whole thing. Gut-wrenching fear stabbed at her, but she fought it off. "First of all, I'm giving my written report to the hospital administrator. Then, depending on what action he takes, I'm sending it to the college. I already spoke to King." Alex shook her head and gave a humorless little laugh. "Naturally, he denies any responsibility."

Becky nodded. "You probably won't get far with the administrator, either. Perkins and King are fishing buddies. And the coroner, Sid Drysdale, is Olinda's cousin, so as far as he's able, he'll just verify what Doctor King says."

"But what about Mrs. Williams?" Alex felt a thread of hope. "Surely she'll question her husband's death? If it were me, I'd get a lawyer and launch an investigation. These days, it's almost unheard of for a young man in reasonably good health to die from something as basic as a gall bladder operation. Everybody must know that."

Again, Becky shook her head. "I'm willing to bet she won't do anything. Dr. King helped Laura get her mother into a nursing home last year. The old woman was senile and she was driving Laura nuts. King was also responsible for Laura getting her job with the municipality. He's been their family doctor since she was a kid. She sees him as her personal savior. She'd never question anything he says about what happened to Johnnie."

"I see. Well, I guess it's up to me, then." Feeling defeated almost before she'd begun, Alex got to her feet. She'd asked to speak privately to Becky, so they were in the seldom-used front room, and she could hear Emily wailing from another part of the house. The smell of food cooking reminded her that it was late, that she should let Becky join her family for supper.

Becky, too, got up, again wiping her eyes. "I know how badly I'm letting you down, Alex. I'm so sorry. I feel like such a traitor." There was torment in her voice.

Alex tried for a smile and couldn't quite manage it. "Hey, I understand. Like I said, I'm sorry I've put you in such a difficult position. Say goodbye to Sadie for me, will you, and give Emily a kiss." She moved toward the door, wondering if she'd ever be invited here again and welcomed as a friend.

"CAMERON, I REALLY NEED to talk to you." Alex stood in the doorway of the garage. The room was brightly lit and the air reeked of gas and oil. Cameron was sprawled on his stomach holding a wrench, and David was on his back with only his legs and feet protruding from beneath the frame of the old car.

"Be with you in half an hour or so, hon. We're trying to get the muffler off. The bloody thing is rusted and burned, and it won't budge." He didn't so much as glance her way.

The desperation that had been increasing every inch of the way home overwhelmed her, and she lost control. "I don't give a damn what you're doing, Cameron," she shrieked. "Just for once, would you listen to what I have to say when I need to say it? I've got to talk to you *right now*."

He looked up at her, surprise and concern on his face. "Okay, okay, I'm coming. Dave, I gotta go. I'll be back soon as I can."

A mutter of assent came from underneath the car as Cameron laid down the wrench and got to his feet.

Alex turned away, hurrying down the path that led to the wharf. She needed to be outside, in the clean fresh air. She needed to feel that something in the world was untainted.

She could hear Cameron's footsteps behind her, crunching on the gravel, but she didn't turn around or wait for him. She felt more alone than she'd ever felt in her life.

AS HE FOLLOWED HER down the path, Cameron's sense of apprehension grew. Something was terribly wrong. From the tone of Alex's voice and the expression on her face, he knew there was an emergency of some sort. She was also mad at him, and with a sinking feeling in his gut, he tried to figure out what new calamity might have occurred.

The sun had set long ago, and the lake was like pewter in the dusk. A few yards away a fish jumped, and somewhere far off a loon laughed insanely. It was ironic, Cameron mused, that they'd lived in the apartment in the city, with all the noise and confusion of a busy street a few yards away from them, and yet they hadn't experienced half the turmoil they'd had since they'd lived in this idyllic setting.

Alex walked to the very end of the small wharf and sank down on the weathered boards, drawing her knees up and hugging them to her chest, staring out at the water.

"So what's up, Doc?" He tried to sound upbeat, but he knew he sounded wary. The last thing he needed or wanted just now was another confrontation with his wife.

She spoke without looking at him, her voice a monotone. "A young man died in the operating room this morning. I was giving the anesthetic. It was a gall bladder operation, King nicked the liver and the man bled out." Her voice suddenly became passionate. "A gall bladder, for God's sake. Nobody dies from a simple gall bladder operation anymore." She struggled for control, and he waited, trying to assess the problem.

Her voice became flat and hard again as she related every terrible detail of the operation and its macabre outcome. But as she explained it all, telling him exactly what had been said in her confrontation with King, the emotions she'd been holding back gradually overcame her, and she began to sniffle and then to cry openly.

"The thing is, it's my fault, too, Cam. I knew after that cesarean that King wasn't fit, that something ought to be done to stop him from operating." The tears increased, and she gulped and fumbled for a tissue, blowing her nose and wiping her eyes. "But I—I didn't say anything. King is—he's so—overwhelming. He can be so nasty and sarcastic, it's been pure hell working with him at the clinic, and now there's this." She rested her head on her knees and sobbed for several long moments.

Her tears tore a hole in his heart. Cam reached out a hand to touch her soft, curling hair, but he realized at the last moment he was covered with grease. He felt helpless, witnessing her grief, and utterly appalled that he hadn't known exactly what was going on or how hard it had been for her.

And once again, it was all his fault.

She blew her nose and said in a tear-choked voice, "We'd—we'd just started getting along a little, enough so that I didn't hate going to the clinic so much and—and having to confront him every day. And I'd fi-finally started getting a few patients. Things were getting easier, and I didn't want to rock the b-boat. And now this poor man is dead, and I could have prevented it. I could have—" She lowered her head to her knees and sobbed as if her heart were breaking.

All of a sudden, Cameron was deeply, horribly angry, at himself, at circumstance, or fate—at whatever malevolent force had put in motion the events that had brought them here and caused such heartbreak.

"I guess I didn't understand before just how much you hate it here in Korbin Lake." His voice was rough. "Why the hell didn't you tell me King was being such a bastard to you?"

Her head snapped up and she glared at him. "What could you have done about it, Cameron? Punch him out? Tell him not to be mean to your little wife?" She shook her head. "The one valuable thing all this has taught me is that I can fight my own battles." A sob caught her breath. "It's been bad enough knowing my father bent someone's arm just to get me hired here—I was right about that, by the way. King used it against me tonight. The last thing I need is my husband protecting me at this late date." She looked at him, her eyes streaming, her nose red, and there was defiance in that look instead of the love that had always shone there.

The pain in his gut was so overwhelming he nearly doubled over.

"See, I've grown up, Cam. I don't need you to defend me anymore. You've taught me the hard way to stand on my own two feet. Every time I've needed you lately, you haven't been there for me."

He loved this woman more than life itself, and it was evident that he'd failed her completely, in every way, beginning at the moment he'd decided to do something about Perchinsky. And now, when he realized the extent of her despair, he couldn't see what he could do to help her, and his sense of helplessness devastated him.

More and more often lately, he'd questioned the decisions he'd made that had landed them here in Korbin Lake. Maybe he ought to have turned his back on what was going on in the drug squad, let matters take their course. After all, Alex was the person he loved most in all the world, and he was all too aware that his decisions had seriously affected her career. His gut knotted again, and he felt nauseated as he admitted the rest of it to himself.

Not just her career. Their marriage, too, was damaged.

Alex was talking, and he had to make an effort to hear the words over the clamor inside his head.

"You've gone away to a place where I can't reach you, Cameron." She sounded exhausted, without hope. "You never really hear what I have to say, you're not home when I need you, we don't talk about anything that really matters. Even when we make love there's a barrier between us."

His terrible sense of guilt, his awful fear, made him defensive. "I'm having a hell of a time with this transition

from Drug Squad to general duty. You're not the only one
with a demanding job. This is a two-man detachment. I
practically have to live in my bloody uniform, you know
that. And when I'm not working, I'm right here. We talk.
We're talking right now.''

But he knew it *was* his fault. It was because of him she
had to work in a backwoods mining town and take crap
from a has-been who wasn't fit to call himself a doctor.

Cameron had to control the rush of blind fury that
made him want to seek the man out and beat him sense-
less for what he'd said and done to Alex. What stopped
him was knowing that what he'd done to her himself was
just as bad.

"Did you speak to Harry Perkins about this?" His
mind was racing, desperately trying to figure out what was
best to do, how he could best help her.

She shook her head. "Not—not yet," she gulped.

"Why the hell not?" His tone was accusatory, although he didn't mean it to be. "You've let a whole day
go by, and the person you should have gone to right away
was the hospital administrator, for God's sake.'

"I know that, Cam. But he wasn't in this afternoon, so
I made an appointment to see him first thing in the
morning."

His brain went furiously from one option to the next.
He needed to help, wanted to make it better for her, yet
knew that this time he wouldn't be able to. "And what
about the guy's widow? Can't you talk to her, let her
know what King did? Seems she has a right to know exactly what happened to her husband."

Alex shook her head. "I can't do that, Cam. It's not
ethical, and besides, it's just my word against King's."

"Hogwash. You two weren't alone in that operating
room. The nurses saw what happened."

Alex nodded. "They did, but Shirley is King's mistress, and, and—" She swallowed painfully, and her voice was bleak. "Becky won't back me up. She needs her job—she has too many responsibilities to jeopardize it. I asked her for help, and she refused."

God. He knew exactly how that worked. Oh, he knew. All those men he'd worked with over the years, men he'd had to trust with his life, and not a single one of them had backed him when he needed it.

He could hardly bear the thought of Alex feeling that same sense of betrayal. There had to be something . . .

"Ask for a full investigation by the College of Physicians and Surgeons. They hire ex-policemen as investigators. They'd sure as hell figure out in short order that King—"

All of a sudden, Alex scrambled to her feet, startling him. Her face was tight and angry, her voice cold. "I don't need you to tell me what to do, Cam. I told you, this is my problem. I know what steps I need to take."

He swallowed, and his hands curled into fists.

"Then what the hell *do* you want from me, Alex?"

She looked at him, her deep blue eyes signaling disappointment, resentment, utter despair. "If I have to spell it out, it isn't worth much, is it, Cameron? There was a time when you didn't have to ask what I needed from you. God knows I still love you, but for me, this marriage just isn't working anymore." Her face crumpled, and she turned her back to him and ran up the hill.

Shocked to the depths of his being, frightened half to death, it took him several minutes to act.

"Alex. Alex, wait just a damn minute." His furious voice echoed off of the mountains across the lake, and the kitchen door slammed shut behind her fleeing figure.

Cameron tore up the steps to the back porch and threw open the door, meaning to take her in his arms and shake her, or kiss her, or just hold her—something, anything, to ease the awful sense of fear and loss her words had created. But she was already up the stairs, and before he could catch her, the bathroom door slammed and the lock clicked home.

He knocked. He banged the old wooden panels dangerously hard with his fist. "Alex, let me in. Let me talk to you, please."

"Go away. Just leave me alone, Cameron. I want to have a bath."

The water started in the tub, drowning out any possibility of conversation.

Cursing, helpless, longing to strike out at something tangible, he made his way back outside again and into the garage.

David was cleaning his greasy hands on a rag. He looked over at Cameron and frowned. "Trouble?"

Cameron nodded but didn't elaborate. "You get that muffler off?"

David shook his head. "We need a blow torch, and I promised Becky I'd take a look at her washing machine, so I'm not messing with this muffler anymore tonight. I'm heading in for a shower."

"You're seeing a lot of Becky." Cam did his best to keep his tone neutral, but David was instantly defensive.

"So?"

"So I wonder just how well you know her, that's all. Whether you could maybe have a talk with her, get her to see reason on something. There was a situation in the operating room this morning—a guy died because King made a mistake. Alex called him on it, but Becky won't back her up. Alex figures King shouldn't be operating anymore, but she needs Becky's help to stop him.''

"And you want me to see if I can change Becky's mind about this?''

"Yeah." It was the only thing Cam could think of that might help his wife. "I happen to know how convincing you can be with women."

David gave him an inscrutable look and then, to Cameron's amazement, he slowly shook his head. "Sorry, but I won't do it, Cam. If Becky doesn't want to be involved, then I respect her decision."

For a long moment, Cameron just stood and looked at David as the meaning of his words slowly sunk in.

"Without even hearing Becky's reasons, you support her?" The anger inside Cameron erupted all over again. He didn't stop to consider who it was directed toward. "David, every single time you've been in a jam, I was there for you." He spat out the words through clenched teeth. "Now, when I need your help, you refuse. Where the hell's your sense of loyalty, *brother?*''

As always in his dealings with David, he realized too late that he was going about this all wrong, that in another instant David would lose his own temper and storm off, the way he'd always done when he and Cameron had a disagreement. But David met Cameron's steely look with one of his own, and in spite of his anger, Cameron glimpsed something different in his brother at that moment, a strength and sense of purpose that hadn't been there before. And even more surprising, instead of stomping off in a rage, David held his ground.

"Alex is your wife, Cam. You'd do anything to help and protect her. Well, I feel the same way about Becky. I'm in love with her. I have been since the first moment I laid eyes on her. I intend to marry her if she'll have me.''

CHAPTER NINETEEN

CONFOUNDED, CAM COULD only gape at his brother. "Marry her? Godalmighty, David, do you even begin to understand what you're saying here? You've never even had a—a pet to take care of, and you're thinking of taking on a family? And a tough one at that?"

"You figure I'm not up for the job?" David's tone held a note of warning, but Cam had rescued his brother from too many avoidable scrapes to heed it.

"You're not ready, no," he said flatly. "What happens when the novelty wears off a few months or years down the line, and you want out, just the way you've done so many times before? Grown-ups are one thing, but jeez, David, that little kid of Becky's needs stability in her life. You must realize that. You—you're still on probation from that last caper you pulled. You've got ladies phoning you from Vancouver, you haven't got any savings, you've only just started this new job—"

"I know all that." David's voice was low and earnest. "Becky knows it, too, because I told her every last rotten thing about myself I could think of. And she's scared. Who wouldn't be? It's gonna take me a long time to prove to her that I can be responsible, but I intend to do it."

Cam had long ago given up hoping that would happen. His temper snapped. "Don't give me any bull about being responsible, David. I know you, remember?" His voice rose, echoing in the enclosed area. "Damn it, I've yarded you out of more jams than I can count over the years. When you get tired of playing house with Becky and decide to move on, an innocent baby's going to get hurt because of you, and this time I won't be around to pick up the pieces.''

"Maybe it's about time.'' The words were quiet, the tone icy. "Maybe I don't want you picking up the pieces anymore, Cam. I've done a lot of thinking since I met Becky. In my whole life, I've never had to face the consequences for anything I did, because you were always there fixing it for me. From the time I was a little kid, you fought all my battles, so I didn't have to. Don't get me wrong. You've been the best brother a guy could have, and I'm grateful, but it's past time I grew up.'' He drew in a deep breath and gave a rueful grin. "It's hard to know where to start, but I figured I should at least get out on my own. It *has* dawned on me it's not so good for you and Alex to have me hanging around.

"I've found myself an apartment to rent. A guy at work's moving in with his girlfriend, so I'll be moving out in a coupla days. I'm really grateful to you and Alex for letting me stay this long, but from here on in, I've gotta be independent, do things my way. If I make mistakes, I'll deal with them myself.'' His voice deepened, and Cam heard again that new note of determination. "I'll make plenty of mistakes as far as Emily's concerned—what the hell do I know about kids? With Becky, too. I don't know all that much about women, either, when it comes right down to it. But I'm gonna do my best.''

He met Cameron's skeptical eyes and didn't flinch. "They won't be the kind of mistakes you think, Cam, so don't look like that. I'll learn as I go along. Which is exactly why I won't try to talk Becky into doing something she doesn't want to do. See, you just gotta let people make their own decisions. If they're the wrong ones, at least they got to make 'em themselves.'' He tossed the greasy rag down, embarrassed by so much sentiment, and awkwardly gave his brother a punch on the shoulder. "That's about it, then. No hard feelings, right? Gotta go. It's getting late. See ya later.''

Cam watched him lope across the yard and take the back stairs two at a time. He had the strange feeling that part of his life was ending and there was nothing to take its place. Slowly, moving like an automaton, Cameron put all the tools away and carefully cleaned his hands in the bucket of solvent on the workbench. He heard David come out of the house, whistling cheerfully, and get into his car. The motor of the old Chevy roared to life, and he drove away.

Cameron closed and locked the garage doors and made his way into the house and up the stairs. The door to their bedroom was closed, and he could hear Alex moving around inside. He thought of going in to her, but he was filthy from the garage.

He went to the downstairs bathroom and stripped off his greasy work clothes and stepped into the shower, letting the hot water beat on his skull.

"You were always there fixing it for me—"

He'd never stopped to think that maybe that wasn't the best thing. He'd grown up knowing his role in life was to take care of those he loved, and that meant trying to make things right for them.

Didn't it?

"You gotta let people make their own decisions—"

He knew he'd forced decisions on Alex without even explaining why. Uncomfortably, he remembered her saying she didn't want him telling her what to do or trying to solve her problems for her. In some peculiar way, she and David had sounded a lot alike tonight.

He rubbed shampoo into his scalp, forgetting that he'd already washed his hair.

"There was a time when you didn't have to ask what I needed from you—"

What had he done before in their marriage that he wasn't doing now? He had to figure it out, and fast.

"This marriage just isn't working anymore—"

After a long time and a lot of hot water, it dawned on him. He'd stopped listening, just as she'd said. He'd been obsessed with his own problems, but he hadn't dared share them with Alex.

He turned off the water and stepped out, and in spite of the steam, a cold shudder coursed through him. How could he have allowed things to go this far astray? How could he have put his marriage in danger?

He toweled himself dry and pulled on jeans and a shirt, and suddenly the single most important thing in the world was to find his wife and talk to her, really talk, right now.

He swallowed the fear that rose in him. Talking would mean letting her see how imperfect he really was; it would mean showing her all his inadequacies, revealing all the secret fears he'd denied to her and to himself. If he told her what it was like in the depths of his soul, never again would she view him as her hero, and that hurt terribly.

It was a terrifying prospect, letting Alex know how he'd failed her—and himself.

But David had done it. *I told her every last rotten thing about myself—*

Maybe his little brother was a hell of a sight braver than he was, Cam thought ruefully. He wrapped a towel around his middle and headed for the bedroom, determined to repair the damage he'd inflicted.

He tapped, opened the door and froze when he saw the packed suitcases on the bed. She was dressed in jeans and a sweater, and she was stuffing silky underwear into a plastic bag.

"Alex, what are you doing?" He could hardly get the words past the constriction in his throat. She didn't answer right away, and he moved into the room toward her, reaching out and grasping her hand. "C'mon. This has gone far enough. I'll get dressed, and we'll go downstairs and sit down. I really need to talk to you."

She stepped back, away from him, deliberately removing her hand from his grasp. She sounded calm and distant.

"How many times in the past weeks have I said that to you, Cameron? I needed to talk to you, too, and every single time I tried, in one way or another, you refused." He heard her draw a deep breath and expel it. "Well, now *I* don't want to talk. I have nothing left to say to you."

He'd expected anger. This quiet resignation terrified him.

She turned and walked toward the dresser, gathering up her watch and several pairs of earrings, dropping them into her handbag.

She was slipping away, and he couldn't bear it. He grabbed a pair of faded jeans from the closet and tugged them on, and in two quick strides he caught her by the arm, turning her into his embrace.

She didn't resist. Instead she stood like a wooden carving, her sweater soft against his damp skin, her body stiff and passive. After an agonizing moment, he released her again. He had to try, somehow, to reach her. The only thing he had left was the ugly feeling connected to the events that had led them both here to Korbin Lake, and at last, in utter desperation, he blurted them out to her.

"I left Drug Squad because I got labeled a bad narc, Alex." The words were so simple now that he'd voiced them. "Part of me believed that was true, that I was wrong, no matter how right the reasons were for what I did. Cops have this code of honor, and the worst thing a guy can do is break it. You know all about that, Alex. You doctors have it, too.

"The other guys turned against me, and they let me know it in all sorts of ways. They weren't there for me when I needed them, because I was a fink, not to be trusted, not one of them any longer. I couldn't do my job anymore, but by asking for this transfer, I felt like I was running away instead of facing up to the problem." He struggled for words that would convey what that sense of defeat had felt like, but he couldn't find any. "I just couldn't talk it over with you. I figured you'd think less of me, start seeing me the same way the guys on the squad did." He sighed. "I never meant to hurt you, Alex, but I know now I did. All I can say is, I love you. You know I do."

"Do you?" The depth of sadness in her voice tore at him. "I used to think so, but now I'm not sure anymore. Obviously you didn't love me enough to trust me, Cameron, to talk to me about what was really bothering you. What did you think, that I was only in this for the good times, that I wasn't tough enough or resilient enough to weather the bad? That I'd blame you for doing what you had to do?" She gave a sad little laugh. "Isn't it ironic that now I'm in almost the same situation you were? I've got to turn King in, just like you did with Perchinsky, and it would have helped so much, Cameron, *so very much*, if you'd shared how you were feeling before now."

She was silent so long he thought she was done. He struggled against the habit that silence had become, but before he could speak, she added in a desolate voice, "Now, I'm not sure of anything, Cam. I don't even know if I want to stay in this relationship anymore."

A quick jolt of panic raced up and down his spine. He had to stop this, he had to, before it went any further and something inconceivable happened.

"Look, you're exhausted." He thought of the man who'd died that morning on the operating table, the confrontation she'd had with King, the way he himself had acted, and he felt mortally ashamed. "You're probably hungry, and you're tired, love. C'mon down to the kitchen. I'll make you something to eat and then you can get a good night's sleep. We can talk this out first thing in the morning. I'll take the day off. We can spend it together, just the two of us."

"No, Cameron." She spoke very quietly. "Yesterday, the day before, last week... Lord, I'd have given anything to hear you say that. But not now. Now, it's too late."

Too late. The words sent icy fear slicing like a knife through his every nerve ending. "For God's sake, Alex—"

Her voice didn't waver. "I need some time on my own. Completely on my own. I don't want to stay here with you any longer." Now he could hear the pain that lay just underneath her rigid control. "I had such dreams for us here. I thought things were going to be wonderful. This place is beautiful, peaceful—yet I've been so unhappy. It hurts me too much to stay. So I'm taking a room at that motel just outside of town, the Slumber Lodge, or whatever it's called."

The words stunned him. "Alex, please. Don't do this." His hands were fists at his sides, but he knew the barrier he'd created between them wouldn't yield to force. He fought down panic. "We can work our way through this. I know we can. I know it's my fault, but I can make it up to you. Just give me a chance to try."

"I'm sorry, Cameron. I just can't. I'm all out of chances."

She looped her handbag over her shoulder and picked up her suitcase.

He wanted to beg. He wanted to weep. He wanted to sweep her into his arms and make love to her until neither of them had the strength to walk.

But he looked at her face, the mobile, animated face that revealed her every mood, and he saw there was no use. He'd never seen her look that cold, or that detached.

"You'll take care of Pavarotti for me, won't you?"

He nodded and watched the distance between them stretch into infinity. "Yeah, I'll do that. And if you need anything, I'm here."

She nodded.

He stood in the upstairs hall and listened to her footsteps as she went down the stairs. He heard her open and close the door, and a few moments later, he heard the motor of her car.

Gravel scrunched in the driveway.

Cameron closed his eyes and cursed himself for a fool. Then he sat down on the stairs, and for the first time since he was a very small boy, he wept.

CHAPTER TWENTY

"YOU ARE HEREBY notified that your admitting privileges at Korbin Lake General Hospital have been revoked subject to review by the hospital board, effective this fifteenth day of September..."

Two endless, miserable days later, Alex stared down at the letter that Ruthie had just placed on her desk with the rest of her mail. Typed on heavy bond, it had Harry Perkins's letterhead in ornate script at the top, and she read the words for the fourth time, still unable to believe them.

It was outrageous. It was totally unfair. It was exactly what she should have anticipated after her interview with him early Wednesday morning.

She'd spent a sleepless night after checking into a room at the Slumber Lodge Motel. She'd barely locked the door to unit 24 and laid her suitcase on the bed when the telephone on the bedside table buzzed.

"It's me," Cameron had said in a gruff tone. "I just wanted to be sure you got there safely."

The sound of his voice threatened to unravel the twisted skein of determination she'd wound around her emotions.

"I'm fine, Cameron."

"Good." There was a long, long, silence, filled with unspoken misery. Alex could visualize him so clearly, standing in the kitchen, leaning on the counter, scowling at the blackness outside the window.

"Well, I should go," she finally said. "I've got to settle in. Good night, Cam."

She'd hung up, and she hadn't allowed herself to cry, because she knew once she started it would be impossible to stop. She'd unpacked, put on her nightshirt, and then lain wakeful hour after hour in the strange room, her brain replaying every word of the conversation she and Cameron had finally had.

"You'd think less of me," he'd said. *"Start seeing me the way the guys on the squad did."*

As if she ever could see him as anything but what he was, an honorable man. Her heart ached for him, but at the same time, the agonizing hurt he'd caused by shutting her out was still in her heart, deep and insurmountable. He hadn't trusted the depth of her love.

He'd needed support and solace, and he hadn't come to her. He'd agonized and suffered the tortures of the damned for weeks—months—and he hadn't had enough faith in her to tell her what was bothering him. He hadn't shared any part of himself with her, his wife, supposedly his beloved.

So what did that say about their relationship, about the love she'd thought they'd shared, about the life they had together?

She couldn't bear to think about it anymore, so at three in the morning, she propped herself up on pillows and turned the television on to an old movie while she finally fell into a troubled sleep.

When morning came, she showered and dressed and was waiting in Perkins's outer office when he walked in.

Her heart sank, because she knew by the wary expression on his face that King had already talked to him. In a quiet and, she hoped, rational voice, she described the previous day's operation and its tragic outcome. She outlined the other disturbing things she'd observed, and concluded by saying that she couldn't ethically administer anesthetic again for any of Dr. King's procedures. She stopped short of saying there should be a full inquiry into the death of Johnnie Williams, but she implied it. When she was done, she laid her carefully prepared written report on his desk.

The whole time she'd been speaking, Perkins had fussed with a stack of papers on his desk, arranging and rearranging them. He'd never once looked up, and when she was finished, he cleared his throat several times, still staring down at his desk blotter.

She waited.

"These are serious allegations, Dr. Ross. I hope you realize that."

Hysteria rose inside of Alex. *Really, Perkins? And here I thought we were just indulging in trivial gossip.*

"Of course I do," she managed to say. "This is a serious matter. A patient died." Again she waited, and for the first time, he looked up at her, and now she could see the overt triumph in his eyes.

"And the others who were in the operating room, Dr. Ross? They're prepared to substantiate what you've just told me?"

Becky had been absolutely right, Alex thought. Perkins intended to do nothing at all. She'd turned without another word and walked out.

Now, however, holding his letter in her hand, she realized how wrong she'd been about him. Instead of doing nothing, he'd immediately taken steps to get rid of her.

With shaking hands, Alex lifted the telephone and then set it down again. No, by God. She wouldn't do this by phone. She'd go over and confront Harry Perkins in person and demand an explanation. It wouldn't do any good—she understood that—but at least she would say all the things that needed to be said.

With the letter crumpled in one hand, she raced past a startled Ruthie and the sizable number of patients waiting to see her, out of the clinic and over to the hospital. Incensed, she barged into Perkins's office, marching past the wide-eyed secretary to the door of his inner sanctum, only to discover that it was locked.

"He's not here, Dr. Ross," the secretary said in a timorous voice. "He's in Calgary at a conference. He won't be back till next Monday."

It was Thursday. Perkins had timed it perfectly. She'd have three full days to calm down before any confrontation was possible. She'd also have three nights, Alex thought despondently. Long, lonely nights like the two she'd already spent in the sterile confines of the Slumber Lodge. Well, at least now she'd have something entirely new to keep her awake.

Slowly, feeling a hundred years old, she walked back through the hospital, forcing herself to respond to the friendly greetings of staff members, and near the nursing station she came face-to-face with Becky.

They hadn't seen each other since Alex had made her ill-fated visit to ask for her friend's support, and the strain between them was immediately evident. Neither seemed to know what to say next.

Alex was painfully aware of the letter clutched in her hand, aware that Becky, too, looked drawn and weary. Struggling against the awkwardness, Alex groped for something sufficiently neutral to talk about. "How's Winifred doing?" She realized guiltily that she hadn't been in to see the old woman yet this week.

Tears filled Becky's eyes, and she shook her head. "Not good. Not good at all."

Alex suddenly wanted to reach out and wrap her arms around Becky, but she knew if she did, she'd lose the steely control with which she'd managed to get through the past two days. Worst of all, she was no longer certain that her gesture would be welcome.

"I'm so sorry," she murmured. "If there's anything I can do—"

Becky nodded, and then said in a hesitant voice, "David told me last night that you're not living out at the lake anymore." She tried for a smile and failed. "Small towns, no secrets." She looked straight into Alex's eyes and said earnestly, "Please, Alex, come and stay with us. Mom and I want you to know that you're more than welcome."

The offer was so unexpected, so touching, that Alex had to struggle hard to control herself before she could reply. Even so, her voice was thick. "Thanks, Becky. More than I can say." She swallowed hard and battled the sobs that rose in her throat. "Your offer—it means a great deal to me, but I—I have to be alone for a little while, to—to try to sort myself out. You understand. Please tell Sadie how grateful I am, won't you?" She added miserably, "And give Emily a big hug for me."

Becky nodded, a worried frown creasing her forehead. "Em had a sore throat and a bit of a temp this morning. I'm afraid she's getting the flu."

Alex opened her mouth to offer any medical aid Emily might need, and then closed it again, reminding herself that Hollister was their family doctor. And, she thought bitterly, tightening her hold on the envelope, she no longer had admitting privileges at this hospital, which meant that her days as a family physician here in Korbin Lake were coming to an end—right along with her marriage.

The pain she was keeping locked inside nearly overwhelmed her, and she had to struggle hard before she could say, "I should get back to the clinic, I have patients waiting. Thanks again, and I'll see you soon, Becky."

But as she walked quickly away, she knew it was unlikely she'd be seeing Becky anytime in the near future.

Sometime in the past hour, Alex had made a decision.

She was going back to Vancouver. She wasn't sure what she'd do when she got there, but there was nothing left for her here in Korbin Lake.

CAMERON WAS WAITING when Alex left the clinic that afternoon. He was sitting in his Jeep, parked beside her car in the nearly empty lot.

He got out when she came walking slowly across the pavement, and he realized that his legs weren't quite steady as he moved toward her. The way she looked shocked and frightened him.

She was pale, and there were dark circles under her beautiful eyes. More than that, however, was the absence of vivacity. Alex never just walked; she moved with purpose, with a sense of absolute energy and grace. Now, that animation was gone. She seemed hardly able to put one foot in front of the other.

She hesitated a moment when she first saw him, as though she might actually turn and go the other way. More than anything else had, that hurt him. Cam had to clench his fists to keep himself from reaching out and grabbing her.

"Hi, Alex. I wondered if you'd like to have some dinner," he said as casually as he could manage. He was wearing his old leather jacket for luck, but underneath it he'd put on dress slacks and the silk shirt she'd bought him.

He'd traded shifts with Greg so he'd have the whole evening free. He'd made reservations at the best restaurant Korbin Lake had to offer, a new place overlooking the lake. He'd vowed that he wouldn't beg her to come home—he had his pride, but seeing her now, he knew that pride wasn't important at all.

Every hour, every minute since she'd left, he'd resisted the impulse to go after her. He'd wanted to give her time, if that's what she needed. He'd give her *anything* she needed. He loved her more than life itself.

"I wanted to talk to you tonight, Cameron, but I don't think I have time for dinner." Even her voice was lackluster. "Maybe we could grab a sandwich back at the house?"

For an instant, terrible relief made him dizzy. God, she was coming home.

She must have seen the burgeoning hope that flickered in his eyes, because she added in a less-than-steady voice, "I want to pick up Pavarotti and the rest of my clothes."

She took a deep breath and then said in a rush, "I'm leaving for Vancouver in the morning. I've decided to go home for a while."

Home. Her use of the word slammed into his gut like a fist. He'd always thought that home was wherever they were, together.

"I see." He didn't see at all, but nothing really mattered now. "What about your practice?"

Her lips tightened, and her eyes were bleak. "Perkins has withdrawn my admitting privileges at the hospital, so there's not much point in pretending I can go on practicing here in Korbin Lake."

Hot rage rose in Cameron, and his fists clenched.

Perkins. He'd kill the son of a bitch for doing this to her— But she'd made it clear that what was happening was her fight, not his.

"Let's go back to the house." He was dully surprised at how normal he sounded. "Your car needs an oil change before you start on a long trip. I'll do it while you're packing."

It was the only thing left he could think of to do for her.

An hour later, with Pavarotti complaining at the top of his lungs from the carrier on the seat beside her, Alex drove up the driveway, on her way back to the motel.

Out of his life. Cameron went inside and called the detachment.

"Greg? Look, I'm giving you the night off. I'll be in to take over as soon as I get my uniform on."

He had to have something to do tonight or he'd go mad.

Alex was deeply asleep when the telephone rang. Dragging herself to a sitting position, she fumbled for the receiver and dropped it. Managing to locate the light switch on the bedside lamp, she finally retrieved the telephone. From the cozy nest he'd made on the other pillow, Pavarotti awoke and gave several insulted yowls before he quieted again.

"Yes?"

"Alex, it's Becky."

The clock read 2:53. Immediately, Alex thought of Winifred.

"Becky, what is it? Is it your grandma?"

"It's Emily." Becky's voice was edged with hysteria, and her words spilled out, one on top of the other.

"Alex, I think it's epiglottitis. She can't breathe. She's choking and tripoding. David and I are at the hospital with her now. I don't want Dr. King touching her. Please, Alex, please come. Hurry."

Acute Epiglottitis. Sudden respiratory obstruction caused by a rapidly progressive infection that could be quickly fatal. Children assumed the tripod position, leaning forward and hyperextending the neck in a desperate, futile attempt to breathe.

"Move her to the operating room. Set up for a tracheostomy. Don't touch her any more than you have to."

Thank God emergencies didn't require admitting privileges. Alex fought down her own panic as she threw on jeans and a sweatshirt, grabbed her keys and her medical bag and ran for her car.

She burst through the doors of the emergency room a scant seven minutes later, and at top speed streaked straight down the hall to the operating room. The first sound she heard as she slammed into the room was the high-pitched, wheezing noise Emily was making as she struggled to draw air into her lungs. The tiny girl was on her hands and knees on the table. Her face was scarlet. She was drooling copiously, obviously in severe respiratory distress.

David and Becky hovered helplessly, one on each side of her. The night nurse, Pam Walker, stood nearby, and all three of them turned to Alex with profound relief.

Alex threw her coat off and, dragging on a pair of gloves, reached out to gently touch Emily's arm.

"Poor little sweetheart. Let's have a look—"

And at that precise moment, Emily stopped breathing.

CHAPTER TWENTY-ONE

WHEN EMILY'S BREATHING stopped, David's own breath caught and held in his throat.

Don't die, sweetheart. Please, please don't die—

He watched Alex deftly take charge, and with a combination of horror, utter terror and finally, humble and profound admiration, David saw his sister-in-law save Emily's life by opening a tiny hole in her windpipe and inserting a tube for her to breathe through. Alex was cool, efficient and expert at what she did, and David was nauseous and dizzy.

He knew he didn't have to stay here and watch—Becky wasn't even aware of his presence. She wasn't conscious of anything at this moment except her daughter. He could easily step through the operating room doors into the hallway, but he didn't. He stayed, and afterward, he marveled at the cool control all three women displayed as they labored over the fragile, unmoving little figure on the table.

But while the procedure was going on, all David could think was how superficial his life had been up to this moment. He couldn't remember ever really praying before, but he prayed then, asking humbly, over and over, for the life of the tiny girl he'd come to love as though she were his own. Maybe he'd never prayed because he'd never known, clearly and exactly, what he wanted out of life.

He knew now. He wanted Becky as his wife, and he wanted Emily as his daughter. And he wanted her to live more than anything in the world.

In the past, he'd paid scant attention to children like her. Oh, he'd seen them now and then, and with indifferent, casual pity, dismissed them, forgetting their very existence the moment they were out of his sight, but now he knew Emily's special sweetness, the recognition that dawned in her fathomless dark eyes when he walked into the room, the unconditional love that was her gift. He knew the feel of her delicate arms looped lovingly around his neck. He'd taught her to wink, and she'd taught him about trust.

He wasn't aware of holding his breath until at last the operation was over.

"That's it, angel." Alex sighed. "We're all done here. You're such a brave girl. You're going to feel much better now." Rotating her stiff neck, Alex stepped back from the table and stretched, allowing Becky and the other nurse to lift Emily's small, limp figure off the operating table and place her into a crib.

"We'll start her on cephalosporin IV. She'll need restraints to keep her from pulling at the tube."

As Alex gave quiet orders for the care of her tiny patient, David moved hesitantly over to stand beside Becky, looping his arm around her and drawing her close.

She looked up at him, and now that it was over her eyes filled with tears and her face crumpled. "Oh, David. Thanks for being here with us," she whispered.

He couldn't even reply. He simply held her, and both of them looked down at the crib.

Emily lay on her back, exhausted but completely relaxed now, blessed air easily filling her lungs, the neat white band holding the pediatric tracheostomy tube firmly in place around her neck. Alex had done the procedure under a local, and Emily's eyes were open, confused and blurry, but aware.

"Hey, princess, how ya doin'?" David swallowed back the lump in his throat and leaned down to stroke a satin-smooth cheek with the back of one finger. Even after all she'd been through, Emily tried her best to smile up at him.

That tiny smile was his undoing, and it was Becky who comforted him as he sobbed.

Watching them, Alex saw David's shoulders heaving, saw the tears that slid down her brother-in-law's strong features.

He truly loved Emily, and for the first time, Alex realized that David could be responsible, that he had depths of compassion and an ability to love that she'd never suspected. Becky and Emily were safe with him. That conviction, and the knowledge that she'd kept Emily alive for both of them to love brought an enormous sense of giddy relief to Alex.

I can't wait to tell Cam. He'll be so pleased and proud and surprised—

The thought was instinctive. It took an instant to remember, to remind herself that she and Cameron no longer shared such intimacies, and with the realization came the pain that was becoming so familiar, the constant pain of missing the other half of herself.

She loved him, she'd always love him, but love alone just wasn't enough. There had to be communication, as well, the kind of togetherness David and Becky were experiencing at this very moment, a sharing so deep nothing was held back.

Alex turned and hurried out of the operating room. She'd simply have to get used to being alone. She remembered something Verna once said, and it brought an ironic smile to her lips, a sad smile. She'd be a woman alone, with an eccentric cat for company. A terrible cliché, Verna had called it, not realizing she was foreshadowing Alex's future.

She drove back to the motel just as a pewter dawn was beginning to tinge the valley with the first hints of daylight.

She wouldn't be able to leave today, she realized with weary resignation. It would take three days at least before Emily recovered enough to have the trach tube removed, and of course Alex wouldn't think of leaving until the little girl was truly on the road to recovery. It complicated everything, however. It was agonizing to be this close to Cameron, and this far removed. She'd counted on actual distance to make the break easier.

There was also a new development in her complaint against King. She'd had to tell Becky about having her admitting privileges taken away. Technically, she'd administered emergency treatment, which was her right—her duty—but, as she'd explained to Becky, she had no legal way of admitting Emily to the hospital for further care.

"She's going in with Gram right now, and she's staying there," Becky had stated with fire in her eyes. "And as soon as I get home I'm writing out a full report of what went on in the ER when Johnnie died. I'm giving copies to Dr. King, Harry Perkins, and the College of Physicians and Surgeons. I realized tonight how wrong it is of me to go on letting King operate on others when I wouldn't allow him to touch my own child."

She gripped Alex's hand painfully tight in both her own. "I was so wrong to refuse you, Alex. I'm ashamed and sorry, and I hope you can forgive me."

Alex had simply hugged her tight, her heart swelling at the thought that Becky would, after all, support her in her struggle with King and Perkins.

Maybe it was a good thing she couldn't leave town today, she told herself, pulling the car into the motel parking lot and wearily making her way to the doorway of her unit. Becky would need support now.

She fished in her bag for the key and unlocked the door. *Pavarotti would be beside himself. She hadn't left him any food—*

"Pavarotti?" The cat was nowhere in sight.

"Pavarotti?" She knelt on the floor, checked under the bed, looked in the closets, even turned back the bedcovers, but it was evident he wasn't in the unit. He must have slipped out when she left for the hospital, she decided at last, trying not to panic. With the flashlight Cam insisted she keep in the car, she went out to look for her cat.

An hour and twenty minutes later, shivering in the early-morning chill, her feet soaked by icy dew and her voice hoarse from calling, Alex finally admitted that Pavarotti was lost.

Terrible visions of her beloved cat under the wheels of a truck on the nearby highway or trapped somewhere, unable to escape, overwhelmed her. She slumped into the green armchair beside the motel bed, and she felt like howling. Losing Pavarotti seemed the final, awful culmination of a series of disasters in Alex's life.

She'd learned, in these past difficult weeks, to be more independent, and even more confrontational, than she'd ever been in her life. She'd stood up to her mother for the first time, she'd dealt with Hollister King on her own, she'd made major decisions without procrastinating, completely without Cameron's support—but losing Pavarotti was not something she could bear alone.

She picked up the telephone and dialed the RCMP office, and in twelve minutes flat, Cameron was there.

He didn't try to take her in his arms or talk about their separation or beg her not to leave. He simply listened as, nearly incoherent with worry and weariness, Alex babbled out the story of Emily, of how long it must have been since Pavarotti left the motel, of how she blamed herself for not being more careful about the door.

"I love that cat—your mother gave him to me. I can't bear the thought of losing him," she moaned.

When finally she ran out of breath, Cam rummaged in her suitcase for warm, dry stockings. He knelt at her feet and tenderly stripped off her wet ones and then bundled her into her warmest jacket and a dry pair of boots and loaded her into the squad car.

"We'll find Pavarotti," he promised, and Alex believed him, because in spite of everything else, she'd never known Cam to break a promise.

Officious in his uniform, he went to the motel manager's door and knocked until the wizened man appeared, grumpy and disheveled in a ratty blue housecoat, angry at being disturbed so early in the morning because of a cat that wasn't supposed to be in one of his motel units in the first place. Cam ignored his complaints and insisted every unused unit be opened so Alex could search.

There was no sign of Pavarotti.

They drove up one street and down the other, stopping constantly to examine abandoned sheds, building sites, stretches of wilderness, open garages. Cam contacted Greg when he came on shift at eight and had Louise notify the local radio station and all the schools.

But no one had seen, or even more disturbing considering his considerable voice, heard the cat.

As the hours passed, any initial awkwardness Alex might have felt faded, and gradually she began to talk to Cam of other things besides Pavarotti. It was warm in the squad car, and unless she talked, she was afraid she'd fall asleep.

First she told him about David and his vigil at the hospital, and they had the kind of discussion married people have about families. That led to a long, satisfying conversation about Wade and Thea and their marriage, and Alex's newfound courage in standing up to her mother.

About that time, Cameron pulled into a fast-food outlet and bought them substantial breakfasts, and over coffee Alex related every detail of her difficult first days at the clinic, and Cam told her about the clever trap he'd set at the mine to catch the thieves.

"I had it in my head that small-town policing would be boring, but it's not at all," he confided. "I remember the magistrate telling me when I first got here that there was nothing as satisfying as being the law in a little town, and I'm beginning to think he was right. I like getting to know everyone and I enjoy working with Greg. He's becoming a close friend, something I never had time for in the city."

Their conversation was erratic, interrupted by the radio and numerous stops to search a new area, but gradually they related all the events they'd neglected to share over the past months.

They went on looking for the cat, but as the hours passed, Alex grew less certain they'd ever find him.

"He's just a cat," she told Cameron despondently, trying to control the wobble in her voice. "I have to keep telling myself he's a cat. It's not like it was when Wade was hurt, or—" She stopped abruptly. She'd been about to say, when I left you.

"Or when you left me," he supplied in a soft voice. His dark eyes were eloquent when he turned and looked at her. "You know, I'd rather die than lose you, Alex. I've been doing a lot of thinking the past couple of days, and I understand how I hurt you and why. Ever since we left the city, I kept thinking that what I did, turning Perchinsky in, was wrong. I was ashamed of it. Then when you told me about King, I saw you going through the same thing. You did the right thing, Alex. You really had no choice. And right about then it dawned on me that I didn't have a choice, either. What I did had to be done. All I did wrong was hide my feelings from you."

He gave her a sidelong glance. "I figured if I told you, you'd finally see through me. You'd see that I wasn't really as tough or sure of myself as I pretended to be. And I knew when that happened, you'd stop loving me."

Completely stunned, she turned to stare at him, and she remembered David telling her of a little boy who had to play at being a man before he was ready, who somehow got it into his head that it was his strength that was lovable instead of his soul.

There was no trace of that child now, but the feelings were still there, that conviction that he had to be always in control, always on guard. Something hurt in her chest when she thought of how difficult that must be for him.

Cameron's face was like granite, and he was looking straight ahead. "Ever since I was a kid, I've pretended to be a tough guy, when all the time, inside, I knew different. It always scared me that someday people would find out I was a fraud. I couldn't let you get too close, because if you did, you'd be the one to see—" He stopped abruptly and swore.

"See what, Cam?" Her voice was gentle. "See that you're human? See that you're vulnerable? Don't you think I already know those things about you?'' She drew a quick breath and added bravely, ''Don't you know that I love you because of them?''

He turned toward her, fighting for control, his face ravaged, his voice breaking. ''If you could give me another chance, Alex, I swear to God I'll never hide another damned thing from you as long as I live. I'll show you all my weak spots and I'll talk your ears off. And I'll listen, really listen, to what you have to say.''

The words went straight to her heart, but it was the look in his eyes, the naked vulnerability and terrible, lifelong need that broke down the last of the barriers. She lifted her hand and gently touched his lean, rough cheek with her palm.

''You need a shave, Copper.''

''My razor's back at the house.'' He sighed, a hopeless, bitter sigh. ''And we haven't found that damned cat yet.''

''Maybe we should go home and rest awhile. We could look again later.''

''Home? You mean—''

She nodded. It took another instant to register, and then a look of pure joy spread across his face. He picked up the radio, and in his voice was all the authority of the head of the detachment. ''Korbin Lake, 851. I'll be 10-7 at my residence.''

There was suspicious moisture in his eyes, but he gave her the crooked grin she loved. He came close to breaking several of her ribs when he unhooked her seat belt and dragged her across the seat and into his arms. His kiss said all the things he still hadn't learned to say in words, but Alex didn't mind at all.

They exceeded the speed limit by an astonishing amount on the way out of town, and gravel flew when he steered down their narrow driveway.

"We're here, my love," he whispered.

Alex remembered clearly the first day he'd brought her here. Her breath caught in her throat just as it had then at the wild beauty of this, their first real home.

"Alex." Cameron's voice was suddenly filled with laughter, and with wonder. "I'll be damned. Look there, on the front porch."

She looked, and there was Pavarotti, sitting regally on the top step, cleaning first behind one ear and then behind the other with a front paw. He waited until they tumbled out of the car, and then he raised his formidable voice in welcome.

EPILOGUE

DAVID AND BECKY'S wedding took place on a windy afternoon in April, in the quaint old wooden church on Korbin Lake's main street where Becky's mother and father had been married years before.

Of course, Alex and Cam attended the wedding. And they had been at this church not long before.

Winifred's funeral had been held here two months ago, on a bleak, snowy morning in early February. The old woman had held on to life tenaciously during the uncertain and worrying time that followed Becky's suspension from her job at Korbin Lake General Hospital.

Winifred was worried about her granddaughter, and she had good reason. The battle that raged after Becky's testimony to the college and her report to the hospital board about the death of Johnnie Williams had been both violent and nasty. Becky had been verbally reprimanded and immediately suspended by Perkins, as well as castigated in front of other staff members by Dr. King.

Inevitably, the whole messy situation became common knowledge among the townspeople, and many old-timers rallied behind King—but even more staunchly supported Alex and Becky. It took two months for the college to hire an investigator, and all of December for them to examine every detail surrounding the death of Johnnie Williams. Finally, ten days after Christmas, the college released its report. Although it didn't recommend criminal charges, it strongly suggested that Dr. King no longer perform surgery.

King had lost the battle. He resigned and immediately left town with his wife.

Shirley Boyd also resigned, and it was rumored that her long-standing association with King was over. She stayed on in Korbin Lake in spite of the gossip that raged about her role in the Williams affair, although it was said she'd become a recluse.

King's resignation was the signal for a massive rebellion among the members of the hospital board. Late in January, Harry Perkins was forced to resign, and a much younger man, a stranger skilled in business administration, was hired in his place.

Immediately, Becky was reinstated, Alex's admitting privileges were restored and applications were invited for the hiring of a second doctor, subject to Alex's approval.

She and the board agreed on Larry Kajinskji, a genial young GP with notable surgical skills. Larry had become a friend, and it was a pleasure for Alex to go to work each morning.

And so, with her family once again secure, Winifred died peacefully, in her sleep. Her huge funeral here in this church had been a testament to her life in Korbin Lake.

Alex remembered that day so well. Just as now, the pews had been filled to overflowing, the air redolent with the piercing sweet smell of flowers and beeswax, and the powerful notes of the old organ had reverberated through Alex's very pores.

Today, however, the tears that blurred her vision as she walked ahead of the bride down the aisle were tears of joy. She smiled through them, responding to the warm expressions on one familiar face after another as the congregation turned en masse to welcome the bridal party.

It wasn't a typical procession by any means—Alex, the maid of honor, was carrying the tiny flower girl, who'd had an attack of desperate shyness at the very last moment.

Just a few minutes ago, Emily had plumped her round, padded bottom down on the threadbare carpet in the vestibule and, like a little turtle, pulled up her ankle-length blue satin dress until it completely covered her head. Alex had lifted her and managed to coax her into smoothing down the pretty dress, but Emily wasn't about to walk down the aisle on her own two feet, so Alex had swung her up in her arms.

The church was filled to overflowing with patients, family, co-workers and out of town guests. Alex grinned at Morgan Jacobsen, who'd arrived just hours ago in typical Morgan disarray. The airlines had somehow lost her suitcase on the two-hour flight, and Alex had scrambled around to find a patient as tiny as Morgan from whom to borrow a dress suitable for the wedding.

Actually, she concluded fondly as she winked at her friend, Morgan looked better in the borrowed amber silk suit than she probably would have done in her own garments. Alex knew from experience that every scrap of Morgan's clothing seemed to have a mysterious stain of some sort, undoubtedly originating from the delivery room.

Old friends, new friends; all were gathered here for this occasion, and as Alex led the way in the traditional walk down the red-carpeted aisle, she had the strangest feeling that Winifred, too, was invisibly present this afternoon to witness and bless her granddaughter's marriage to David Ross.

There were other guests also conspicuous by their absence. Alex's parents were spending the winter in the Bahamas and had sent their regrets. Nor had Wade and Thea been able to attend, but the reason for their absence sent a thrill of excitement through Alex.

Wade's rehabilitation had progressed steadily. Her brother was able to walk now with canes, and he was studying hard so he could enter college the following semester. He'd decided he wanted to be a counselor for others with spinal injuries.

The fact that Thea was six weeks pregnant and too nauseous to travel was proof positive that her brother was recovering in all the ways that mattered, Alex had told Cam in bed early that morning. "I just can't wait to hold my niece or nephew. It's like a miracle, Thea getting pregnant so quickly."

"We could try again for our own miracle, Doc," he'd suggested, nibbling her neck. "We don't have to get up for at least another half hour. Mom's down there taking care of Pavarotti and making breakfast for everybody."

"Well, all right then." She'd sighed with mock reluctance, giving herself up to his loving.

It was only five weeks since they'd decided to try to have a child. Alex thought there was just a faint possibility they'd already been successful, but she found she was embarrassingly superstitious about her own possible pregnancy. She didn't want to do any tests just yet. Paradoxically, she wanted her body to signal the news instead of a test tube. And it was far, far too soon to raise Cam's hopes by saying anything.

She nuzzled Emily's neck and thought of babies as they progressed slowly down the aisle, and the little girl giggled and grew brave enough to peek through her fingers.

Her small square face split in a huge grin when she spied her mother close behind. Becky was breathtakingly lovely in an ivory satin suit, carrying a rich bouquet of spring flowers.

"Hey, Mummum, hiya!" Emily's surprisingly powerful voice rose above the organ, and a ripple of laughter erupted at her delighted exclamation. More confident now, she loosened her stranglehold on Alex's neck enough to gaze all around her. When she realized that everyone was smiling lovingly at her, she grinned and planted a huge, sloppy kiss of sheer exuberance on Alex's cheek, prompting another burst of amusement from the congregation.

"Gamma, hiya!" Emily waved frantically as she spotted Sadie, sitting next to Verna at the very front of the church, and as Alex drew abreast of their pew, Emily wriggled like a little eel to get down.

Alex bent, setting her on her feet, and the small girl hurried over to where her grandmother and Verna were seated.

The two older women had ignored the traditional rule of seating guests on either the bride's side of the church or the groom's, choosing to sit together for this occasion. They'd become fast friends during Verna's visit to Korbin Lake at Christmastime, and Sadie had accepted an invitation to visit Verna in Vancouver after Winifred's death. Both welcomed Emily now, making a space for her to snuggle down between them.

With Emily settled, Alex straightened her dress and smiled at the three men who watched and waited at the altar—David, Cameron and, of course, the pastor. David was resplendent in his tuxedo, but to Alex, it was Cameron who dominated the group.

As David's best man, he wore red serge, his close-fitting tunic emphasizing his broad shoulders and narrow waist;

the blue pants and highly polished congress boots of his dress uniform highlighting his long, strong legs.

He caught his wife's admiring glance, holding her gaze with his own, and a thrill coursed through Alex at the naked admiration and raw sexual desire she saw reflected in his dark eyes. Wickedly, he gave her a lascivious wink, and Alex had to grin, even as she shook her head a tiny bit, reproving him for having what were obviously lewd thoughts in church.

"Dearly Beloved, we are gathered here..."

The majestic words of the traditional service rolled out and over the congregation. Alex looked at Cam and silently echoed each sacred promise along with the bridal couple. She knew by the expression on his face that Cam was doing the same. He looked steadfastly back at her, and she could feel the power of his love touching her very soul.

"—to love and to cherish from this day forward—"

"—in sickness and in health, for better and for worse—"

Alex's mouth curved in a wry smile, and Cameron's lips, too, tilted up in his signature one-sided grin, ruefully acknowledging that over the past year, they'd had a whopping dose of worse.

They'd come through it, however. Whatever was wounded had healed and become stronger than before. Alex knew that the relationship they now shared was infinitely richer for the stresses it had endured. She knew by the somberness in the depths of her husband's eyes that he, too, was thinking of how close they'd come to losing each other during those first troubled months here in Korbin Lake.

"—pronounce you husband and wife. You may kiss your bride, David."

Reverently, David drew Becky into his arms. She tilted her face up for his kiss, and as they embraced, Emily let out an outraged roar and slid down from her seat beside her grandmother, making her determined way toward the group at the altar.

"Em kiss, too, Dabid," she said in an indignant tone, giving David's pant leg an insistent tug. Amidst a ripple of laughter from the congregation, he bent and scooped her into his arms.

Crowing with delight, she cupped his face in her tiny hands and kissed him exuberantly, smack on the mouth.

Through the tears that accompanied her laughter, Alex looked at them, the strong, handsome man holding the fragile child, and her hand moved unconsciously to her abdomen.

In that moment, in that holy place, she knew that she carried Cam's baby, and along with the ecstasy of knowing came a flutter of uncertainty.

Wife, mother, doctor—would she be able to fulfill with grace all the demanding roles she'd chosen in her life?

The organ music swelled into the strains of the wedding march. The congregation surged to their feet, and the bride and groom and Emily started their triumphant journey back down the aisle.

Cam reached out in an old-fashioned, courtly gesture, and with a tiny bow, offered Alex his arm. She placed her hand on the bright scarlet serge, aware of the corded muscle beneath the cloth, the utter solidity and goodness of this man who was her life's partner.

She was strong and capable and confident, but it was comforting to know that her husband was there to support her along the way, should she need support—just as she was there for him.

Dearly beloved...

Side by side, in perfect unison, they walked down the aisle.

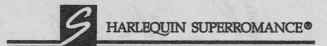

HARLEQUIN SUPERROMANCE®

WOMEN WHO *Dare*

**They take chances, make changes and
follow their hearts!**

40 TONS OF TROUBLE
by
Connie Flynn

Move on down the highway... That's all Cat DeAngelo wants to
do, but it's getting harder and harder.

That's because *someone's* trying to ruin DeAngelo Transport.
Cat's trucks have suffered a rash of break-ins, and a slimy
competitor keeps underbidding her and offering to buy her out.

Worse, Cat's at odds with her young sister and brother.
They want her to get out from behind the wheel and take
over the day-to-day running of the family company—from
behind a *desk!*

Then Cat takes on a six-foot-five certified "hunk" as a
temporary co-driver. That's when her problems *really* escalate.

Right along with her heart rate.

**Watch for *40 Tons of Trouble* by Connie Flynn
Available in February 1997
wherever Harlequin books are sold**

Look us up on-line at: http://www.romance.net

WWD-297

Heartbreak RANCH

Four generations of independent women...
Four heartwarming, romantic stories of the West...
Four incredible authors...

Fern Michaels
Jill Marie Landis
Dorsey Kelley
Chelley Kitzmiller

Saddle up with Heartbreak Ranch, an outstanding
Western collection that will take you on a whirlwind
trip through four generations and the exciting,
romantic adventures of four strong women who
have inherited the ranch from Bella Duprey,
famed Barbary Coast madam.

Available in March,
wherever Harlequin books are sold.

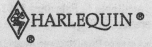

HARLEQUIN ®

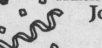
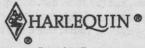